I0656857

John McGovern

**Daniel Trentworthy**

A tale of the great fire of Chicago

John McGovern

**Daniel Trentworthy**
*A tale of the great fire of Chicago*

ISBN/EAN: 9783337027476

Printed in Europe, USA, Canada, Australia, Japan

Cover: Foto ©Andreas Hilbeck / pixelio.de

More available books at **www.hansebooks.com**

"Hurry up there, Bill!"   Page 33.

# A TALE OF THE GREAT FIRE OF CHICAGO.

By JOHN McGOVERN,

AUTHOR OF "BURRITT DURAND," "GEOFFREY VAN LIEB," ETC.

CHICAGO:
RAND, McNALLY & COMPANY, PUBLISHERS,
148, 150, 152 AND 154 MONROE STREET; and
323 BROADWAY, NEW YORK.
1889.

# DANIEL TRENTWORTHY.

## PROLOGUE.

HUMAN history must deal with human interest. Events thought to be unimportant in their day may tower up with the ages—as the death of Shakespeare. Events great as a royal marriage may be buried as deeply in a library as they could be inhumed in oblivion; for what is oblivion but lack of interest by the living? All is for the living; nothing for the dead.

Let us then deal candidly with events, subjectively as to their merits, objectively as to the interest they arouse, at once and forever. By that means we may perhaps claim that in three centuries there have been but three events in the first class of human interest—namely:

Seventeenth century, the works and death of Shakespeare.

Eighteenth century, the French Revolution.

Nineteenth century, the destruction of Chicago.

I shall tell a simple tale of the nineteenth century which may hold the reader's attention because of the august presence of a kingly event. I shall ask the man of keen sympathy and sound imagination to pass through days that must seem longer than days. To a spectacle from which men will never turn away, I shall try to give the color it had in its own age; yet, like Shakespeare, it was not for an age, but for all time.

Madame de Sévigné made herself famous by writing a short letter: "I am going to tell you," said she, "a thing the most astonishing, the most surprising, the most marvelous, the most miraculous, the most magnificent, the most confounding, the most unheard of, the most singular, the most extraordinary, the most incredible, the most unforeseen —the greatest, the rarest, the most common, the most public, the most private, and the most brilliant; in short, a thing of which there is but one example in past ages, and that not an exact one, either; a thing that we cannot believe in Paris —how, then, will it gain credit in Lyons?"

And what was it that this clever woman told? Only the engagement of marriage between a princess and a nobleman! She thundered in her index, and gained an immortality not altogether to be despised.

Can there be any prologue whatever for that chronicler who, having the Event of October, 1871, for his theme, addresses a human interest that grows only the keener as decade after decade laps and whispers on the beach of time?

---

## CHAPTER I.

### JOHN TRENTWORTHY.

THE Bank of El Dorado had a capital of ten millions. No depositor trifled with the time of the institution who could not draw his check for $50,000. No stock company hoped to have the confidence of the Pacific slope if it had not secured the permission of the officers of the Bank of El Dorado to refer to them.

The directors of the bank were men of unlimited means; and by "means" they meant gold coins, for the greenbacks of the United States had never seemed quite good enough for the Bank of El Dorado. They might be good, and again they might not. Gold would be good. No one doubted that.

Not only had the Bank of El Dorado unlimited means, but it had a man. "Arms and the man, I sing," said the poet. "Gold and the man," sang the lauders of the Bank of El Dorado. Gold was very well, but a financier was even better.

John Trentworthy was the financier.

Men said he was Midas. Whatever he touched turned to gold.

"I am more fortunate than Midas," he would reply. "I do not have to eat gold."

Is it not an extraordinary thing to be pivoted in the center of confidence? Round about John Trentworthy clustered fifty millionaires, each dreaming of the happy moment when Trentworthy would start from some reverie and say: "My boy, I can use three or four and turn it over in sixty days."

"Three or four" meant millions. The more it meant the more gleefully did the lending millionaire seek his down pillow that night.

A Niagara of molten gold was thundering over a precipice into an abyss of credit. In a frail bark, plying between two crags, John Trentworthy would carry such of the imploring millionaires as his fancy prompted him to favor. They shivered in agony as they looked up at the flood, but they were the envy of the craving host back on the hither crag.

"He'll go down yet," the millionaire would say as he saw John Trentworthy land a rival millionaire safely with an added fortune. "He'll go down yet."

But that was because the disappointed millionaire had not himself been taken across the abyss.

Is it not an awful problem this—"How shall I make money?" Thus our disappointed millionaire has but five millions. He sits down, writes a little on paper, and presto! he is a poor man! Ah! may God forgive him; his wife must dismiss her servants and do her own housework; his children must clamor for the advantages that other children have; there will be no travel, and there will be the nethermost pit of impatience where one man with infinite faculties must attempt to please another man with infinite faculties.

No, no; it is a dream. The millionaire has *not* written on the paper. He is safe! But is it any wonder that cold sweat stands out upon his brow?

John Trentworthy sits down and writes a few words on paper. Five millionaires have given him a million apiece. Presto! it is ten millions. Is it not easy?

Ay, that it is, if only John Trentworthy be the man who does it. Still the millionaire who carries his bags of gold to John Trentworthy must have pangs and terrors. The ways of the magician are not the ways of the meek-spirited millionaires. Everything he does outside of his money-making frightens the rich men and amazes the populace. Hence, perhaps, a portion of his financial power.

He learns how far a man may drive the fastest trotters. At the end of that measured line he erects a palace. There he keeps a room and a plate ready for each of sixty guests, whether one or none or sixty be present. If a king or an ambassador, a head man in the Orient or a fashionable statesman of the Occident, be at the Golden Gate, the Golden Gate opens only to the hospitable doors of John Trentworthy's palace.

From the palace to the city there stretches, as the crow flies, a costly drive—"an incredible drive," said all previous horse-owners. And daily does this strange man ooze the excitement out of his body through the ribbons that hold his flying steeds to their swift gait. Perhaps that vent gives him his coolness when he handles millions.

In every part of the world the voices of the noble, the glorious, and the fortunate go up in recital of the wonders seen at John Trentworthy's palace. And all these stories, while they may vary as to the things seen, end with the same averment. The most wonderful of all the wonders was the man who closed his eyes and saw millions which the greediest people on earth had not before espied; the man who drove fifteen leagues to his daily business; the man whose word was law at the Bank of El Dorado, at London and at Vienna.

"I wish we had him here," said each of the Rothschilds.

"Commerce is developing wonderful financial genius," said the Barings.

But the poor millionaires at the Golden Gate were too near their man. They would have felt easier had he lived in a small back room and done nothing else save close his eyes and see millions for the big four, or the big eight, or the big sixteen.

Speculation—it is a strange word. "Thou hast no speculation in those eyes," cries the wretched Macbeth. Speculation—sight—to see—to see where it is not, but will be. And perhaps not to be at all. Thus, speculation—to see what others will deem probable. Thus, a town may be a city. To see that first is a fortune. The town may never reach a city's dignity. To see that last is ruin.

The millionaires peered. But there was no speculation in their eyes. They must have the terrifying John Trentworthy to see for them—John Trentworthy the greatest speculator in the history of finance.

## CHAPTER II.

### BAD FOR DANIEL TRENTWORTHY.

ONE memorable week the owner of the palace has eaten with an especially large crowd of mandarins, dukes, princes, sergeants, kings, poets, and statesmen. He has driven in from the palace in a road time unprecedented. He has crossed under the molten flood in the cockle-shell of his credit with an unusually large number of trembling millionaires. He has heard a chorus of prophecies from the stupid and the disappointed—all to the effect that he will go down.

"Mr. Trentworthy, you seem more than commonly excited, or absent-minded," a favored friend would say—some expert judge of a horse.

Generally a close student of men appreciates a student of some excellent animals.

"Yes," Trentworthy would smile. "I have had news that my son is doing well at Harvard College."

For John Trentworthy had a son, a lad with perhaps the most enviable prospects of any young man in America. He was thoughtful, handsome, amiable, and ambitious to learn. It was expected that he would graduate from Harvard at an age which would permit him to take a course at a foreign university. Bonn would be super added to Harvard. Travel and the best of society would fit him for the close companionship and confidence of the magician at the Golden Gate.

Can we blame the poor young men at Harvard that they looked upon this heir of all good things, and questioned: "Why is it not so with us?"

Yet, so envious is man, the comrades of young Daniel **Trentworthy** had all that he had, except expectations. For the magician at the Golden Gate had often said that there was but one way to make a man, and that was by hard knocks. To spare his only son—to make him soft and effeminate—would be to leave John Trentworthy without a successor. At the father's knee the boy heard this gospel of toil and attrition. At college the faculty preached it from constant and anxious letters they had received.

Daniel Trentworthy's comrades did not covet his brains, his good nature, or his quiet spirit. As a matter of fact, it came about that he had nothing else they really wanted, for, one day, the president called the lad into a private room.

"Mr. Trentworthy," the president said, as he glanced at a dispatch, "have you received any news from home to-day?"

"No, sir," said the lad, growing uneasy.

"Then it is my sad duty to say to you that your father is dead."

"Is that so?" said the lad, mechanically, all his words, and all his thoughts, and all his blood coursing in a strange way through his body.

"Yes: my dispatch puzzles me. It reads: 'Tell Trentworthy Bank of El Dorado closed, and John Trentworthy dead. Directors.'"

"My dear boy, have you no other relatives at home?"

"None," said the boy, with a swallowing sound.

"Well, well, well," said the kind old scholar. "Leave it to me, and I will ascertain the particulars by telegraph."

Now this had happened: A depositor, having need of a few hundred thousands, drew a check for the amount on the Bank of El Dorado—a trifling matter. How handy are these banks! You draw your check; that suffices; your creditor is paid.

The check was presented. It was not paid. What was the matter with the check? Nothing. What was the matter with the bank of El Dorado? Ah! there you reach it!

Now, imagine such a thing. No money in a bank with ten

millions.   No money in John Trentworthy's bank—and he—

How many thousand people stand in that cross-like crowd in the streets ?   Enough to lift up that stone structure, if they could get hands on, as Ramesis made the children of Israel catch hold of the obelisks.   It is truly an angry crowd.   Plenty of Argonauts there.   Dukes, royal drivers, palaces—magic !   It fills the host with a demoniac sarcasm. Where is this magician ?

Truly, where is he? he has driven his leagues to-day, as usual, for the hostlers have scraped his steeds.   He bathes every day, for his health is of prime importance—or was. Perhaps he is at the bathing place.

Yes, he has gone down into the water.   They will follow him.   They want his life—that which they deemed the glory of the coast but yesterday.

But they cannot get his life.   It was too proud to wait for them and their impotent wrath.   John Trentworthy is drowned.

He has gone down under the molten flood, before the very eyes of the millionaires who would so gladly have sat with him in his cockle-shell.   It gives the little groups on the hither and thither crags a shock that brings them to their senses.   Speculation comes to an end.

Now the Bank of El Dorado is greater than any magician after all.   The honor of fifty millionaires is a very substantial financial fabric.   The Bank of El Dorado opens the moment the dead body of John Trentworthy has been found.

But they are a sorry lot of mourners.   They mourn their gold—millions of it.   Anything that John Trentworthy had is the bank's—theirs.   Strange that they could not see through his magic—so they say now.

And yet John Trentworthy had simply lost in a game where one must win all the time.

They telegraphed to Harvard : "Tell young Trentworthy that his father dies a debtor to the bank of El Dorado for millions. We have taken possession of everything. We fear the young man will be left without support."

They did not fear it, they knew it, but one of the most knowing of the stupids said it would be much better to say "fear." It was. They pitied the boy. But think how sad they were! Think how they pitied themselves!

"My son," said the president of the college, "I cannot express my sorrow for you. I have never seen great expectations swept away so suddenly or so completely, although the same kind of misfortune has often visited us here. You are left without money, and I believe your father's creditors mean to deny you to the last cent."

"What shall I do?" asked the young man.

"In the present state of public feeling you would not want to go to San Francisco. You can earn your own living, can you not?"

"Yes, sir."

No young man ever doubts this. It is strange that nothing but experience will teach a man that life is hard.

"I think you had better seek some thriving Western city. Are you favorably impressed with Chicago?"

"Yes; I will go there."

"I have personal influence which may aid you in getting a foothold; I cannot tell you how glad I shall be to put it at your service. I hear there is no place in the West where there is so good an opening for a young man. Wait here till the year is out."

"No," said the young man, "I will go at once."

How could he stay and face the scornful pity of the other young men whose fathers would not fail until the next panic, or those others whose fathers would never fail at all?

So he took the letters of the kind old president and rode toward Chicago. The city filled him with curiosity. That is, the gathering of metropolitan forces at Chicago had been so sudden as to become the talk of the world. The real estate speculators had concocted a glowing scheme. The star of empire had itself moved in the very zodiac of their scheme. What they had expected to make the world believe through the power of their enthusiasm, the world was forced to accept as fact through the imperious caprice of a nation's commerce. If Daniel Trentworthy picked up a newspaper his eye rested on some tale of Chicago, and that tale was sure to be the most wonderful thing in the day's news. Men loved to read of the gold-diggers of the winter of '49 and spring of '50. But there was not enough of those chronicles. Here, however, at Chicago, there was a wonderland that crowded the rest of the world out of the columns of the daily press.

The war was over. The boom was on. Real estate was held at the prices which it brings to-day, in 1887, when the city has 800,000 souls. It was the metropolis of Lincoln's State ; therefore when the body of the martyr lay on its cata-falque, in the Court House, all the Northwest came to hold the hand of Illinois as she sobbed over the greatest of the Western dead. The tomb of Douglas was here ; therefore Andrew Johnson swung around the circle and saw with his own eyes. Here were gathered the adventurous, the enthu-siastic, the crowded-out of the whole world. And they con-tinued to do wonderful things. They set great brick palaces on jack-screws ; they tunneled two miles under the lake for water that a dozen generations might drink ; they fathomed the descent of their river, and set at work to turn its flow backward. They raffled away their opera house, and a new owner came riding on his horse out of the West. And to this day that opera house has hardly been equaled for its qualities as an auditorium where the rich and the poor could alike hear and see with ease.

Even the murderers and the suicides rose to the spirit of public performance that was on the inhabitants. The bar-ber packed his wife's body in a cask, and became the proto-fiend of all that sort; the saloon-keeper cleared away the midnight glasses from one of his tables, ran a hose from the gas-burner to the table, lay down on that table and breathed out of the gas-holder far away on Adams street. The papers of the world were full of it.

The wonderful city said: "We will have oil." They bored and struck the first of the artesian wells, that spouted for the world's amazement.

The city that had built the wigwam, and caucused Honest Old Abe on the nation as its President; that had nominated McClellan; that had mustered Ellsworth and Mulligan; that had the lumber and the grain and the cattle of the continent for sale—this city seemed to call all young men; and the tide of buoyant and expectant life that rolled toward her showed the power of her allurements.

Daniel Trentworthy rode around the lake-shore; he crossed other lines of railroad and lines of telegraph poles that seemed hurrying to one center; he gazed with falling spirits over the foggy marsh out of which the second Rome had risen. It was so level, so flat, so watery, so rainy! Why did the scream of the outflying locomotive startle him as it rushed away? His woes came on him then, and he wept a little for his great father, the lamp of whose life had been extinguished so suddenly. In what darkness had it left his son!

But, as he came forth from the depot beside the beautiful lake, he saw a long cavalcade and procession coming up the leading street of residences. All spectacular processions took that route.

"What is it?" he asked.

"It is Weston, finishing his walk from Portland, Me.," was the reply.

Yes, Chicago was the end of the world for Weston, as it seemed for every other mortal. Daniel Trentworthy gazed on the little man as he bowed to his tens of thousands of admirers.

"If he can walk here, I can at least ride here," he smiled, and was happy that he belonged to the "bright Christian capital of lakes and prairie."

---

## CHAPTER III.

### NO DANGER OF FIRE ON DE KOVEN STREET.

As Daniel Trentworthy had left the train and crossed the dead-line where he became the legitimate prey of the hotel-runners, a man in gray, with a massive mustache which failed to hide a square chin—a man with a cold gray eye betokening vast experience, and with a ponderous steel badge pinned to the lapel of his coat—this formidable man fixed his cold steel eye and his cold steel badge on the young adventurer.

"The Girard House," said the man, speaking not as a scribe, but as one having authority.

Of course the young man did not want to go to the Girard House.

"A dollar and a half a day," said the great man sternly, as though the visitor had harbored thoughts of foolish expense. Expense was to be avoided. That was the look of the gray eye.

"But where is the Girard House?" The young man's voice was getting faint. He was losing ground rapidly.

"Right here," and the thumb went behind the immense badge. Surely enough. It was clearly a decoration of which the austere courier was proud. The doubt implied in the young man's query had been overwhelmed.

"How far do we go?"

"It is right here at the end of the depot. Close to the depot. Near by the depot."

He of the stern eye had said his say. It was sufficient. Daniel Trentworthy was led away to the little Girard House, because it was adjacent to a depot which he would not again use. That argument had won the day.

So, down at the end of the nastiest street this side of Erzeroum ; down at the end of a double row of chicken crates nearly a mile long ; down at the end of an avenue where green grocers' wagons, packed like sardines, carried away only a portion of the green things that must wither and mildew in a day ; within a few feet of a sewage lagoon that had not yet been drained into the Mississippi River—to such an inn the boy was forced, by the power of one man over another, to go. However, he need not stay, for the great man's work was done when he led the guest to the register. Daniel Trentworthy wrote his name, and the glorious runner went back to the dead-line.

It was easy enough, after dinner, there being no other great man at the Girard House, to pay the bill and seek a hotel in the region of the Court-house.

How imposing is an edifice with a great dome, if it stands in the middle of a square, with an iron fence around it and the heart of a wonderful city at every gate.

And if a solid line of hackney coaches surround it on four streets, how shall the mind escape the conclusion that there is a funeral of some hero within, or a Webster, or Clay, or Douglas, or Lincoln charming all those who can crowd into the rotunda ?

Boom ! strikes the deep bell on the roof of the Court-house ; again, one, two ; one, two, three.

Yes, it is doubtless a funeral oration. How thick the mist ; how insufferably thick the air ! It is a fitting day for such an event.

" Why, my dear sir," exclaimed a bustling Chicagoan, " that is the hack-stand. The bell ?—why, yes, that is at box 123, on the North Side."

2

" What's that ? "

" Oh, yes, I see.  You are a stranger.  It is a fire—nothing but a fire."

Ah, well, Daniel Trentworthy thinks it would take a very hot fire to burn much of this damp region.  He feels as though he were in a cave.

He hears much of " the North Side," " the South Side," " the West Side."  The glibness with which an inhabitant, uses local terms always offends a new-comer.  So Daniel buys a map of the city, and fixes these divisions in his mind.  He finds that he may take a sheet of common note-paper for the site of Chicago.  On the right edge is Lake Michigan ; on the other edges the low and level prairie.  Two sluggish bayous lie lengthways of this sheet, in the center—that is, one runs southward to the middle, and the other northward to the middle.  Draw a line up and down the centre of the sheet ; the junction is at the middle of the sheet ; or, to be exact, about two rulings above the middle ; thence, to the lake at the right, a main bayou lies between ; blacken the right half of the middle ruling of the note-paper.  Now Daniel has three divisions on his paper—the West, twice as big as either the North or the South.

So much adherence, in every-day speech, to this dividing of the city did not seem necessary to him, but the people thought so.  If he crossed a bridge that turned on a pivot in the middle of the river, although he traveled only a hundred feet, he had gone from the South to the West side. It probably came from the days of township government, for the three " sides " embraced as many towns, and taxes are still paid on this theory.  By careful attention to these details of local custom, Daniel Trentworthy came to understand the city.  The West Side was the Brooklyn, or bedchamber.  The South Side had the business, or nine-tenths of it ; the North Side had the oldest trees and favorite houses, and prettiest park, and first cemetery, already abandoned.

Counting across his sheet of paper, from prairie to lake, he found he could have about thirty long streets; counting lengthways of his sheet, he could have about sixty shorter ones. It was decidedly a lake-shore city, twice as long as it was broad in its widest part, which would be the middle of the sheet. He marveled at the peculiar lay of these branch rivers. At their junction a square of land fitted on each side of the main conduit. Vessels coming down either branch turned a right angle as they took the principal channel to go into the lake. The top of the sheet would be Fullerton avenue; the bottom Thirty-first street, the left side Western avenue. Across the sheet would be three miles, down the sheet six miles. All these measurements, of course, were approximate, and yet the sheet of note-paper, with its two lines, one long and one short, represented well enough the great level plain of say eighteen square miles on which stood the city of Chicago. He fixed the Court-house at a point equally distant from the South Branch, the main channel and the lake. This was the heart of the city. A ring a mile out surrounding this Court-house would strike De Koven street, a humble avenue that was to be greatly exalted in history. A radius pointing to 137 De Koven street, at its junction with the mile circle, would run east of southwest; the corresponding radius, running north of northeast, would reach the northern side of the circle precisely at the water works. The Court-house then was exactly half way, on a straight line, from De Koven street to the water works, at the lake shore on the North Side. A ring three miles out would touch Fullerton avenue, the top of the note-paper. At college Daniel had been in the habit of projecting the outlines of the plans of great cities on his mind. Paris, London, Berlin, Rome, and Vienna were thus familiar to him, and this device of a sheet of note-paper had been the means by which he accomplished a seemingly wonderful (but rather

simple) undertaking. But no city is so easy to lay out in
the mind as is Chicago.

Daniel Trentworthy had suffered a great fall, but he knew
very little about that. He spoke the words as he heard them
spoken. His future had been one of great responsibilities,
so he had thought—a future from which he shrank. Now
he had only to earn his own living. It looked easy and comfortable.

Here was a beautiful city. At the end of the street the
air was pure and blue, for it stood over the lake. The streets
were well paved and noiseless. The buildings were continuous, and five stories high. The men were young. At
thirty-five he (Daniel) would undoubtedly be the owner of a
block, like these others.

Therefore he would see the city before he captured it.
What were its sights ? The Douglas tomb, the Court-house
cupola, the water works, the artesian well, and Lincoln Park.
The artesian well was at the western limits. The tomb was
at the southeastern limits. We know where the Court-house
and the water works stood. Lincoln Park was in the upper
right corner of the sheet of paper. He did not care to see
De Koven street—in those days.

So when he found there were so few things to amuse the
idler he bethought himself that idlers belonged farther Eastward, and presented himself to the honorable gentlemen who
were to take his case in hand. In those days letters of recom-
mendation meant something. The honorable president of the
board, and the honorable deputy superintendent of the force,
and the honorable mayor himself were pleased to hear from
their learned friend. There was room for young men in
Chicago. For, when you have only 220,000 people in a city
with eighteen square miles, you need a great many more people with whom to fill up.

" Put him in with the boys," said the deputy to the president, for that would let the deputy out of it.

" How would you like a place in an engine house ? " asked the president.

" That would suit me exactly," said the son of the president of El Dorado.

So Daniel Trentworthy became a cub in the Long John engine house behind the Board of Trade that had just been finished.

He was obedient and useful. The boys liked him. He did not get " hard."

" It is wonderful how well that young feller knows the streets of this 'ere city," a fireman would observe. " We've got a big machine to haul, but we never take a roundabout way if he's along. He knows every foot of pavement, and he always seems to keep track of even the house-movings. I ain't seein' what we'd a done without him."

From the Long John house to a certain corner was precisely the distance to be traversed by another engine coming up another street. Thus, whenever both crews worked in the same time and drove at breakneck speed toward that point, they would certainly come in collision with dire results. Not long after Daniel got on the rolls, this usual collision came about, a man on the Long John was killed, the engine house was hung with black, and Daniel was given the vacant place. He was now a pipeman, a full-fledged fireman—one of as brave a lot of men as ever breathed fire and smoke, like Apollyon.

One day there came into the engine house a slight man with a pale, narrow face and a weak voice. He spoke as if he had a sore throat. He asked for Daniel.

" Didn't you once live in Lima ? "

" Yes," said Daniel.

" Well, when you were a little boy, and wore gingham aprons or frocks with a belt, do you remember that a printer boy used to print your name on a strip of paper, which you would fasten to your belt ? "

"Yes.   That was Harmon Holebroke."

" That's my name.  I live here in Chicago, and I heard you were here.  Wouldn't you like to take your meals at our house and make your home there ?  We would be glad to have you."

So Daniel went to the house of his old friend, Harmon Holebroke.   There he found the mother and a sister.  Another sister was at school in a New England town.

Harmon Holebroke was a printer on a morning daily newspaper.  He was quiet and good.   He did not drink.   The foreman of the office had little sympathy for men who kept away from saloons, and had possibly given Harmon his situation under a misapprehension.  However, the foreman stood by his man after he had hired him.

" He's harmless, boys," the foreman would say.

The greatest ethnological and convivial authority in the office gave Harmon a careful and effective study.   " Gentlemen," he said, " it's a sheep's-face."   So for a while all the topers called Harmon Sheepface.

But printers, after all, are the most intelligent of wagelaborers.   Would that all leaders of men knew as much ! The great authority met his fate when he made the  mistake of calling Harmon Holebroke Sheepface.   The men, within a month, adopted the  name of " Christian" for Harmon, and " Hogmouth" for the great man.   Once fastened, neither of these appellations was ever shaken off.

Now, " Hogmouth" had dwelt in that office many years. He had rechristened many a wight, and had long evaded the penalty of their revenge.   To be the victim of the  worst of all the nicknames, and to have his comrades seize it with avidity, as if it expressed some thought which had  long sought relief, was  more than he  could bear with stoicism.   One day he met Christian Holebroke and Daniel Trentworthy on the street.   He invited them into a saloon to drink.   They thanked him, but declined.   He  was partially intoxicated, and all his hatred of Holebroke flamed out.

"You will drink with me or fight!" he cried. And Harmon, being more used to these things than Daniel, went into the saloon and pacified the drunken bully. It made a bad impression on Daniel. "You ought to have let me settle with that fellow," he said ruefully.

But "Hogmouth" was only the more dissatisfied. He denounced both Christian and his friend the fireman as men of the white feather, and did not go back to work for three weeks.

Meantime the authorities behind Daniel gave him a little push forward. They appointed him one of a committee to report on the condition of that part of the city lying near West Twelfth street, and within the mile-circle drawn around the Court-house.

He found that the streets had been laid out very closely together, and very narrow. They were solidly built up with cottages that had received one coat of poor paint. Situated in a region near the smoke of the river tugs and planing mills, the cottages had blackened in a year's time. They all looked to be forty years old. The shingles were black, and lolled lazily in a good breeze. These streets were built east and west. The lots were not over 100 feet deep. Back of the cottages were sheds and barns, and board fences joined whole districts together. The alleys were sixteen feet across, but a pile of dry stable-bedding from each barn would meet a pile across the way.

The city had been much frightened by the Lake street fire, where a whole block on one side of this, the principal wholesale street, burned, and set fire to another block on the other side of the street and two blocks eastward. The loss had been $3,000,000. The buildings were so high that the water froze before it reached the windows after leaving the pipe. This had given an impetus to the present inspection.

Daniel, book in hand, and with the badge of authority, was a most unwelcome visitor on De Koven, Forquer and Ewing streets.

"Hogmouth" lived on Taylor. The householders appealed to him. He worked on a newspaper, and therefore was an editor.

"Pay no attention to him," said "Hogmouth." "I'll fix that fellow."

So Daniel entered house after house, and sketched pile after pile of kindlings for a great fire. He was unfortunate enough to ask the old women if they did not feel somewhat insecure.

"Maybe we doos, wid th' loikes av yez ter pit oot oor foires, yez tax-aiting thafe," they scolded. "They're do be goin' th' Coort-hoose bell, now, yez loafer, an' some poor woman's burnin' oot. Divil a bit yez moind phwile yez do be makin' yez pietchures av honest payple's hooses. We'll trun th' loike av yez into th' river av yer shows yer mug here agin at all!"

What filled the inspector with especial fear was the sight of great arks of fine shavings from the mills. Processions of these vast wagons, twice as long and high as ice carts, would file down the lanes and alleys, leaving in the aggregate tons of their contents at the gateways of the inhabitants. The shavings were used for the bedding of both man and beast. After use they were piled in the alleys.

Daniel's report, with drawings and detailed accounts of the fire material on hand, which solidly covered an area so large, made a nine days' sensation in the city. "Hogmouth" went to his two aldermen, and those worthies came down so hard on the young inspector that he was privately cautioned that if he should have any more reports to make he would do well to draw them milder.

This dampened his ardor. Meeting "Hogmouth" on the street, Daniel gave him a mauling, after the fashion approved in the Fire Department.

Now, although this encounter pleased the boys at the Long John house, it resulted disastrously to Daniel, for

"Hogmouth" secured Daniel's arrest, and the authorities reduced him to his ordinary duties.

There was a jollification on De Koven street over the downfall of the inspector.

"Did yez hear phwat that thafe wor a goin' to be doin' wid us? Well, thin, he do be buildin' a wall bechune us an' th' river, ter kape off thin lake breezes. Th' divil take *him*."

This likelihood of fire was a sore subject. It made the denizens mad at the first thought. Why was that?

---

## CHAPTER IV.

### "HURRY UP THERE, BILL!"

"I DO not believe you will stay in the Fire Department," prophesied Christian Holebroke. "The crowd doesn't suit you."

But Daniel was young and hopeful. He liked the service. Besides, he was without the ties of family. The boys in their bunks were his family. He invented an apparatus that threw him out of bed and slid him down-stairs whenever an alarm sounded.

Now, most of us would prefer a bed that had no such tricks. Yet, if we had invented it, perhaps there might be a delicious sense of enjoyment as we found ourselves shooting down the slippery plank.

Anyhow, it was so with Daniel.

The Washington street tunnel, after a history which included the worst wreck that ever was cleared away, was completed with a great show of civic pride. It promptly began leaking, and has leaked ever since. A couple of confidence men stationed themselves at the entrances and charged an extortionate entrance fee.    But nothing could keep sight-seers out.

The passage for vehicles separated at the bed of the river, and there the great arch divided into two arches, with a wall between the teams which passed each other on their way through.   The descent from Franklin street was rapid.   Of course, the head of the center wall was a thing to be avoided by the descending drivers.

Now, firemen, when they drive, avoid nothing.   Everything avoids them.   So, one day, ding-ding went the house alarm, tramp, tramp came the horses out of the stalls, of their own accord—the good old fire laddies—thump, came the boys down the plane, and out went the Long John, like a whirlwind, up LaSalle to Washington, and down Washington, to the tunnel.   Down the tunnel the engine thundered, racking from two wheels to two wheels, square in the center of the way, frightening every up-coming driver well-nigh to death, as might easily be done.

Now, the Long John had never met anything before that it had not knocked over.   The solemn and bellowing ice cart was only a hollow delusion—the Long John, the monster engine, had often demonstrated the flimsiness of all ice carts.   But the buttress at the bottom of the tunnel was a new thing.   The Long John, as we have said, first on two wheels, then on the two on the other side, its horses galloping at full tilt to keep from being run over, its drivers turned into furious demons who yelled that all who loved their lives might vanish into the narrow walls praying to God, and who, thus yelling, clanged on a soul-terrifying gong which drowned even the infernal clatter of the horses' hoofs—the biggest, longest, heaviest engine in the city thus made its first entrance into that swift-descending tunnel.   Dimly the buttress in the center loomed across the path of the terrible visitor.   The demons in

helmets yelled for the buttress to get out of the way, and
then dashed on to overtake it in its flight.

But, alas! the next moment the Long John was a wreck,
its horses were sprawling in the right passage-way, and the
demons were turned into half-insensible firemen—nothing
but Chicago laddies, who wondered how it had come, and
how it had come they were not killed.

The wreck of the Long John brought the "Hogmouth"
to the front once more. The Alderman from De Koven
street set an investigation on foot to "bag" Daniel, but he
escaped the blame, and was laid up at home for a few days,
where Mary Holebroke's mother cared for him as she would
have cared for her son Harmon. Had she not known Daniel
when he was a boy?

"Never mind the engine house," she said to console him,
"Mary will play you the pieces you like."

And Mary's playing did console him mightily. He found
himself buying the Boosey red books—then new in the West,
all the operas, all the masses, the great waltzes that then
were pouring, one a week, on the world—Strauss, Kela Bela,
Offenbach. How strange that we should wait twenty years
for another Blue Danube!

This young lady would take the scores that bothered
Daniel so much, and forth would step the chords and fancies
which eluded him so easily. How did she do it? Who can
tell? She was a musician. She did it naturally.

Now, Daniel was a dumb musician. He had whole masses
in him. He could whistle the "Lohengrin" *vorspiel* for
sixteen violins—that is, he could whistle the part of one
violin and hear the other fifteen in his soul.

"Oh, pshaw!" you exclaim. "Save me from a whistler."
Very true. But are you not sorry for a soul so full of music
and yet so dumb?

Now, Mary Holebroke heard Daniel whistle Ferrando's

bass aria, " Vuelta Zingara," at the beginning of " Il Trov-atore." It astonished her.

"Why, you whistle that just as it is written," she said.

"Of course I do," he said, in a tremor of pleasure, being at last appreciated.

"Let me accompany you," she said.

How extraordinary were his feelings as he chirruped through that mazy aria, feeling the accompaniment beneath his thin performance. He had found his other half.

The girl laughed and laughed. It was the oddest thing she had ever seen. She begged a repetition. There were thousands of tunes before them—"The Monks and Their Convents," "The Wolf," "Why Do the Nations," "Ruddier Than a Cherry," "The Fair Land of Provence," the whole fourth scene of the fourth act of "The Huguenots."

The maid looked out the window. The sun was setting. They had put in an afternoon of it. It seemed but a moment to Daniel. They went below to dinner, and paused in the garden.

"I am glad I was hurt," he said.

"Let me pin a geranium leaf on your coat," she said.

"Put a violet with it, dear," the widow Holebroke suggested.

Was it not a beautiful city and a beautiful world ? Peace, blessed peace ! No more of war. The lake rippling out there. The odors of May fondly hovering over the lilacs of June. The white linen passing by insensible stages into the gleaming silver of the home-table. The gentle face of the Christian, thankful for life, for even poor health, for his sisters, for his mother, for Chicago.

Something was happening to Daniel.

Yes, something was happening to Daniel. It stole upon him cautiously, because young men of his type are not easily allured from the peace of single life.

He fell to asking how he could conform his whistle to the

conventions of society. He ended by concluding that the
same persons who shuddered at the music he made would be
satisfied if he were to whistle through a flute. He therefore
paid $60 for an instrument of this kind. One-third of it, or
one joint, was ivory. Then he strove to breathe all his
tunes into it. Why did hi heart grow so sad, even while a
great hope quickened within him?

"Never mind your flute. I'd rather hear you whistle.
It's *so* odd!" Mary Holebroke said. She looked at him with
her gray eye. It was quarried out of the same agate that
had made the eye of the great man of the Girard House.
Daniel looked deep into it, and felt that he had no power.

He did not like to seem odd, but there was no help for
him. Odd he seemed, and glad enough he was to be the especial object of that young gray-eyed lady's attention. So
he whistled and she modulated and whipped the piano as it
were her slave, and laughed and laughed. She had not
been so amused before.

And on Sunday Mary asked Daniel if he did not want to
go over to the Foster Mission on the narrow Jefferson street,
just below Polk. She had a class there. Did he wish
to go? The girl must have thought so. How swift the
hour went. How well Daniel understood those newsboys and
how little the good deacons knew of them! The tough little
pieces are raising Ned. "Look here, boys," cries the Deacon, "you ain't in no theayter!" That was too good. For
how stern that copper in McVicker's Theatre was, to be sure!
Yet the deacon's idea of a theatrical performance was some
sort of orgy, such as the gamins knew would not be tolerated
anywhere else save in a mission school.

So went the days until the winter season set in; and
though something had happened to Daniel, something of a
more tangible essence was to come. Late one wintry day the
fogs and smoke and dread of the winter's solstice had settled
well down into the South Side. On every hand the yellow

flicker of the gas-lights fought a losing day against the gloom
of it all.

Ding-ding went the gong in the engine house again, and
all knew there was a fire on the West Side, just over the
South Branch.

It was at the close of the working day in winter, near bridge
and tunnel, in a city where a fire was counted a spectacle that
none should miss, where the volunteer spirit was still in the
department, and where men loved to show the fire that was
in them. It was a blaze fifty feet wide by 150 feet long,
three stories high. This was the evening's drama as it
opened.

In that din which delighted them the firemen galloped
their engines into the adjacent streets, the hose was unreeled
in miles, and the ladders were set against the machine shop
that was on fire. The policemen took their places and ran a
rope around the corner. Over the Lake street bridge, nearest
the main channel; over the Randolph street bridge next;
through the Washington street tunnel next, and over the
Madison street bridge next, the home-goers hurried across
the South Branch, and debouched into the streets that were
fronted by the doomed structure. Twenty-five thousand people were gazing at the fire in as many minutes after the engines had stopped at the fire-plugs.

"Kape back, d'yer moind!" yelled the police.

"Hurry up there, Bill!" bellowed the long silver trumpets
of the marshals. A great, hoarse voice—something entirely
indistinguishable, yet terrifying—a bull-like roar, yet husky,
nigh to speechlessness. "Hurry up there, Bill!"—like the
"deep-bellowing caves of the ocean," caves with faulty vocal
chords, truly a cavernous speech. A voice that made the
crowd fall back as no policeman's billy could do. "Hurry,
up there, Bill!"—it rolled away, like the echo of cannon at
sunrise.

"How pretty the wires look!" exclaimed the host, as the

blaze burst through the windows and rested on the telegraph. The rain and fog had frozen on the wires, and they shone white as snow for blocks away.

As the twenty-five thousand faces were lit up all the cries of Milton's demons seemed to come from the lips of the exasperated firemen. The "Hurry-up-there-Bills!" grew into an orgy. The rites became an offering to Baal. "Toot-toot," asked the engines. "Chuffy-chuffy-chuffy," they settled to their monotonous work as the building was seen to be badly off.

And now the horns grow hoarser and the excitement of the multitude spreads to its uttermost limits, a quarter of a mile away.

"My God!" cries a spectator, "they've no right to send men up there! I know that roof. The whole thing is a rattle-trap."

The longest ladder is to be put against the building. It will barely touch the roof. The wires are in the way.

"Cut them wires!" bellows the fog-horn voice through the trumpet.

A man climbs up the nearest pole.

Just then the ladder is let under the wires and raised again. It rests against the side of the building.

"On my soul, I believe I saw that wall shake!" cries the spectator.

"I did, too!" adds another.

"Hurry up there, Dan!" bellows the fog-horn. Daniel Trentworthy seizes the pipe, and three other firemen catch hold on the hose. They are already on the ladder.

"Don't go on that roof!" yell the crowd, now thoroughly of a belief that the building is rotten.

Up the ladder the men toil. The hose is very heavy.

"Come down! Keep off that roof! The wall's shaking!" echo the thousands of throats.

"Oi'll shmash yer face, wid yer!" cries a policeman to a

loud-voiced warner. The officer has seen crowds scared before.

But farther back than the officer could see the wave of warning rolled onward toward the ladder.

"You'll get killed if you go up there! Let the trap burn! Good riddance of bad rubbish!"

"Hurry up there, Dan! Hurry up there, Bill!" resounded the deepest of all the fog-horns.

The little group grasped the parapet. They tugged at the pipe and the hose. They hooked it to the coping. They sprang lightly to the roof.

The vast crowd yeasted and writhed within itself. The cheer surged from block to block. Ah! but a fireman is a brave man—a Chicago fireman!

The man on the pole has not cut the wires. He yells that the boys want an ax. Up goes the ax, and is handed over the parapet. Then the four can no longer be seen. Perhaps there is the sound of an axman chopping. One, two, three. It may be an ax. Still the general noise is all-pervading.

"Oh, they do be pitting a hole t'rough th' roof. An' they be afther havin' it oot now," explained the officer.

Yes; one, two, three. That is the ax. One, two, three! What is that?

"Oh!" breathe the twenty-five thousand, as if it were their last gasp.

For, after the third blow, there is a sound as of wind among pines; a whirring as of sightless couriers of the air. There is a deep red gleam in the home of Orion, who is riding on high over that roof. There is truly an opening in the roof, but it must be a large one. Then there comes a crash that strikes a heavy blow on the walls of every throbbing heart. The roof has gone down. The conflagration leaps to Orion, and Orion, smiting it with his sword, beats it back into its four walls. A million sparks loiter in the skies and

cluster into baleful constellations. Let no babe enter the
world under their empire.

Is it not awful that these _our lads should thus be fed to
Moloch? Yes, it is awful. It spoils the supper of many a
Chicagoan who but a moment ago was impatient to reach
his home. Four brave men have gone down into a hell of
flame.

"Well, the wall stood, after all," says one of the crowd.
"I thought I saw it shake. I guess I was mistaken."

"Yis, yez was mistook," says the officer.

And what is that on the parapet? It is a man's arm!

"Save him! Save him!" goes up on every hand.

"Hurry up there, Bill'" rumbles the fog-horn. Two men
start up the ladder.

It is Daniel Trentworthy up there. He has clung to the
hose and pulled himself to the coping. He crawls on the
stones and lies on his face at full length. He gathers
strength and peers down the outside. He is not far from the
ladder.

"Hurry up there, Bill!" bellows the trumpet.

"Go down! Go down!" Daniel cries to his rescuers.
"You shake the wall. I can come down."

But firemen obey orders.

"*Hurry up there, Bill!*" resounds the deep horn.

It is too late. The ladder's weight has been the last
straw. There is a pendulous movement. The men on the
ladder feel it, and drop at once to the ground.

The wall moves outward as the pressure from the ladder
lessens, and then, as the beams on the inside assert their
weight, the movement begins the other way.

Daniel Trentworthy is on his knees. He is on his feet.
He stands on the coping, a black silhouette clearly limned
upon a background of red flame. It is Blondin, walking before the molten cataract, as the father of Daniel Trentworthy
had done. One moment more the wall will be far off its

3

center, sucked in by the flames. The ladder is there, but it cannot avail.

The young man tarries until the crowd nearly faints with excitement. They ought to wait if he can. And it is necessary to his nature that he should commend his soul to God.

The wall is slowly on its way inward—perhaps a foot, perhaps eighteen inches. Now its motion accelerates.

" He waits too long ! He can't jump now !" they cry.

He bends his knees. He gives a great spring. He is in the air. The wall is at forty-five degrees far behind him.

" The wires ! The wires !" resounds backward to Halsted street.

There are three cross-trees on the tall poles. Each cross-tree or spar carries ten telegraph wires. The climber has clipped only three or four in all.

The three tiers of wires gleam white in the air. Even before the flying man reaches them the ice has melted and they disappear from sight. His arms project over the upper plane of wires. His body curls under as a snake's would, so anxious is the imperiled life to save itself. The three nearest and topmost wires snap under the shock, and the body lies for a moment on the second plane. But the shock has also dazed Daniel. His is only a dumb body, without thought. He has dropped through to the last tier before his struggling, clutching arms and legs feel the resistance of a wire.

But the momentum is out of his body. As he drops through to the under plane a hand seizes a wire. It holds him, but it cuts. The other hand seizes another wire. It cuts, for the blood can be seen in the vivid light. The arms might hold, but the body is afraid to trust them. The legs writhe upward, as if they were also hands, and finally one foot affects a lodgment. Then it slips, and the body swings full and fair toward the wall.

There is a cry of horror. It is an awful tableau. The wall

is down with a resounding blow on the earth, and a cloud of dust and smoke obscures the vision.

But the body has refused to let go, and the two wires have not broken. The hands pull upward and the teeth catch the wire.

" He'll cut his t'roat, sure ! " observes the officer, who has seen many horrid sights.

The ice rattles in showers from Canal to Clinton, to Jefferson, to Desplaines, to Union, to Halsted. The wires groan and chant their well-practiced requiem. The poles sway like masts of "some tall admiral." Twenty-five thousand people grow stony-eyed and sick with terror.

"HURRY UP THERE, BILL !" roar all the fog-horns, as though Jericho's walls had toppled.

----

## CHAPTER V.

### SOME NEWS FOR DANIEL.

IN an incredibly short time a long wagon had rushed under the wires, and a ladder standing straight up was shot, by lengthening apparatus, to the height of the pole. Like a cat a man ran up the swaying ladder, and the crowd, fearing that the machine would fall over, surged backward upon itself. Another climber followed closely after the first rescuer, and as they cried to Daniel a hush went across the sea of faces. In a second that hush swept from Canal to Halsted street, five blocks.

" Hang on, Dan, me boy ! We're here ! " they said.

The crowd heard it far away. But Daniel was only a dumb body, struggling like a wild beast in a snare. The commotion in the wires was something to frighten a stout heart. The athletic body curved and writhed, and sought

some immovable thing.   As the climber touched Daniel he
was aroused to another paroxysm of effort.

The crowd broke forth again: "He'll fall yet!  Get a
rope !"

"Hurry up there, Bill !" bellowed the trumpet.

And, surely enough, up the ladder went another fireman
with a rope.   There was a great noose in it.   As ineffectual
efforts were made to throw the rope upward and around the
flying limbs of the wretched man, the ladder would wave
far from a perpendicular.   The crowd rushed forward and
scrambled on the great wagon to give the contrivance a
steadier base.

At last a cheer rolled in from the outlying ranks.  They
had seen the noose rise up around Daniel and inclose his
body.  He was safe.  Hurrah! hurrah!  The dead were
forgotten in the joy for the living.  But Daniel, as he felt
the rope, supposed it to be only the beginning of the end—
some greater despair that had fastened on him.  Not only
did he struggle to reach some solid support, but he frantically sought to detach the rope.

" Steady, boys !   He's crazy as a loon.  We must go slow
or he'll throw us off."

Daniel hung by the two wires nearest the fire.  His body
ngled.  The men pulled the rope gently, and he, letting
go with one hand to relieve the pain, would clutch a wire
nearer to the ladder.

" Now, when he takes the next wire, catch his hand.  Give
me a firm hold on your belt, my lad.  And you, Jerry, hold
fast to me.  Don't be afraid of the ladder.  It can't go past
the wires."

Thus repared, they once more tightened the rope.  Toward them, with blood-shot, protruding eyes and bleeding
face, came poor Daniel.  He reached a torn hand forward,
with the pitiful fear and doubt of a man who hoped for nothing.  He felt a warm and soft grasp.  Quick as lightning

the other hand clutched for the same strong and friendly arm
and the top man was nearly wrenched from the ladder.

The crowd expected all four men to come down in a mass.
The ladder swung away from the wire; it creaked and turned
on the pole of its axis.

But those brave men had gone up that ladder to save Daniel. They fastened upon him like leeches. "Let him touch
the ladder, boys!" one of them said. And thus Daniel was
quieted into insensibility. Down they came. A stretcher
was at the wagon.

"This is my number," said Harmon Holebroke. "Take
him to my house, 257 South Clinton street."

The nearest of the crowd strove to look at the young man
who had slipped through death's door. Many of them
fainted.

Never had Chicago mourned as she mourned for the loss
of her three firemen. Could money have restored them,
millions would have been poured out. There came a funeral,
the greatest that had coursed the streets since the pageant
of Abraham Lincoln. The police in platoons, the Mayor,
the old settlers, the fire engines draped, the catafalque, the
knights, companions, brethren, and members of every association in the city, and interminable lines of citizens in carriages and on foot. Few men are so remembered. Many
men would die for such a memorial. The great bell tolled
all day long, a truly solemn performance, and one that gave
thought even to the unthinking.

Then after the trappings and the suits of woe there
came the demand, loud and angry, for a scapegoat. The
Board was to investigate the matter. Who was to blame?

Now a political investigation is a bird of a queer feather.
Looking at it as we do, one would not think that Daniel
Trentworthy was to be blamed for the order of his superior
or the rottenness of that roof, yet if we consider that Daniel
was already a marked man, who had bidden defiance to the

"inflooence" of De Koven street, we shall discover that he was
seriously compromised.    Why was he not killed?   So the
relatives of the three other victims asked.   Politically, it was
clear that Daniel promised to furnish an acceptable scapegoat.   The Board erased his name from the rolls, De Koven
street gave its unanimous approval, and the wonderful city,
grumbling a little, settled back to await the next matter of
importance, which was to be the opening of the Pacific railways.

For weeks Daniel Trentworthy could not sleep.   To drop
into a doze of exhaustion was to seize a small wire and dan-
gle fifty feet above the ground.   To close his eyes was to
see the horrid pit of flame and stagger in the heat that leaped
toward him out of the red depths.   He had saved himself
by his nerve, and now, the doctors said, he must suffer the
consequences.

How grand a character is that mother in Israel who pays
little attention to the social "duties" of women, being compelled to visit the sick and lay out the dead!   How often
we say : "I would have been over to your house, but that I
had an important engagement."   Harriet Holebroke, Harmon's mother, had no important engagements.   She went to
no dinner parties.   She spent no evenings in the civilities
of neighborhood life.   But if she heard a neighbor were
ill, she put on her bonnet and went.   Even in summer, when
her strawberries needed attention sorely, when the sparrows
were counting her cherries, she put on her bonnet and went.
If the doctor could not stop the paroxysms, she, with her
great bag of hops, might do it.   Life is a stern thing.   She
knew it.   Yet she never said it.

Into her hands had Daniel fallen.   It was very well for
him.   She went about curing him in her methodical manner.
"Humph!" she said dryly, "he will get well."

And finally, Daniel turned on his couch.  Mary Holebroke
sat at the window.

"Ah!" thought Daniel, "my angel is with me. I felt her presence when I was on the wall. She has nursed me. 'Oh! woman, in our hours of ease!'"

"You are better, aren't you, Daniel?" she said, looking at him with her gray eyes.

"I should have been better before had I known you were here," he said, his face beaming with a smile.

The maid's countenance grew cold. She looked out of the window. She was uneasy. "Oh, what is that in the garden?" she exclaimed, and ran to see.

Poor Daniel! He tried to gather his thoughts. Was not this Mary Holebroke, who had played for him? Were they not lovers? Had she not nursed him? Ah! now he had it. Alas! what a sick man he must have been! He had never whispered a word of his love for the gray-eyed maid. He had blundered. He tried to leap from the bed and look in the garden. He was so lonesome he could not bear her absence. But the exertion showed him his weakness. He fell back with a moan, and Mrs. Holebroke, entering, protested firmly that he must lie still, and that Mary must keep out of the sick-room.

Daniel wondered at that, too. "Surely she has aided in nursing me!" he thought. "Will she ever speak to me again? What a strange fate drove me to open my eyes, feeling that I was in Paradise! What a perverse thing is the heart! It was awake, and the mind was still asleep. A truant heart—a truant heart! I've lost her!" he wailed. "I've lost her!"

He was too weak to bear the excitement of the moment. His forehead broke out in sweat, and he fell into a sleep.

"Mary," said Mrs. Holebroke, "I told you not to disturb Daniel."

"Yes, mamma. I sat quietly at the window. He awoke and spoke to me. I saw his mind was wandering, and ran out as fast as I could."

"Mary," said the mother, "Daniel Trentworthy is a good young man. He has acted as if he cared for you. Do not let him believe you return his feelings, unless you are quite sure about it. You are exactly like your aunt, Mary, and she never married, although she had dozens of opportunities."

"Oh! I shall marry," said Mary, tossing her head. Young ladies consider that affair entirely their own.

"Well, I do not want to see you trifling with Daniel. You hear what I say, do you not?"

"There comes the ice-man. Yes we want ice all summer. Sixty cents a week! Dear me, it was only forty last year. Mamma, forty cents a week!"

Mother and daughter completely misunderstood each other. The daughter rebelled at her mother's methods, economies and ideas of duty.

And Daniel Trentworthy, starting from another short sleep, wherein he had fought against letting the rescuers take him from the wires, found his forehead getting cold and sweaty and his heart thumping until it hurt him, because he remembered how greatly he had erred in supposing that he and Mary had pledged their love for each other.

"She will not forgive me. She thought I took too much for granted. I do not blame her. How could I blame her for anything? I am so glad I was saved. And yet, why was I not killed and the boys with families spared?"

Thus his emotions swayed. He was glad, and now he was sorry. It all depended on Mary.

"She will not forgive me!" the sick man moaned.

The piano poured a gay flood of notes over the house. Daniel was in heaven again.

"M'appari"—"It was a dream." The chords came to him as a message of peace. How often had he whistled the air. He thought of his flute. "I will be a virtuoso yet," he cried. "M'appari! She loves me. I would not have escaped had she loved me not."

"Daniel," said Mrs. Holebroke, "you are not keeping still enough. I shall send for the doctor if your color does not go in a little while."

"I feel much better, Mrs. Holebroke," he said.

The piano ebbed away. It stopped. Mary, portfolio in hand, passed the door. She looked in.

"Good morning," said Daniel, because he dared to say nothing else.

"I am going to write a letter to Mercy. Shall I send her your love?"

"Mercy is a pretty name. Yes, send her my love."

And with that the maiden passed on. The piano had whispered her love for him. But that gray eye! Was it not cold?

Daniel was not so happy. He could only get peace when he thought of the music from "Martha." "Why did she play it? Why did she play all my pieces?" he asked. "Oh, the minx; she loves me. She loves me."

This enabled him to sleep. And sleep is good medicine for weak nerves.

The maid wrote, at her window:

"My Dear Sis: We are still in this prosy city, on this dusty Clinton street, and very little has happened since my last. Daniel Trentworthy, Harmon's friend, is still in bed all the time, and I wish he would get well. You know I told you how we 'played duets' together before he was hurt. It was odd, wasn't it? I couldn't get over it. And he never tired, it seemed to me. Harmon teased me about him until I almost dreaded the sight of him.

"Well, of course, when they brought him home so nearly dead, that was an end of the whistling. And what do you think he had done, just before the fire? Why, to be sure, h. goes and buys a costly flute, on purpose to play with me. You know that boy who drove us wild at Lima, with practicing the flute? That, I thought, was the worst! Since he's

been sick, laws! mother doesn't think there's anybody else
in the house. It used to be Harmon; now it's Daniel this,
and Daniel that. 'You'll wake Daniel!' or 'Wouldn't
Daniel like some of that?'

"He has an honest way about him that I kind o' like.
He's a queer old fellow. Sometimes, when he is so tender
and thankful to me I feel quite pleased. But my! Merce,
you needn't fear that I shall lose my head, even if he does
lose his. He is nothing but a poor young man. Of course,
he's smart. I never saw so smart a fellow. But what is
he? A fireman. Dear me! that was a dreadful escape he
had! And, it seems, he has lost his place on the force.
What he'll do next must be determined. But you know
Harmon. He'd keep the whole fire department if it got out
of a place. Dear me! you and mother and Harm are all too
good for me!

"You know I am not out of high school yet. I haven't
finished flirting with the car conductors on West Madison
street. Some of them are too sweet for any single thing.
There is one who wears a blue coat and has a mustache. I
wish our poor, sick Daniel had that mustache! There I go
again! As I said, I am not yet out of school. And my
heart is set on the tour in Europe. I want a piano lesson
in Europe. I don't care if it lasts only half an hour. A
half hour with Liszt or Von Bülow! I think I could make
it worth something; don't you?

"How am I to get it! Merce, I'm going to marry for it,
as sure as you're born. If Daniel had money—there, you
see! You'll be sure Daniel will get me. But he will do no
such thing, Sister Merce! And I will tell you why. Because
I can carry my eggs to a better market. Daniel is all very
well. I think he aids me with my music. I declare, not
one person in fifty but likes 'Le Sabre de Mon Père' better
than the 'Traumerei!' It's different with Daniel. I am
quite sure I love him when I hear him praising good music.

His tastes are good. He was not always a fireman, Sis.

"And now I *am* going to tell you something that I ought to have written before—so you will say. Who do you suppose is taking me out driving every time he can get a chance? Who took me to see Davenport and Wallack act? Who took me to hear Piccolomini sing? Bouquet, book for the opera, oysters, carriage. Is it not nice? I took the flowers to school next day. The girls were just wild. 'Well, never mind,' you say, 'but who was it?' Who was it? Whom do you think? Why, Alderman Errington, the handsomest, dashingest bachelor on the West Side. The girls adore him. They say he's as rich as a Turk.

"Do I like him? I like him as well as he likes me. When he gets warmer I'll thaw out, too. He is too conceited for any use outside of a circus. He just thinks if he smiles and sends around a note and stops in front of your house with his carriage that the girl ought to be too happy. He asks *all* the girls—all who have any style. He sent me an invitation to go to see the Union Pacific parade. I answered that I must be excused, as we had illness at home. Then three of us girls went down on Wabash avenue and stood three hours, and I was mortally afraid he might come along. That brought him around the next night.

"'Who is ill?' he asked.

"'Daniel Trentworthy,'" said I, innocently, as though he ought to know.

"'Oh yes,' he said. 'I did not know you thought so much of him.'

"'Yes,' I said, 'Daniel is Harmon's best friend. We knew him before he came here.'

"'You did?' said Mr. Alderman, fidgeting.

"'Oh, yes,' I replied. 'Daniel is no new acquaintance. Is it not nice, Mr. Errington, to have old friends—friends of years?'

"'Yes, yes;' he said, 'but you do not mean to say that

you stay in all the time on account of Trentworthy?'

"'Oh, no, indeed. But there was no school the day of the celebration, and I wanted to relieve mother that day?'

"'That's right!' he said. 'But he looked relieved. He's about thirty-five years old, and I'm seventeen. Twice seventeen is thirty-four. Daniel can whistle 'Di Quella Pira,' and Errington came near going to sleep when Brignoli sang it the other night at the opera house. But my new beau could take me to Europe and Daniel would have to whistle for it. The girls all envy me, and the old maids are just green, they are so mad. Mother will not let me go but one night a week. Isn't that like her? He goes three or four nights. He told me he went alone twice, but I didn't believe him.

"Now, Merce, I've told you all. Don't lecture me. It's no use. If you pity Daniel, come home and marry him. Mother says he oughtn't to think of marrying for ten years yet, and you know you think that whatever mother doesn't know can't be picked up at Holyoke or Vassar.

"Good-by, and don't come home till I get my fish landed —that's a good sis. You are too old-maidish for most men, but who can tell but what, with your good looks, you might take my lord's fancy and cut me out completely? No, you had better take Daniel.

"Write me a long letter like this, I am so lonesome without you that I am afraid you will take my nonsense to heart. Your sister,

MARY."

She addressed her letter, closed her portfolio, started from the room, and stopped at Daniel's door. His face lighted up once more. He was so glad she had come.

"What will you do when you get well, Mr. Trentworthy?" she asked—she seemed to say it with her cold, gray eyes.

"I will go back to the Long John engine house," said Daniel.

"Didn't you know they had put you off the force?" and her eyes grew larger.

"Is that so?" said Daniel, and he fell backward off the parapet, just as he had meant to leap for the wires.

---

## CHAPTER VI.

### "GOOD-BY, DANIEL."

It is a serious thing to jump from the parapet of a side wall. It is a terrible thing to save one's self by the teeth among a hundred treacherous wires that snap and cut and wriggle as if they were snakes with poisoned fangs. It is a pitiable thing to lie weak and distracted on a sick-bed, just alive and little more. It is a cruel thing to see one's beloved willing to stay away from the bedside of the stricken one. It is a bitter thing to be told that Aldermanic influences have taken advantage of a sick man's helplessness to oust him from a place he had filled with bravery and fidelity. And how barbaric is that fate which puts the word of misfortune into the mouth of the angel for whom the sick man would willingly once more stand on the wall and confront the leaping element!

"Something happened to him, mother. I know it," said the gentle Harmon. "He was improving. Now he looks bad again. Did any one call?"

"No," said the mother. "He saw Mary for a moment. I heard them speaking casually. There was no protracted conversation."

"Daniel thinks too much of Mary," said Harmon.

"Yes, Daniel is foolish, like all honest young men," said

the mother. " I declare I feel as if the scapegraces were the
only young fellows who know how to win the graces of a girl.
Mary is too young to think of anything serious for five
years."

" She is seventeen, isn't she ? "

" Yes."

" You married when you were fifteen, I've heard you say."

" Harmon, that was years ago, in York State. My daughters shall never do it."

" No, I guess they will never marry that early, mother."

They walked toward Daniel's room.

" Yes, Doctor," Daniel said, as he tossed about. " I'll
have to leave college. I would go to Chicago, but they have
put me out of the department there. An Alderman named
Errington has pursued me relentlessly to oblige a con-
stituent. No, I can't go to Chicago."

" How does he know he's off the force ? " asked the son.

" That I don't know, Harmon."

" Who saw him to-day ? "

" Mary, you and I."

" You didn't tell him, did you ? "

" No, of course not. I was leaving that for you."

" Then Mary told him. Mother, Mary is the coldest-blood-
ed girl I ever met, if she *is* my sister."

" Mary is a queer child, my son. But she is a great deal
to us."

" Yes, yes, mother. Don't worry for her. Wasn't she
out with Errington lately ? "

" Yes."

" Well, that accounts for  the milk in the cocoanut.
Mother, I'm sorry to see that man come in our house."

" Daniel, we must be civil."

" Well, you know Mary. She is too ambitious. She has
absurd notions. She is bright, and plays well. They puff
her at the church concerts until she loses her head. She

goes round selling tickets, and in that way gets acquainted with many people whom she ought never to know. Errington bought fifty tickets to the last concert."

"Yes."

"Now, he had no use for those tickets. He has no friends in the congregation. He merely did it to please Mary. The concert, I think, profits at her expense. I don't like the man. I don't believe he is sincere, and he has misused that poor boy to oblige the crowd over there on Jefferson street. I am going to talk to Mary."

"I wish you would not, my son. She does not take advice well."

"Indeed, I do not," said the gray-eyed maid, who had entered rather noiselessly.

"Mary," said Harmon, "between you and Errington you have pretty nearly killed that poor boy in there."

"Now, Harmon, don't be silly. Mr. Errington is a gentleman, and I hope you will let him see we also have some manners."

A high school miss hisses the word gentleman. She uses it very often, and very often she has little use for a man who has earned the title, even without great emphasis.

"Mary, where do you pick up these ward politicians? I never see you at the primaries."

"Be kind enough to keep your insults, Mr. Harmon Holebroke. Mr. Errington is coming to take me to the new South Park this very afternoon."

"Harmon, is that you?" asked Daniel.

The mother, son and daughter started, almost guiltily.

"Why, yes, God bless you, Dan! I'm so glad to see you in your right mind. I'm so glad."

"Harmon, they have put me out."

"Never mind that, Dan. I have another place for you as soon as you are well. But you're a strange patient. This morning, they say you are all right. A half hour ago your mind was wandering. Now you are as straight as a string again."

The soft chords of Chopin's Moonlight sonata began to pervade that humble home. They all liked Mary's playing. They were all proud of her. She had a strange magnetism that attracted young and old alike. In a new country talent brings a big price.

"Yes, I feel very much better."

"She plays for me," he thought.

"I ought to play this more," she thought. "I will, when Daniel gets out of the house.

"Harmon, when I get well, I feel like going over on De-Koven street and whaling two men, just to let off steam."

"Oh! pshaw, Dan. I'm glad you're out of the engine-house. You would have been a bully in a year."

"That man whom the printers call 'Hogmouth,' and his Alderman, a flashy politician named Errington—you know him. Those are the two men who have been after me ever since I ran against the first of them. Harmon, does the best man always get the worst of it in Chicago ?"

"No, Daniel."

"Well, do you think that a ward-heeler like Errington ought to triumph over a decent fellow like me ? Do you think that I ought to stand it ? Do you believe my father ever stood such a thing ?"

The door-bell rang.

"Miss Mary, it's Mr. Errington, with his carriage," yelled the hired girl.

The Moonlight sonata ceased.

Daniel's eyes were again protruding from his head. He reached forward and closed his torn hand with a fearful grip on Harmon's shoulder.

"Say, Harmon," he swallowed, "that girl said it was Errington."

"Yes, Daniel, that was what she said,"

"And she called Mary."

There was nothing to deny.

"Are you ready? Mr. Errington wants to know. He can't come in and leave the horses," the girl screamed, so that the girls in the next house might not by any chance miss the fine spectacle.

"Tell him I will be there in a minute," said a low voice. But Daniel could have heard it had she whispered.

"It is true, isn't it, Harmon?. It is Errington himself, and he has come to take Mary out riding. Did I deserve this?"

"No, God bless you!" Harmon could not talk. It seemed to him that if Daniel knew Mary better he would not suffer. But Harmon could not say this of his own sister.

The sick man fell back on his pillow. His temples beat like the drums in war-times. It was a trial to live—simply to live.

A fresh and joyous face appeared at the door, a jaunty spring hat, a glove button in mouth, a glove that would not button. "Thou knowest my favorite ward, Hal. Here stood I." That is the favorite ward of a maiden who has something to say. She works as though she were defeated, and talks as though it were "on the side"—a secondary thing.

A moment before, the sick man had lain exhausted on his pillow, and Harmon had cast his eye toward the bottle of restorative. Now Daniel's eye brightened. It was the picture of the being he loved. He loved her, though she loved him not. Yes, he loved her. There was none like her. Had he not scanned all the women in Chicago week after week? She was not only young and beautiful; she was innocent and good. She was his, because he loved her. His eyes gathered upon her as a dog looks at the master who has returned from a long journey. He had forgotten the man out in front.

A moment before he had believed her perfidious. Now

4

she was an angel. Had she been a fury, he would still have
been her slave. A moment before he had done with her.
Now he strove to detain her, if only for a moment. She had
a right to ride if Errington chose to take her. He could
not have suspected Daniel's affection. Yet he could, for all
men must love her. Had not Daniel pitied all the married
men he saw because they could not even hope to have his
Mary? And was he not, even now, better off than any
married man?

"Good-by, Daniel," she said. "I'm going riding with a
friend."

He must conceal his feelings. Jealousy would destroy his
hopes. He smiled his approval, and the beads of perspiration
from weakness stood on his white forehead.

"Will you go riding with me?" he said. "After I get
stronger, I mean."

"Of course I will," she smiled.

He was again happy. But she saw it.

"I would go riding with anybody who had a nice turnout,"
she said, demurely.

There was a rattle of light wheels, and Harmon slipped
out of the chamber. The coverlet began rolling forward on
Daniel, the trumpets began their harsh commands, the wires
swayed toward the flames, the tunnel loomed up far ahead
of him, and the man with the wide jaw, and with Mary's
calm, gray eye fastened the boy's attention on a great badge,
and led him off to the Girard House, where the smell of garlic
acquainted him with a new horror of city life.

That is a fever. Great would be the physician who should
be able to diagnose the suffering of his patient and stop that
in-rolling from the windows and toward the pillow.

Thus went the afternoon. At last a strain of music stole
up the stairs. It was a tarantelle, fanciful, odd, like the gray-
eyed maid. The coverlet began to roll back where it belonged; the trees of Cambridge began to send out their per-

fume ; the white-haired poet came by, and the children ran to be kissed.

Mary was home and Daniel slept well.

---

## CHAPTER VII.

### IN THE TOILS OF LOVE.

A YOUNG man, without father, mother, brother or sister, lives for himself until he falls in love. His first impressions of the grand passion are agreeable.

When Mary Holebroke pinned the sprig of green on Daniel's coat that calm afternoon the young man had gone back to the engine house with the feeling that he had something worth keeping. He was inclined to boast that he had a girl—a best girl, as the saying went. He felt that in many ways it would add to the enjoyments of life to take her on his arm and challenge, as it were, some one to make faces at her or in any way to reflect discreditably on her looks. These thoughts took more definite shape the very next time he whistled at her piano. She had been a little late, had been what she called *distrait*—all high school girls delight in being *distrait*, or calling it that. She had told him she intended to go to Europe, and had given him about the year—say 1870 or 1871— that would suit her best. Altogether, Daniel had been scared. He went back to the engine house, and when the boys alluded to " his girl," turned the subject as adroitly as he could. The feeling was coming on him that the maiden had a mind of her own, and would undoubtedly exercise it with regard to the man she might honor. He knew her because he lived at her mother's. The advantages he enjoyed grew out of this chance alone.

A young man in a great city, without family, approaches the natural state of his species. Daniel gazed on the demure Mary Holebroke and felt that the proper thing to do would be to carry her off. It seemed to him that it was unfair to place him in the predicament of necessarily pleasing her ladyship. To abduct her and ride in triumph back to his own tribe would be a brave act, and would surely win her love. What odds, though, as to her love? He would love her.

But this civilization to which mankind had attained, clothed the gray-eyed maid with powers that were to startle poor Daniel as he came to plead before her august tribunal. From the moment that he bought the $60 flute my lady eyed him with a peculiar set of her head. It was not hostile. It was possessive. Yes, she would play—if Daniel wanted it. The queen was graciously pleased. She played, and Daniel whistled.

One day he passed the corridor of the Sherman House, then the largest hotel in the West. A great crowd stood in a circle. In the center was the puss of the office. A little mouse had fallen in her clutches. She lay on her side, and dosed in a clever, false fashion. The mouse rose, peered at his horrible captor, and sprang away. The hind claw moved an inch, the great forepaw gave him a blow that stunned him, and the cat, rising, bristled with furious feelings. Then she calmed herself, purred, petted the mouse, and again turned her attention completely away from her victim. He did not move, and the disappointed cat gently urged him. He gave another spring, and the tiger leaped out of the captor at every hair. The crowd yelled with laughter. The cat again dozed.

"Oh! she's asleep!" said one.

"Yes, it's a good time for his nobs to run away," suggested another.

Daniel went home. He opened the piano. He found the aria in the book. Mary came in. He was glad.

"I do not feel like playing to-day," she said.

Daniel's heart throbbed in apprehension. His pride came up strong and mighty. He went to the engine house. He ran a block or two on the way. But when he stopped, the captor had him safe.

"I am a miserable mouse," he said.

That is love. It differs as an emotion from an inexperienced young man's idea of it. It is nature, despotic nature, lashing him to the destinies of life.

This was what had been happening to Daniel all through the fall and winter of 1868. His experience at the corner of Washington and Canal streets had come upon him just as he was entering the cat-and-mouse stage of love for Mary Holebroke. She had him. She knew she had him. She had begun to take an interest in the struggles which he would make to get away from her.

For the first thing a young man does when he is in love is to try to get out of it.

The illness of Daniel had come and had greatly diminished Mary's interest in him. She had her music and her school, and the two engaged her whole attention. Experiments with her heart were wholly intellectual. Her heart did not yet exist. She was living with a heart which she had borrowed from books. Perhaps that, also, was the way Daniel had stumbled into love with her. Had he known that love was a strong coil of inert force that would suddenly leap with power within him he would not have touched its spring so jauntily. He would not have gone to the engine house and bragged that he "had Harm. Holebroke's sister dead to rights."

And when Daniel had regained his hold on life, and turned to the gray-eyed maid at the window, and forgotten that they were not yet pledged lovers—then she had been as unpleasantly recalled to the book flirtation that she had carried on with Daniel. She had at times been very sweet with him, merely to draw him out. The eagerness with which he met her gracious moods angered her. Mr. Errington, with his invitation to the opera, had come on the scene. The girl's ambition had been whetted. The sight of Daniel's weak face, breathing its devotion, frightened her. She had run away.

Now, Daniel was well, and at work. Harmon and many other printers had organized the Chicago Printers' Co-operative Association, with 1,000 shares at $25 a share. No one could own over a limited amount of the stock. In this way $11,000 in money had been raised by subscription and a mortgage of $2,500 given. The company secured the printing of the city directory. Daniel began as a canvasser of names. He ended as a proof-reader and indexer. He was now in receipt of a good salary, and he had better hours. He was at less disadvantage as to Mary.

As that young lady grew capricious, Mrs. Holebroke became more kind. She liked Daniel, and Harmon Holebroke, who had never loved, marveled that Daniel did not regain his handsome form and color. So marveling he would try to engage Daniel's interest in the great co-operative scheme which was to revolutionize the labor system.

There was to be another concert. The young lady next door and Mary were to play the overture to "Tannhauser" as a duet on the piano. Morning, noon and night, the piano would go. The girl loved to practice while Daniel was at table, and eat after he had gone. This punishment would teach him a thing or two.

The young man would go away in wrath. He was a fool. He would show that snip of a girl that he had something in him. He stayed down town to his supper.

At breakfast sat Miss Mary, bright and smiling:

"Oh ! Daniel, we missed you so last evening."

"Yes, Daniel," Mrs. Holebroke would say.

"We are very busy with the directory," he would remark, gloomily.

Then he would hurry through his meal and spurn that gray-eyed siren. But he would not stay away at supper-time. Neither would she. Her eyes would wreath with smiles, and his heart, giving one or two great struggles, would escape the chains he had put on it and leap toward her eyes.

She would wait on Daniel in a thousand little ways—so he thought. The supper was good. It was nectar and ambrosia, poured by the fairest of the dwellers on Olympus.

Then as the happiness neared its fatal maximum, the maid:

"Oh! Daniel, aren't you coming to our concert! The tickets are only 50 cents."

"Certainly."

"Oh! we girls are just selling oceans of tickets. Mr. Errington took fifty of me again."

The little mouse had regained its feet. It had dragged itself to the utmost reach of the velvet paw. It was time that the blow came and came swiftly.

Daniel looked up as if he had been shot.

"I will take fifty," he said dryly. "Do you want the money now?"

"Oh no! Isn't that perfectly lovely? just think, mamma, I have sold 113 tickets, myself alone."

"Yes, I suppose so," said the mother, as dryly as Daniel had spoken.

As for him, he could eat no more. His cheeks flamed inside and looked white without. He found that the supper was but half through, and that the only thing he could do would be to sip water. Cold water he could retain on his palate. It felt cooling. He would like to plunge into the lake, and drown his doubts.

What an evil, indigestible lump one has in the throat when some other man has one's best girl!

At the earliest opportunity Daniel rose. Could he not stay and go over to the rehearsal? Mr. Errington and lots of other young gentlemen would be there. A girl delights in calling an undoubted bachelor a young gentleman.

No, Daniel said; the directory would need his time.

He went to his room before taking the street car.

"Mary," said Harmon, "I think you are too selfish to belong to our family."

"Why?" asked the simple maid in astonishment.

"Does it strike you that Daniel ought to take fifty tickets to your concert?"

"He ought to if he wants to—if he's silly enough."

"Let him do it," observed Mrs. Holebroke. "It's too late now."

A half-hour later Daniel entered the music store. The proprietor was glad to see him.

"We have the scores of six more operas," the worthy lover of art said, rubbing his hands in gleeful expectation.

But Daniel laid the flute on the counter. He opened the case and exposed the beautiful instrument.

"I paid you $60 for that," he said, "Have you another?"

"I have just ordered one."

"How much freight was there on this one?"

"Very little, I assure you."

"Then I can make it an object for you if you buy this back again."

The proprietor's face clouded.

"You had better keep it, Mr. Trentworthy."

"I have no use for it."

"But I fear I cannot buy it of you."

"Why, are you ashamed to own what the profit was?"

"Oh, no! Yet you could not afford to part with it."

"Did you make more than $35 on it?"

"Are you ashamed to own what the profit was?"   Page 56

"No."

"Will you give me $25 in cash, now?"

"Ye-yes."

"Let's have it," said Daniel, with a great feeling of relief. "I need the twenty-five."

---

## CHAPTER VIII.

### TWO LOVERS.

RALPH ERRINGTON'S real name was John Flint. The name had not caught his fancy, and as he did not tolerate things he disliked he dropped it.

He found Chicago a field for a smart young man not over-scrupulous. While less observant newcomers sought a boarding house on West Washington street or some cross thoroughfare thereabouts, Errington went down Halsted street. He started a beer garden near Twelfth and Jefferson. He easily became chairman of the ward delegation of his party. He obtained a place on the Board of Education. When a site for a schoolhouse was bought he managed to get enough options and commissions to clear several thousand dollars in the trade. Men who courted political favor asked him to spend their money. He spent it at his own place and made a fair profit.

Having carefully amassed $100,000 in two years, he went on the Board of Trade and bought 100,000 bushels of wheat. The next day he sold 100,000 bushels. He made a quarter of a cent, and paid an eighth to the broker—he made $250, and paid $125 to a broker who had pulled hard to get him on the Board of Education.

He thereupon announced that he had won $75,000 on the Big Board, and gave an "opening" at his saloon, where he dispensed $200 that a Congressional candidate had asked him to "place."

The "opening" was because he had sold out. That is, he had transferred the saloon business to a clerk. He was ambitious, and was going to become respectable. Easy to do—in Chicago.

He went to the Alderman and told that worthy he wanted the place. The Alderman protested, but accepted a seat in the State Legislature.

The papers printed the names of the ring in the Council, and put Errington's candidacy on the reform basis. He went in as a patriot who was "to stop the shameless scandals that had given our city the name of a modern Babylon." That is what the editors said—who knew nothing about it.

But that was not what Errington went in for.

He had learned enough about civic corruption in the Board of Education to warrant him in the belief that there was a plum worth picking in the Council.

In the Council there were thirty-six Aldermen. Nineteen would make a ring. Errington organized this inner body during the first fortnight after election.

The city press congratulated the electors on the overthrow of the conspiracy to rob the city, and the opening of the Pacific Railway. California pears were already on sale.

The leading corporations were promptly touched by Errington. Was there anything more they wanted? If so, how much was it worth to them? One little favor could be had for $20,000.

On the night of the day that the papers printed their last "ringing editorials" on the overthrow of the machine in politics, the following performance was undertaken at a committee-room in the City Hall:

The agent of the corporation stood at the door of a locked room, outside. An old woman brought a basket of California pears to the door. The agent relieved her of the basket, and knocked on the door. Errington, a large handkerchief in hand, opened the door. It proved to admit to an ante-room.

"Put down your basket," said Errington.

"Show me the closet," said the agent. "You said there was a closet."

Errington led the agent to a locked closet. He opened it, put the basket inside, locked the door, and said:

"Now I am ready."

"You are a suspicious fellow," said Errington.

"Yes, I've been here before."

Errington bound the agent's eyes with the handkerchief.

"What's that?" asked the agent, in surprise.

"Oh, that's a little cap the boys want you to put on, that's all."

The agent was absolutely blindfold.

"I don't believe I'm safe in doing this," said the agent. "How do I know there are nineteen of the boys in there? They can change around on me."

"You'll have to do it," said Errington.

"Well," said the agent, determinedly. "You tell those fellows to stand awful quiet. I must rely on my ears to make out that there are nineteen there. I want every mother's son to get his share."

"Come on," said Errington.

"You go on," commanded the agent.

Errington went to the door with the agent. The agent felt him as he passed in. Then the agent groped his way back to the closet. He opened the closet door and took out the basket. Under the California pears were twenty packages of paper. Each package contained a thousand dollars in $5 notes.

He groped for the door in the inner chamber. He rapped. Errington opened the door.

"Do you want to buy some California pears?" he said. "I am blind. Please do not cheat me."

"Come in," said Errington. "How much are they worth?"

"Fifteen cents apiece. They are the first ever sent across the continent. Please buy one."

"Here are your 15 cents."

"Reach down and take your pear," said the blind man.

"Try the next man on the committee," said the friend of the blind man.

"Fine California pears, 15 cents a piece. Reach down for the good ones. Where are the 15 cents? Thank you."

Around the room went the agent. Each man took out a package of paper, and the sharpest also took one of the biggest pears. Eighteen pair of aldermanic eyes fastened on each purchaser as he bought and took his pear.

As the agent completed the circuit of the committee-room, Errington opened the door and followed the fruit vendor out.

"Here, let me go down in that basket," he said.

The agent pulled the cap off his head. "That's a hot thing," he muttered.

"You need not have looked so soon," said Errington, as he put the twentieth package in the tail pocket of his long coat.

"What do you think we give up an extra thousand for, if it isn't to see you take it?"

"Well, I suppose you must see a little. Do you know those fellows are beefing terribly over that 15 cents? It's just like a corporation to strike them for the price of those pears."

"Blast their thieving stars!" cried the agent, "I was a fool or I would' have charged them a dollar. I could a-done it."

The old woman who had brought the basket was peeping through the keyhole, and saw Errington take the package. The old woman was the president of the corporation, with a shawl, a bonnet, and a calico skirt on. The agent and the president went home together.

The agent had attended the committee meeting on the

ordinance to give a corporation something for nothing for ninety-nine years. On account of the arguments of the agent thus made, the ordinance passed the Council that night, 19 to 17. The city press confined its congratulatory remarks to the opening of the Pacific Railways, and the presence in the Chicago market of the most luscious Bartlett pears that the midland palate had ever tasted.

Errington took the $2,000 and went to a real estate office.

" Fifty feet at $200 a foot are $10,000," said the agent. " He will take $2,000 down, balance one, two and three years. My commission ought to be something liberal."

" You'll get no commission at all."

" That is hard ! "

" Well, that is what you will get."

The real estate agent had had a hand in the school deals.

The finest homes were on Wabash avenue. The fathers strolled down its shady walks, asthmatic with satisfaction at the way things were going in Chicago. The town was booming.

" What's that ? " they cried, as they espied preparations for a building close to the street.

An accommodating man stood there to explain. Alderman Errington was going to erect the finest livery stable in America.

Everything in Chicago was to be the finest in America.

Now paterfamilias is as glad to have a livery stable on his street, next door, as political bosses are to get into jail. A committee of property-owners waited on Errington.

" How much do you want ? " they said. He showed them his prospect of profits. Ten thousand dollars extra would let him out whole.

The real estate transfers next day showed that Ralph Errington had sold to paterfamilias fifty feet on Wabash avenue for $20,500.

"I had to pay the agent the $500 as commission," he explained to paterfamilias.

It may thus be seen that Chicago was a fruitful field for Ralph Errington. He could afford fifty tickets for Mary Holebroke's concert.

He piled up another $100,000. It was his whim to buy buildings on leased ground. In this way he became "a great landlord"—great in proportion to his means. In the region of the South Side gas-house, on Wells street, and on the North Side, wherever he could buy a cheap frame building, he set up as landlord over a miserable tenantry. But it was practical. It increased his political influence. He meant to go to Congress.

Nibbling at the bait of a gray-eyed maid, who was not yet out of High School on the West Side, who lived at 257 Clinton street, a little south of Van Buren—nibbling at her hook was this formidable fish. And she was as likely to land him as he was to bite. He already took his little punishments with wry faces. He flirted tremendously with all the girls of her class. Old hawks love young chickens. He was not an old hawk exactly, yet he preferred young chickens. For every school miss whom he took riding, Mary chastised him. She generally used Daniel Trentworthy for her scourge. This man Errington, with fiery, large mustache, with great, sandy eyebrows, with pompadour gray hair that had been red, with his air of the world, which comes with successful politics, with his handsome establishment of buckskin horses and light harness, could be twisted around the figure of a maid who was not above smiling sweetly at the handsome conductor on the West Madison street car.

Was it not strange? Yes, love is always strange. That is why we read love stories.

Why did Daniel tolerate the presence and assumptions of Errington ?  For answer, why did the peers tolerate the sainted John Brown, who served Victoria so faithfully yet so offensively to my Lord Duke and my Lord Bishop ? Because it was the Queen's gracious pleasure.

It was the gracious pleasure of Daniel's sovereign, the gray-eyed maid, to visit her favor on Alderman Errington. Let all subjects look well to it ! Manifestly Daniel must obey.  It was humiliating, but what is left to a lover when he loves—when he cannot eat or sleep unless his lady smile ?

The city directory was out, and Daniel was a proof-reader on a morning daily paper.  This was the hardship of the engine-house over again.  It took Daniel off the scene every evening.  How many times had the lover tried to nerve himself to the sublime act of leaving Mrs. Holebroke's altogether. One day he had risen to the deed.  He came home to supper, for he worked in the afternoon three days in the week.  He listened for the piano, thinking the maid was again displeased with him.

"Where is Mary ? " he asked.

" She has gone to Hyde Park to stay all night," answered Mrs. Holebroke.

The earth was out from under him once more.  Perhaps it was well for him that he was to know what absence from Mary meant.  He left the house without once looking at it. He cast no loving eye at the house near by where she had rehearsed.  The holy spire under which she had gained so much applause spoke not of heaven and hope.  In the morning after that fearful night of waiting he took the street cars and rode to Cottage Grove, then again the dummy southward to Hyde Park.  He wondered which was the sacred roof. He returned late in the forenoon.

" I was worrying over you, Daniel," Mrs. Holebroke said, for she was a good soul—a great, brooding soul, with wings to cover all about her.

"Are you not afraid to let Mary go away all night?" he asked.

"No; Mary's friend Ida has moved to Hyde Park. I suppose the girls will often be together this summer.

That was dreadful news to go to bed on. The bell rang. A man brought a handsome basket of flowers with a note. The poor boy sought his pillow in that kind house and felt that God might forsake him after all. Yet he had hope. He prayed for help to bear his trouble, and prayed for Mary. "Thou knowest she is too good and pure for me," he moaned humbly.

But he also thought she was too good and pure for Ralph Errington.

At 3 o'clock he should rise. He dreamed he sat with Mary at "Ixion." The bower opened to the sweetest strains, and, as the fairyland came full in view, he felt Mary's arms about his neck, as he had seen her clasp Harmon, and heard her tell him, Daniel—Daniel, the despised and rejected—that she had tried him and found him true. And as the bower closed and the gleaming purple and silver faded away, he woke. The dreamy chords of the Moonlight sonata trembled and faded away. There came a magic knock on the door—a maiden's knock.

"Daniel, mamma isn't at home. She said be sure and wake you at 3 o'clock."

"Thank you," said Daniel, and gave thanks also to God. How could he leave that house?

## CHAPTER IX.

### THE MOUSE KNOWS HIS DANGER.

THE days of whistling at the piano were over. The oddity of it was gone. The battle was beyond it. The combat deepened. How Daniel regretted the happy moments—regretted that he could not live once more those long hours when the sun shone down into cooling air, and the maiden's laugh rippled away like a brook down by a camp. The girls in Mary's class vowed that she used her laugh shamefully to attract men's admiration.

Could Daniel play the flute like the young man in Theodore Thomas' orchestra, which was just then a new thing and had performed before a hundred people at Farwell Hall—could Daniel play the flute like that young man, how easily could he command her time! How rapt had been her enthusiasm over that young flute-player!

And then Daniel, dressing, grew sore over the subject of the young man with the flute, and over the flute particularly. What stoic would not get uneasy in remembrance of an episode so clearly inglorious? Thereupon Daniel marched angrily down-stairs and out to the street-car.

The maiden had determined to be absent when Daniel came down. Yet, hearing the front door close, she was not contented.

"Daniel," she called, "would you please buy me a skein of red chenille. Here is a quarter, and the sample."

He took the piece of fractional currency moodily. How he disliked to let her pay for it! It seemed wrong to him. He said little. Yet, when he was on the car, he could not banish the great joy that had come upon him. She surely loved him! He took the money, wrapped it in paper and put it away among his most valued possessions.

At the supper table his queen was again most gracious. She hung on Daniel's every observation. Her musical laugh thrilled him, and he ate as if he had never tasted food before.

"Have another piece of the pie, Daniel," said Mrs. Holebroke, "it's so seldom you eat since you were hurt."

And yet she did not know he was twice hurt.

"I made that pie," said Mary. "I'm glad you like it."

Marvelous being! His queen in the pantry! They rose from the table. The girl stood in the doorway, obstructing Daniel's path out of the dining-room. The boy did not know enough to put his arm around her. She was too good to be touched, e'en by a devotee.

But he walked on the air as he left the house. He was wild with happiness.

"Daniel is too mortally solemn for any single thing; oh, he would kill me!" grumbled the girl.

It is probable that she was displeased with Errington that night, and had tried to like his rival, who was more nearly her own age. It is difficult to foretell the verdict of a jury; but it is still more difficult to read the opening heart of a young girl.

Daniel awoke at 2 o'clock the next afternoon. He lay there until 3, hoping that Mary might wake him. The knock was her mother's.

One, two, three.

"Yes," said Daniel. "She's out," he thought, ruefully.

But when he passed the parlor he found Mary sitting pensively at the piano. She was looking at a new piece of music. On the cover were the compliments of Ralph Errington. Daniel's sorrow was on him once more.

"Mary," he asked, "will you go with me to hear Nilsson?" He had no thought of a refusal, yet he was no less unhappy.

"I don't know," she said, dubiously.

The lover was all excitement.

"Why, what's the matter, Mary?"

"You know mamma lets me out only one night a week, and I'm going with Mr. Errington to-night.

She was all snavity and explanation. Clearly it was not her fault. That was the idea she wished to convey.

Here, at last, was the issue. Daniel had already lost his idol. He had forgotten the basket of flowers and the note.

"Would you go if your mother were to consent?" he gasped.

"Of course, I want to hear Nilsson all I can."

"Very well; I'll ask her if you can go Friday night."

"Friday night? Let me see. Yes, I guess I could go Friday night—if mamma said so."

Oh, that was bitter to a young man's pride. Already he was forced to court her through her mother. Already he would be reckoned among those household influences that a young girl of spirit detests so openly.

So she would be at the Nilsson concert to-night. He went to the office and arranged for a substitute at his desk. This cost him $5. As he sat in the opera house, before the performance, a lady and gentleman entered the row of seats before him.

It was Mary and Errington. She nodded to him, and so did Errington.

He felt awkward. Yet it was natural he should be there. All the city was there.

He sat and wondered what a young man in his predicament ought to do. Rival lovers often assassinated one the other. "A cowardly trick!" thought Daniel, who loved a fair fight. Then came the old feeling of nature, that he ought to seize the maid and carry her away to his own tribe. Alas! he had no tribe whither to carry her. He had no means to support a wife. She was courted by a man reputed to be fabulously wealthy.

Christine Nilsson came on the stage and sang "Angels Ever Bright and Fair." It was a voice famous all over

Europe. This was the first time that marvelous pipe had played in Chicago. Daniel's heart throbbed. Tears came into his eyes. By what transformation did that seraphic voice become the voice of his Mary? Why should despotic nature clothe that gray-eyed maid with the charms of all the nymphs and the voice of Christine Nilsson?

"I was a stricken deer," the boy wept, knowing that the barbed arrow of love, the archer, was deep infixed. "There was I found by one who had himself been hurt by th' archers." These sweet words of Cowper were ever in his ear. He was particularly cast down to-night. He loved Nilsson for that she unfolded Mary to him. He craved advice from some one. He sighed for his dead mother. Yet as he thought of mother even that loved heart dissolved to his view, and Mary, sitting like Marguerite at the window of Faust's vision, gradually took the mother's place.

"I am lost!" he cried, as the audience thundered its pleasure. "O God, hear my prayer!" and his soul repeated the blissful tone that still hung upon the scene. Yes, music is an art divine. It gives the lover expression in his agony, when dumbness might consume his life. The young man sat in stupor the rest of the performance, except when Nilsson sang. As the audience rose, he felt a tap on his shoulder.

It was Errington.

"Come home with us. We have two extra seats. Have you any one with you?"

Daniel looked at Mary. She appeared to regard the matter as settled. He ought to have refused, but he had been too much surprised to devise any excuse.

"Come on, Mr. Trentworthy," pleaded Errington, as if he cared nothing for Mary, or to be in her company alone.

The boy was no match for the man of the world. He meekly followed. He entered the carriage. He was crestfallen. Errington must be a good fellow, after all. He went to his room at least four hours earlier than was his bed-time, and read and fretted till 4 o'clock in the morning.

" I guess I've spiked Mr. Trentworthy's guns," thought Mr. Errington as he drove homeward that night. " Lord, how that concert did bore me ! "

And to tell the truth, these honest common folk have a deal of common sense. It is a wonder it doesn't affect popular opinion to a greater degree. Four dollars for two songs by Nilsson are enough to pay, without dragging it from 8 o'clock until 11:15.

The papers contained a fine notice of Ralph Errington. " It will be remembered," they said, " that Mr. Errington lately made a good purchase in Wabash avenue business property, doubling his money in two weeks. During the past week he has bought a magnificent residence on the North Side. Mr. Errington is already one of the largest landlords in the city."

Daniel read these things with increasing alarm. He felt like an old man. He had entered the twilight of his love. The black night was coming on. Never again would he stand by the maid and carol and twitter, and never more would she ripple with laughter. It was a duel. She fixed her gray eye on him and defended herself resolutely.

"Dan," said the foreman, " weren't you off Tuesday night ? "

" Yes."

" Well, if you are going off Friday night again, why don't you throw up the job ? "

The " job " was $30 a week. It was Daniel's estate. It was his feeble weapon with which to fence with Errington's million-dollar rapier. It was the narrowing of the net of destiny. Now he knew what love was. To escape from it he would have surrendered his life, and self-destruction was the only thought that gave him any refuge.

So, with his $5 for a substitute, his $5 for a carriage, his $2 for a bouquet of roses, his $8 for two seats in the stalls,

and his $2 for refreshments at Wright's restaurant after
Nilsson had sung "With Verdure Clad," Daniel had his
Friday night with Mary.    She talked to him of Mr. Errington's beautiful house, which she had been to see that afternoon, and he aroused himself to an appreciation of her cruelty,
and sought for escape from her toils.

The maiden knew what he was thinking about.   "You
are a solemn old fellow," she said in a provoked tone.

"I was happy till I met you, Mary," he said rashly.

"Why don't you let me alone, then ?"

"I don't know ; indeed I do not."   He was so sad he
thought his heart would burst.

"You are one of the smartest young men in Chicago.
Everybody says so.   But I can twist you round just as I
please.   Do you think I don't see that ?"

The cat was purring with fury.   The mouse must lie quiet
or die then and there.

Besides, it eased his torn heart to hear that vain girl admit
that the poor proof-reader was a talented youth.   She might
yet rebel against Errington's illiteracy.   He had his invita-
tions written at the hotels.

And, besides, if she knew Daniel loved her and was her
slave she acknowledged her ownership.   She had not cast
him off.

Alas ! a dog has claims upon his master, but a mouse has
no claims that a cat must acknowledge.

"Wasn't Mr. Errington kind to be so courteous last
Tuesday night ?   I always told you he was a perfect gentleman."

"Indeed, he was kind," averred the wretched slave.   The
slave must be prompt with his recognition of this fact.   He
was no poltroon when he was unchained.   Errington had
been kind, for a fact.

And thus, the mouse lying very still, the cat, though
seething with inertia of the chase, was forced to lie and doze,

The house was reached, the carriage stopped, and Daniel handed his queen to the sidewalk.

"Good night!" she said briefly.

"Good-night, Mary," he said. He thought of the look of pity the old president of the college had given him, when the boy did not feel the need of pity. He thought of Jesus of Nazareth, on Calvary, "Father, forgive them; they know not what they do." She, too (Mary), knew not. No one could knowingly be so cruel. The flames and the sharp wires had seemed less abhorrent than that wicked carelessness toward a human love—a tribute of the man, body and soul, honor and manhood. "Oh, God," he moaned, "be merciful to that man led on to evil deeds by her whom he must obey." He was a noble young man, after all, for he tried to think of others. He was thankful that Mary was a good girl, who asked no murder at his hands.

"How well she might play Lady Macbeth!" he said.

He could not sit alone until 4 o'clock. He returned to the proof-room, fearing they might be behind. He took hold with a will.

"Did you have a nice time?" asked the foreman, glad to see Daniel back.

He nodded.

"I'll bet he blew in twenty-five," said the copy-holder.

"I'll go you," said a proof-reader, who was eating his midnight lunch.

"How's that, Dan?" asked the foreman. "Come, now, how about that? I'll bet you didn't do it on the cheap-john plan."

"Well, it cost me about twenty-two dollars in all."

"We knew it. The Rank was up here to borrow five, and he saw you come in a hack with an awful pretty girl."

"Oh, we're onto you, Dan, old boy!" went the chorus of lunch-eaters.

"If I'd a-known she was all-fired pretty I wouldn't a-kicked at your going," said the foreman, in extreme good nature. "Oh! you rascal, you've got the inside track on all the boys at that house."

For the boys knew where he boarded.

"I guess so," said Daniel, wearily, settling to an account of the English Derby the previous Wednesday, and praying that God might help him out of his troubles.

---

## CHAPTER X.

### MERCY'S BROTHER-IN-LAW.

Ralph Errington was a man "in thorough harmony with the people." He was a "popular idol." He espied the fact that the people of Chicago wanted wooden houses, and he said at once that the voice of the people was the voice of God. Some of the capitalists were putting three-story mansard roofs on five-story buildings, making eight stories in all. This would make a fire of wood far above the topmost stream of water that could be thrown upon it. A strong attempt was made to stop this form of balloon building, but Alderman Errington was eloquent against any move that would "harm the future of our glorious city."

In furtherance of his views that the people should have what they wanted, Mr. Errington leased a number of blocks on the North Side, near Lincoln Park. One of these, between Linden and Center streets, on Larrabee, was a quarter of a mile long. Two others, on Wells street, at North avenue, were an eighth of a mile each in length. On the Larrabee block it was possible to squeeze at least a dozen extra houses on the lots.

Other men "on the make" around town began the imitation of Errington's balloon operations. A barrack an eighth of a mile long, without an alley, is a money-making contrivance. Barracks sprang up all over the city. A forest of pine joists shone in each morning's sun. At night the houses were closed in. A week later they had tenants.

But the conservative element liked it not. The Council had been elected on a pledge for a fire ordinance, and the project of city law was before the Committee on Fire and Water. On the night of the Council meeting at which it was feared the fire ordinance would go through, and building with brick alone would be permitted within the city limits, a great mob set out from Halsted and DeKoven streets, and bore down on the City Hall. Banners and drums and brass bands and bad whiskey filled the air. The mob invaded the Council Chamber and Errington stood forward as their champion.

It was on this occasion that the Hon. Barney O'Hallaghan, of DeKoven street, made his celebrated speech against brick and stone. Pronounce the *a* in *want* as if it were the *a* in *bad* or *fat :*

"Oi," said the prosperous colleague of Ralph Errington, "kin build av bhrick, or Oi kin build av sthun [pause] av Oi want *tew !* But moi khonchtit-*chew*-wants they says Wod! And Wod says Oi."

His vote would go for wooden buildings.

An Alderman, who already understood that he was in the seventeen helpless outsiders—who knew that Errington had already formed a ring of nineteen—led the fight on the "firebugs," as the wooden builders were called. The reform leader denounced Errington as a man who was growing rich on fire-bug principles; exhibited plats, showing that Errington owned 200 worthless wooden shanties, on which he collected their value in rents each month, and backed his statements with so much force that Errington called him a liar, and was hit as soon as he had said it. This precipitated a great scene of disorder, in which many people were hurt,

The police cleared the chamber, the meeting was adjourned, and Errington was taken to his boarding-house by the mob, a hero, but badly used up.

The fire ordinance, however, was killed. A five-story building had burned the night before because it was out of the reach of the department. In restoring it the owner at once added two stories, all wood. The glory of Chicago, like the beauty of Sara, Abram's wife, spread abroad and filled the whole earth.

Mrs. Holebroke put on her bonnet and went to Mr. Errington's boarding place. She found him ill-nursed, and obtained a trained attendant. She made mutton broth and sent it by Mary. And that lady, making the best of things, appeared in the light of a very attentive and dutiful friend of the unlucky fire-bug Alderman.

"Where have you been?" the sad Daniel would ask.

"I took Mr. Errington some spring chicken that mamma broiled for him," she would say. And then she would be so kind and good that Daniel would forget his great sorrow and keep no chronicle of his hours that night.

Still, he could not forget that when he had lain sick of a fever the maid had never set his food before him. Never had she smoothed his pillow. He had said to himself that she was too young to be in a sick man's room. Yes, the days when the October haze had wafted lazily, and the girl had leaned toward him and begged him to shake that note well in "Di quella pira"—such days would never come again.

Instead of those hours, there now marched the insupportable nights of suspense. Daniel would be at his desk. "Corn closed weak at 38c to 38½c for No. 1 free on track; 34c for No. 2 do; 25c for rejected." Thus the weary figures would repeat themselves in his proof-sheet, and in his journal of sufferings he would jot: "9.30 p.m. How shall I feel at midnight? Will I be alive next Tuesday night at this hour?"

It eased his rack of pain to do this thing. He wanted

Mary Holebroke so intensely! He wanted escape from Mary Holebroke so much more. But neither course seemed possible. Nature puts a pitiless whip upon her children.

Mary never asked him to go on Sundays to the Foster Mission now. She bent her energies on Errington. That friend of religion would contribute famous sums but he vowed it wouldn't do for him to sit up to any such game on Jefferson street.

Lately Daniel had become interested in a wee child, who would soon be a newsboy. The crowd called him "Big Bill" because he was the smallest of the year's brood of waifs.

"There used to come an awful pretty girl to this school," he said to Daniel. "I guess she was Mary's sister. I wish she'd come again."

Daniel wished he were Big Bill. He envied the eyes that could see beauty in any one else than Mary.

"Daniel, come with me to Mr. Errington's. I must carry him these eggs that mamma's hens have laid."

And Daniel went. He was very proud to be on the street with her.

Mercy is coming home next week," said Mary. "I had a funny letter from her to-day."

"I shall be glad to know her," said Daniel.

Now what caused Daniel the utmost self-questioning was the fact that Errington liked him. The sick man appeared to be as glad to see the young man as he was to see the young woman. Why did Errington continually close his eyes to the fact that Daniel loved Mary? But close them Errington did.

Daniel loved Mary. Yet he hated her. He knew she made him unhappy. But his heart almost went out to this man Errington, who, having all to fear from him, feared nothing. He was a brave man, Daniel thought, "and if I had seen Errington at the concert the night I had a carriage, would I have invited him to ride with us? Ah, no,"

And with that the boy came to the wise conclusion that it was idle for him to compete with Errington in the way of expense to be lavished on Mary.

Daniel was in the twilight of a grand passion. The girl saw it, and, perhaps, was kinder than she would have been otherwise.

"Harmon says I will take to Mercy," he said. "I should like to read her letter."

"I should like to have you," said Mary. But she hurried to her room and forgot to give the missive to him. It ran as follows:

"June 30, 1869. My Dear Sis:—The news you send in your last letter, that you have told Mr. Errington that you will marry him, and that he has bought you a lovely mansion on the North Side, of course, caused me the greatest excitement. Harmon has written me that he and mother have not encouraged Mr. Errington, and, sis, in the very last letter before this your whole epistle led me to suspect that you thought more of Daniel than you did of the Alderman. You want me to come home and break the news to Daniel. You are afraid he will do something foolish, and so forth.

"Dear me, haven't you put yourself in a nice boat! And your intended is sick in bed. I imagine the Florence Nightingale mission doesn't give you much comfort. Still, when, one nurses one's future husband it must be different from nursing Daniel. And Daniel goes with you to his house. He does it, you say, so as to see a thing or two, if he has any eyes. And Harmon and mother know nothing about it all. And how do you expect poor Daniel to know it? I declare I am sorry for him. I am coming home, and I will send him away. They say it is not safe for a woman to pity a man. Yet I do not believe I am likely to pick up your leavings. Dear me! Grandpa used to call you a little hussy, long years ago!

"I hope you'll be happy as a great lady. You always said you would be one. I'll be home next week, and get Daniel off your hands. Be good to him till then. But I never heard tell of such doings in my life.

"Your loving sister,                    "MERCY."

And Daniel was well treated. Through unparalleled discipline—through the writing of a thousand entries in his diary of sorrows—he had learned that the heart lived on. He had found that he was more peaceful when he did not see Mary than when he did. When the wasp stings the flesh nature sets up a quarantine whereby the blood is refused entrance to the infected quarter. So with the hurt heart. There is a time when nature begins the process of atrophy of the affections. The life itself is of more importance than the mating.

Daniel was in this black night of diary-keeping and approaching atrophy when Mercy arrived. She was a stately girl of twenty years. No man had ever arrested her attention. She was beautiful, and knew it, but was not proud of the fact, except that it should keep away pretentious admirers. Her hair was as black as the raven's wing and swept almost to her feet. Her forehead was white and noble. Her eyes were deep and belied her whole nature. They looked rich with pity. But they covered a haughty soul. The gray-eyed girl had said well when she begged Mercy to wait until she had ensnared Errington. That clever lover of all good things came to 257 South Clinton street as soon as he was out of bed. He cast one look at Mercy and was ready to surrender.

"Whew!" he said to himself. "I didn't know women were ever so handsome as that!"

"But it would do him little good. Women true to the core with eyes twenty fathoms deep were not for Ralph Errington. He accepted two or three of her lessons in manners, and settled back to his old love.

"Egad," he declared, "it's an honor to be her brother-in-law! There'll come a time when I'll be in the family. She'll be my sister Mercy."

It already flattered his vanity more to be the brother of Mercy than it did to be Mary's husband. How strangely that fact would have struck poor Daniel!

How bitterly that would have rankled in the gray-eyed woman's heart.

"Merce is just lovely—that's all there is to that," she would often say to herself. Perhaps that spurred the younger sister to her triumphs of music and magnetism. And sometimes the most beautiful women do not have the greatest number of admirers.

Yet, though beauty be only skin deep, it often outlasts enthusiasm and a desire to evoke applause. "Magnetism" is a performance. Beauty is a fact.

But Daniel, being stone blind, could not see Mercy's peerless beauty. He loved Mercy, because she was Mary's sister, and he was not terrified in her presence, as the coming of Mary terrified him. He loved all things that appertained to his august sovereign, and in his natural freedom and lack of constraint with Mercy—in his sweetness of disposition that had come with unrelieved suffering—he was certainly an object that attracted Mercy beyond all human beings whom she had seen.

If he arose and felt disinclined to go to the city, Mercy was always about the house. "Her voice was ever soft, gentle and low, an excellent thing in woman." She had no whims, But the door-bell rang very often. Would Miss Holebroke go riding? Could Miss Holebroke come over to the church and take the Goddess of Liberty's part. Could Miss Holebroke attend the opening at Riverside?

No Miss Holebrooke was just home, and tired with over-study. She would not go out for the present.

Daniel would sit at the window and pity the young men who

were flying like wickers around this new light. He would smile
sadly at Mercy, and her eyes would seem very deep. Yes,
Mercy was a delightful friend. Daniel felt easier, because
he instinctively knew that Mercy knew his sufferings and
did not blame him. Mercy did pity him. He seemed so
like a child. He was so different from all other young men
she had known. But she had never before seen a young
man in love with any one save herself.

So she found an innocent pleasure in going to the parks
with Daniel, for he had three or four afternoons each week.
He had once been a confirmed student. Now, he could not
read; Mercy gave him comfort. He loved her name. He
would have felt relief in death, of course. But he would
have gained his surcease also could he have put his head
upon Mercy's breast and told her of his troubles.

Sometimes, as they sat on the bench in the park, Daniel
would find those great eyes full upon him, looking a toleration
that it seemed to him only his mother had shown to her little
son.

"Ah! Mercy," he said, one of these afternoons, "you are
as cruel as Mary. The young men are waiting impatiently
for you to go back into your old round of social events. I
never saw a girl who had so many admirers."

"I am tired out," she said; "I am like you, Daniel."

"No, you can never be like me," he sighed. "No one can
ever be as unhappy as I am."

And thus in his unhappiness, he passed a very happy
afternoon, albeit no less than five of Mercy's admirers drove
or walked within nodding distance of the pair.

"They are not afraid of her now," the boy thought. "I
wonder if she would ever scare them as Mary scares me?"

At night:

"Seems to me," said the gray-eyed sovereign pointedly,
that Daniel and Merce spend a great deal of time in the park."

"Yes," said Daniel, gloomily.

" Yes, " said Mercy, and her great eyes blazed with a light that Daniel had never seen before, and that quelled his gracious sovereign instanter.

" Daniel," said Harmon, " you know our friend Mrs. Trenton, of Fullerton avenue ?  You have been there lately several times with Mercy."

" Yes," said Daniel.

" Well, she wants to know if you do not wish to come there to board.  It is in a delightful spot near the grove and the park.  Mercy is always there as much as she is here.  We are a little crowded here now.  Next winter you can come back here, if you wish to.'

This was exactly what Daniel had been vowing he would do.  Mrs. Trenton was a rapt admirer of Mercy.  She liked Daniel.  She had suggested the change to Daniel, but he had told her he did not know how to leave the roof that had given him a home.  A word to Harmon had brought this about.

" Mary, you haven't been over to see Mrs. Trenton for four months," said Mercy.

" Is it as long as that ? " answered Mary.

" I shall be sorry to have you go," said the mother.

" I shall be sorry to go," said Daniel.  And now that he was turned out, although he had connived with it, he was truly a miserable man.  He looked in Mary's eyes for pity, but she was only bent on making herself agreeable.  Her laugh rippled over the table, and Daniel at last turned to Mercy, who seemed to him the embodiment of all goodness.

The mouse lay nearly dead.  The cat was assiduous in her attentions.  Life must be restored in the fainting thing. The paws were all velvet now.  The touch was the tenderest. The life gradually returned.  There would still be another attempt to escape.  The puss purred and dozed.

Daniel sat at that pleasant board, and marveled that he had not been more thankful for the blessed privilege.  Yes, he would go up nearer the cemeteries. Soon he would rest. He felt that his forces were ebbing away. But never did he rest. Never was the background of Mary's necromancy absent from any web of thought he wove.

He would go. But his heart was breaking.

"I'm very sorry we are to lose you," said Mary, as he left the house.

He was angry with himself that this speech should ease him so. His intellect was clear. It was his heart that was the stupid. Shakespeare's picture of the bird caught in the sticky preparation of the hunter was ever in his mind:

> O, limed soul, that struggling to be free,
> Art more engaged !

And to show the depths of her sorrow, and the keenness of Daniel's knowledge of Mary, it was fated that Mary should at once open the piano and strike the great chords of Mendelssohn's "Wedding March."

"Yes, she's sorry !" wept Daniel, as he heard the notes. He looked back toward the house. A carriage drove up. The march ceased instantly.

A house with a belle and a beauty needs no *porte cochère.*

---

## CHAPTER XI.

### THE MOUSE ESCAPES.

THE house at 639 Fullerton avenue, which ran at the top of Daniel's sheet of note-paper, was situated near what was then the corner of the Green Bay road. Now it is North Clark street. If the reader will take the sheet and clip about twenty degrees from the upper right side of his sheet, letting the radius begin at the mouth of the river, he will have the trend of the northern lake shore. All of the north and south streets of the North Side at the river run into the lake within three miles.

Between Mrs. Trenton's house and the Green Bay road were three vacant lots, or seventy-five feet in all. A picket fence, the pickets three inches wide, ran from the house to the corner and then southward toward the next cross-street, or Belden avenue. The region was finely shaded with trees. It was a delightful summer residence.

Daniel had nerved himself for his supreme renunciation. All of us dislike a change in our habits of life. The prospect always displeases us. Often the realization is much more satisfactory. Daniel had left a region of the city that was utterly prosaic. The nearest trees were at Twelfth street. It seemed that Chicagoans were merely staying in that quarter until they had earned enough to live elsewhere. The sun would beat down on a dirt pavement, and the rosin would exude from the sidewalk, and the dust would gather on the dun-colored sides of the houses until the very ideal of human discomfort had been reached. The fish man would tear the word "Fresh" out of his mouth as though it were calico a yard wide. The straw man would say "Boots!" in an insidious thunder, and the general gender of purveyors, organ-grinders and scissor-sharpeners would keep up a heat-lightning of entertainment while Daniel slept away the hot forenoons. This had been his heaven.

He was now suddenly translated to a couch that over-looked a bower of creepers, where real birds built their nests, where the street-peddler rarely came, and where the grass was accorded rights of its own. The new boarder rose and ate a lunch of Vienna bread and strawberries and cream. Mrs. Trenton was a lady who believed that wives owed a duty to society to care for homeless young men. That is an idea worthy of consideration.

What Daniel had dreaded proved to be all pleasure. Nature exposed her charms to his famished eyes, and he felt once more a desire to live. Mercy came over, and the young man and the young woman passed a delightful afternoon. His feelings had been too tense. A few strings had snapped, and the strain was relieved. Three young men called to take Mercy home. She left Daniel and went with the third one.

"There goes the handsomest and the best girl in the whole world," said Mrs. Trenton.

Mercy was the best girl he had ever known, Daniel thought. But, as for the handsomest, she had no gray eyes, nor laugh, nor cruelty, nor "ways"—and thus the poor lover found himself wandering off into the realm of Mary's faults. We often love people for their shortcomings. Novels have been written about characters who were worshipped for their crimes.

The change was, to Daniel, a reinvigoration. He went to bed the second morning with a consciousness that he could live without Mary. It plagued him, for he had said in his heart that his was no base love. He had sworn eternal affection for Mary. He had determined to win her by patience and long-suffering. This life without Mary was a phenomenon with which he had not expected to deal. Yes, he could forget her. He would forget her. She did not love him, and he did not want her to marry him—now. He shuddered when he thought that he would have seized her and run away, once upon a time. Yes, a woman should love her husband. Thus, in the least misery which he had seen for many months, he dozed away in his new home. The nighthawks coursed the dawning sky; they scoured downward a thousand feet and turned upward with an unearthly sound; the robins called loud and clear; the maple leaves fanned the dust and drank the dew. Daniel slept. The march of day brought nothing uncomfortable. The trees gave back their dew, the noon went by on high, and Daniel dreamed. He was with Mary. "I have come," she said. "I have fought against you. I had not thought my master lived. Thou art my lord. Whither thou goest, there will I go also." He turned; his face beamed with a peace that it never knew waking. Some-

thing was bringing him back to sentient life.   He woke with
a start.

"It was all a lie!" and his face was that dark one might
have taken him for a pirate.   Oh! that assassin dream!

And yet his spirit told him there was something real to
this thing.   He was sure he had heard music—had not
dreamed it.   Paganini was sure he had heard Zamiel play
The Devil's Dream.

Yes, yes; his face lit up with joy.   Oh! thank God!
The notes of the Moonlight sonata stole out among the maple
leaves.   The long, luxuriant, entreating chords came upward and salved his hurt heart once more.   She had come.
She could not live without him.   He was her master.   Because that he loved her so.

He went down-stairs.   Mrs. Trenton was all smiles.

"Mary is here," she remarked.   How wise women are!

"Is she?" said Daniel.   And in his heart he kept thanking God.

It would be churlish to make her come to him.   Had she
not already come three miles and a half?   And she had not
been here before this summer!   He entered the parlor.   She
sat at the piano.

"Oh! Daniel," she cried merrily, like a child, "you're
still alive!   We're so lonesome without you.   We're so sorry
you've gone away.   I told Mrs. Trenton I had come to take
you back."

It was like Indian summer, with the girl begging him to
whistle "Vuelta Zingara" just once more.   He chatted with
her in an ecstasy of ease.   His conversations with Mercy had
improved him—so Mrs. Trenton said—a capable judge.
They went over to the park.   He found a four-leaved clover.
They sat and gazed at the clouds.

Magnificent clouds in Chicago!

It was the only happy afternoon the young man had ever
known.

"You are such a queer old fellow," she said. But the cat was not now bristling with electricity. It was safe for the mouse to stir. Daniel was flattered. He talked and she listened. They spoke of each other's peculiarities. The clouds arose, white as alabaster. One cañon was like the Colorado's; one glacier was greater than Alaska's.

"It's going to rain, I am afraid," she prophesied.

"It will blow, too," he prophesied.

So they ate in a hurry, for it was time to go, and then he took her home. It was a ride of two miles and a half to the Clark street bridge, over the main bayou. They sat on an open street car. The gray-eyed maid was his. The clouds rose on all sides. Over the Clark street bridge to Randolph street and they were on a Clinton street car. The driver hurried his horses as if the trip would be his last. The gale was coming from the north. They reached the Randolph street bridge. The gale came sweeping down the North Branch. It caught a schooner that stood in the river and dashed it against the east end of the pivot-bridge. The car was in the center of the structure. The latch broke, and the bridge swung lengthwise of the stream. It was a perilous moment. "Turn those brakes!" cried Daniel, and the brakes of the car were made fast. The horses reared. Daniel was at their heads. "Sit still, Mary!" he said, "I know you are brave." And she sat still and spoke not. He could not see her, for the very air seemed too thick for sight. The dust rose a hundred feet. Would the bridge blow off its pier? A moment more and the worst was over. But the car was at the center, where the bridge-key was turned. It was not safe to move the load off the center. The passengers were taken down the stairway in the bridge, reached the pier, and were transferred to the dock in a schooner's yawl. Daniel took that gracious sovereign in his arms. He brooded and purred over her, and many a poor sewing girl took note of it.

"Mary," he said, "I knew you were brave."

"Humph!" she replied, "there were plenty of other women as brave."

They took another car and left the bridge-tenders to get the bridge shut as best they could—mainly by swearing.

Now, why should that startling episode provoke his sovereign? Why should she, as the car turned down Clinton street, suddenly withdraw her smiles? Why should she leave him at the door to pay his respects to Mrs. Holebroke, and permit him to depart without thanking him for his kindness to her?

Ah! the Queen accepts no kindnesses from her subjects. She merely punishes them if they do treasonable things.

Daniel reached his office wet to the skin.

"Hi! Dan, I thought you knew enough to come in when it rained," remarked the foreman, for this is not a sympathetic world.

Still it was a triumph. It was the only battle he had ever won. She might well be angry with herself for showing her love for him. So thought Daniel. He blessed the day.

Precisely three afternoons thereafter Daniel awoke once more to the strains of Mary's sonata. It was monstrous strange how much Mary had suddenly come to think of Mrs. Trenton and her lovely home. So Mrs. Trenton, good woman, made bold to admit to Daniel, for it pleased him to the tips of his ears. He had fought such a losing battle on the West Side that he could be pardoned for his gratulations, now that he was winning.

A Senator once visited his home in Ohio when it was reported that a disappointed lieutenant was about to knock the Senator out. The Senator spoke so smoothly to the *chef* of the political *claque* that all was well within three days. A horde of newspaper correspondents came down on the Senator. He blandly told them that the fences were down on his farm, and that he had left Washington rather hurriedly in order to put them up.

Mary was over at Lincoln Park nowadays to put up her fences. This was Daniel's profound opinion. He said: "I have been too anxious to please my queen. I will appear rebellious."

He entered the parlor cold. The maid did not appear to notice it. She took up the guitar and begged Daniel to teach her to play "that exquisite fandango." He told her he must go immediately to work. Her brows came together with a provoked look. "Now, Daniel, that is too mean for any single thing!"

He wished he had let the work go.

"When will you be over?" she asked poutingly.

"When shall I come?" he asked. Plainly the campaign was over.

"Come Monday," she said; "mother will want to see you."

Mother—the witch! It was Mary who wanted to see him! Well, let her have her little subterfuges. Daniel was thankful to go. He had conquered. What odds if the disappointed maiden did seem to play Mrs. Trenton's grand piano with such vim—a stroke like that of Carreno, the Brazilian demoiselle who was just then starring through the United States.

Monday—it was Saturday. The young man walked in the air again. Now that he was to marry Mary, he began to wonder how he should support her. He regretted his night work. He said: "I will abandon it."

On Sunday he was tempted to go on the West Side. He only went as far as the Van Buren street bridge, and looked across. The factories were in the way, and the viaduct beyond was high.

"Anyway," he thought, "she has not seen me." Somehow he connected Mercy with his change of fortunes. "How hard it was for the minx," he smiled. "How faithful such a heart will be when it does surrender!"

For he had heard the foreman say, who knew nothing about Mary, that a gray-eyed woman would lick a man's boots if once she loved a man. Daniel was pleased that his mistress had wanted to be sure of her own heart.

"Was ever woman in such humor won?" asked Daniel, thinking of Richard III. and Mary. Had Daniel thought of George Washington or Napoleon, Mary would have stood hand in hand with him.

At 4 o'clock Monday morning Daniel was unwilling to sleep. "I should like to stay awake," he admitted. "But I should look like a ghost. So he slept.

He dreamed that he entered the Sherman House corridor. A great number of men roared hilariously. The cat had pounced on the mouse, and was striking it ten blows a second, first with right forepaw, and then with left. He awoke with a start.

"Pshaw!" he said. And yet his heart beat furiously, and he was weak with apprehension. So much depended on this afternoon that he was like the wedding guest. "I am afeared," quoth he to the Ancient Mariner. Now that the time had come the young man was unwilling to go. How should he keep his fears from Mary? Would she not persecute him, then, another half year?

"Fudge!" he said, "I've got her. She's fooled me too long already. He reached the Clinton street abode in a tremor of mingled apprehension and joy. Here was the house. How good it looked! He had come back at her request. He rang the bell.

"The hussy!" he whispered. "She might have had the door open. I've seen her do it for Errington." He smiled and then he did not smile.

Mrs. Holebroke opened the door.

"Why, Daniel! Come in. The girl is hanging out her clothes, and both Mary and Mercy are out."

That was unromantic, was it not? But was it not life—real life?

And stern as destiny are all the years.

"They call it July, August, September," thought the forlorn man. "I call it Disappointment, Agony, Death—that is the calendar I must live."

"Aren't you going to come in?" asked the mother, for Daniel was petrified with horror. He had thought he was risen out of hell. He had thought it was the third day, but it seemed it was only the descent. Easy is the descent.

"Certainly. I'll wait till she arrives," he stammered, wondering what Mrs. Holebroke had thought of him.

"Mary?"

"Yes."

"Well, I hardly think she will be back soon. She has gone out for the afternoon."

He sat down in torment. The mother was busy with a tailor's goose, ironing out some cloth. The air of the room was pleasant. Daniel watched her, and there came upon him a great light.

Her features beamed with goodness, and yet with common sense. As Saul of Tarsus went up toward Damascus, so now journeyed Daniel toward the truth. There came a desire to question this mother-heart.

"Mrs. Holebroke," he said, his heart breaking with disappointment, "I think Mary loves me, and doesn't know it."

"I hope she does," said the ironer.

"Don't you think so?"

The ironer ironed.

"Don't you believe that she is so young that it will be a year or so before she will show any degree of womanly affection?"

"Mary is a strange girl," said the mother. And then: "But Mary means all right."

The light fell full on the wretched young man: "Saul, Saul, why persecutest thou me?" It was useless to hold back the main idea. He leaned both elbows on her ironing-board and looked into her face with the gaze of a strong soul who had suddenly seen that the book of the future was at last open to him.  He stopped her work.

Mrs. Holebroke peered into his face.  Many a face must have looked that way as it lay under the guillotine.

" You are a good woman.  You believe in God—in Christ —that he died for us.  Now tell me, do you think I will ever get Mary ? "

The face was still on the block.  She turned hastily to her heating apparatus.

" Daniel, you don't want my advice."

" I—want—the truth."  The voice was hoarse.

She could not gaze upon that upturned face, for she felt instinctively that she was a priest of Mexico.  She must tear out his heart.  It was worse than the French ax.

" Daniel," she said faintly, " it is my honest opinion that Mary does not care for you, and never will ! "

" You *know* that ! "  The jury was merely being polled.

" I *know* it."

It was and is the jury's true and only verdict.

The queen died that moment.  Or, rather, her realm disappeared.  The heart over which she had reigned was broken for the nonce.

He could not rise in a moment, and the mother tarried with her charcoal.

Then he took her unwilling hand.  "You have been a mother to me," he stammered.  " And you have done me the greatest of kindnesses."

The old lady sobbed.  " Please don't think hard of me, Daniel," she begged.  " I wish it were otherwise."

The young man closed the door gently.  He did not want to hear its noise.  He took a car.  He did not want to walk over the river.  Once across the bayou, he was safe forever. His hurt mended.  He became angry.  He grew furious. It is at such stages that men behead their poor queens.

Daniel's diary of sorrows had been made out of the white ends of proof-slips. The stack was inches in height. He kept no record that night. He gathered the papers together; he put the 25-cent piece and the red chenille with them; he added the leaden curl-piece that he had found; he put in the receipt for the fifty tickets; he added the seat coupons of all the theatre tickets that he had bought for her delectation. He tied up this accursed packet almost gleefully. He took it home.

"She will be over here in less than a week," he thought grimly, as he lay down. He could not pray. He could only live. That was all will-power—to do that.

To his extreme surprise, the strains of the mad tarantelle and the "Vuelta Zingara" broke forth at exactly 2 o'clock. He had asked to be called at that hour.

He rose and was down-stairs in an incredibly short time. He ate no lunch. He entered the parlor. The maid looked up and smiled, and then she did not smile. But she seemed ready for the onset.

"Mary," he said, "you promised to go riding with me. You remember?"

"Yes, but I can't go this afternoon, I am afraid."

"I will have a span of horses here in ten minutes," he said, decisively. "I shall never ask another favor of you."

"Yes, Mary, it is a lovely afternoon," chimed in Mrs. Trenton.

But it was not a lovely afternoon for Mary. She detested scenes. She wished herself at home.

Daniel drove up in a handsome black spider, with milk-white horses. The outfit ought to have been noticeable. It cost him two days' labor.

The packet was under the lap-cloth.

The gray-eyed maid came forth. The lady of the house stood on her veranda and gave approval to the scene.

"They are a fine pair," she said to herself. "I envy you," she said to Mary.

Daniel heard it all, as though it were in the dim distance. His mind was on the packet down at his feet. He desired only to tell Mary the story of the woe she had given him.

"Mary Holebroke," he began, "you possess peculiar powers over young men and old men alike. I do not remember an acquaintance who, criticising you in the beginning, has not ended with a tribute to your influence. You may not be aware of this fact, and I want to tell you just what you have done with me in the last twelve months."

This was by far the most disagreeable prologue to which the girl had ever listened. She looked full of hatred. Daniel had never seen the instincts of self-preservation aroused in her before.

"You know that you were exceedingly agreeable in your conduct toward me as early as a year ago last spring."

"I know no such thing," the gray-eyed maid replied. "I was lonesome. Mercy was gone. I was willing to talk to anybody. I considered you a friend of Harmon's."

"You remember that you depended on my going with you to the Foster Mission. Ah! Mary, almost every spot over there is filled with memories of you. I do not see how I can ever go there again."

"We wanted all the folks we could get at the mission. It was my duty to get you interested. You have often told me your acquaintance with Big Bill alone repaid you."

"Yes, Mary. But why did your duty to take me to the mission assert itself so capriciously? When you were kind to me it was your duty. But when you gave me no chance to go with you, was that also the voice of duty?"

"You knew the way," said the girl, laconically.

"I do not mean to upbraid you, for it must be that you could not be aware of the influence you exercised over me— that is, the glamour, the despotism. I have lived in hell."

The word startled her.

"Please, Mr. Trentworthy," she protested.

"Never fear, Mary. I am in my right mind, and am not blaspheming. The Lord has allowed me to live, but I have lived in hell. I want to show you, to your own eyes, the proof of it. I want you should see that you ought to be careful with young men. You are not to blame, Mary. You are not to blame."

It was hard. He had not calculated upon this utter callousness. The poor boy did not know she could not understand him. She doubted his sanity. That any man of sense should pass through the tortures of love she would not believe. She saw him unfold his packet, but she did not want to see it. She looked across at the lawn that bordered the drive.

"Here, Mary," he said, "you see the first ticket I ever got at the mission. Here is the Chinese fan you threw away one Sunday a year ago. Here are the quarter and the samples you gave me to buy chenille. Here is a lead for your hair."

She seized it and threw it away.

"I should think," she said, "you would have been above such a thing."

"No," he said wearily, "I was not." He had expected more tolerance than he was receiving.

"Trust me, Mary," he said, "I would never have asked to marry you, I would never have married you, until I saw you loved me. I was patient. That was my only crime."

"I think you acted very foolishly."

"Well, other men have been as simple. Perhaps I can be of service to them in showing your influence to you."

"No one else would be so like a calf."

She averted her face. This was Daniel's queen. This was the lady who could not live without him.

And yet he pardoned her. He had made her ride with him. He could not blame her.

"Mary," he said, "here is the record of my sufferings.

Do you doubt them? Here the account is kept—hour by hour. From half-past nine to half-past ten there have always been sixty minutes of torment. Then, as I felt you were asleep, I knew I would not wake you, even were I near you. I never suffered so much after that hour. It is a book of misery."

The pile lay on his lap. With one hand he held the reins. With the other he leafed up the rough pieces of proof paper.

"You were not very neat," the gray-eyed maid said, as the wind carried away a half-dozen slips.

"There," he said, "that one left on top is for the night you said you were coming down to see me. It reads: 'Peace. The background gone.' The 'background' was my feeling of intense longing to be near you, to try and say or do something that would make you smile on me. Look at the very next evening. You brought Errington with you to the office. It reads: 'A cruel hour. Can I live until 1 A. M.? 1 A. M.—I am alive.' Now, the very next day, you were delightful. You criticised Errington, and I, for fear of you, championed him. The entry is, 'Peace—no background.'"

Her lip curled. There was an element of her mother's stern common sense in her.

"The very next day," said Daniel, "I found you had given away the handsome book I had bought for you. '9 p. m.—My soul followeth hard after thee. Thy right arm upholdeth me!' That, Mary, was my cry of deepest despair. Wherever you find that verse in these entries, then I was indeed unhappy."

She did not hear it. She was tired of it.

Inconceivable! that the life of one should be of so little interest to another. Inconceivable! that the creator should forget the created. But it was too far from Mary. She was not responsible for it, even if it had come to pass, which she must ever doubt

He threw it all away. Oh! if it did not keep her attention no one else would stop to read it.

"They are gone, Mary," he said.

She again looked at the horses. She was relieved. She
thought far better of Daniel, now.

"I shall destroy everything I have that reminds me of
you," he promised, thinking that also would please her.

But it did not.

"I have always liked you, Mr. Trentworthy," she said, her
composure regained. "I desire to continue to do so. We
have always been good friends, have we not?"

"I have been your friend, Mary."

"Well let us so continue."

"I do not want to see you for at least a year, Mary—perhaps never again."

"Why, that is the unfairest thing I ever heard of. Just
because you cannot monopolize my thoughts, then I must
lose a friend of years' standing."

Ten minutes before, when she supposed he would always
keep the diary, she would have been thankful to get clear of
him at any sacrifice.

"You have not so many lady friends in Chicago that you
can afford to throw them off in that manner."

What an oddity is a woman's mind—to a young man!
Daniel was puzzled. He was riding his last time with her.
Like a thief to the scaffold, each moment was precious. He
turned his horses down the drive once more. The whirligig
of her caprice also turned.

"Oh! let's go home!" she commanded.

It restored Daniel.

"Yes," he said, "you are right. We will go to Clinton
street."

They rode rapidly northward and westward. They both
were silent. He thought what foolish things men were. It
is hard to tell what she thought. The astronomers say

that attraction affects all bodies—that though the moon must pay court to the earth, the earth must forever acknowledge the power of the moon—that together, like waltzers, the two bodies revolve through space, the true center of gravity lying between them. So it may have been with Mary's influence. She may have worried that her satellite should go at a tangent.

Why had she been passing lovely in his sight? Seeing that she was thus lovely, had not every look and speech received a fictitious meaning? Had not "chops and tomato-sauce" been translated into terms of undying affection?

With the case thus before him, Daniel tried to throw the blame all on himself. Yet some things, like Macbeth's "amen!" stuck i' his throat.

"Mary," he said, "it seems to me that you often used Errington as a foil when you were going with me."

"Mr. Errington has far more to complain of on that score than you have."

"Why, how is that?"

"I have been engaged to marry him for over four months. Can't you see the ring on that forefinger?"

Daniel had seen it, but he had not known its meaning!

They are on the soft soil in front of 257 South Clinton street.

He alighted, reins in hand.

She was quick. She did not want him to touch her. He was glad. He bowed, but did not look at her. He did not love her and he did not want to look upon her.

"I am much obliged," she said, civilly.

He bowed, was in his carriage, and around the corner like a Jehu.

Over the Madison street bridge and over the Clark street bridge he went. The grade rapidly descended to Kinzie, and the railroad crossed the street. There was then no viaduct there. He looked vacantly at a train that was passing.

It might have run over him had he reached it at the right instant.

As he passed northward at Illinois street he saw a number of men rush out and grasp the bridles of his horses. The eyes of the men protruded and they strove to make gestures. He turned his head. It was too late. A runaway team, frightened by the cars, was on him. The team veered to the left slightly, but insufficiently. His light vehicle was lifted and he was thrown to the right. He saw himself approaching the edge of the stone sidewalk. He judged it was death. He was ready to die so far as earth was concerned.

> My God, my father, and my friend,
> Do not forsake me in mine end—

he murmured, and struck the pavement. The blackness of night came with a great noise.

---

## CHAPTER XII.

### A GRAND WEDDING.

DANIEL's head had not struck the stone pavement. He had fallen just inside the stone. A wooden block well incrusted with pebbles had received his head; but the block was loose. A gas company had dug a ditch, and in replacing the pavement had left this block on a cushion of sand, without the plank beneath it.

Daniel was taken to a drug store to die, but he did not die. The blow on his head had not been a fatal one. The druggist knew the livery rig; the liveryman knew Daniel, and Daniel was soon at Mrs. Trenton's house. That lady was in great agitation. Who would not be? Yet she had her senses about her. "Where is the young lady?" she

7

asked. There was no young lady in the spider. That cheered her. A lady of points always considers herself responsible for the welfare of every young girl whom she patronizes. Mrs. Trenton sent word to the office that Harmon's friend Daniel was badly hurt. The doctors told her to do so. The counting-room sent up to the foreman and the foreman sent the news over to Harmon.

"Mercy," Mary had said on arriving home, "Dan knows I am going to marry."

And Mercy had gone to the window just in time to see Daniel whip around the corner. She wished he had come in. "Still, how could he?" she asked herself.

"Well, Mate," Mercy had replied, "he knows more than anybody else. You had better tell mother and brother, if every one is to know it."

"Humph!" the capricious maid had said. "Time enough for all that!"

And now, within so short a time, the message came that Daniel was perhaps fatally hurt; would Harmon come at once? The gray-eyed maiden turned ash-color.

"That is awful!" she said, and was unhappy—perhaps the most unhappy she had ever been in her strange life. It was the gravitation of human lives—the debt they owe each other. Life is a solemn thing.

"Bring me my hat, sis," said Harmon, doing two or three things at once.

And Mercy, when she brought her brother's hat, came also prepared for a sudden journey across town.

"I shall go with you," she said.

"Yes, Mercy," said the mother, "perhaps you can be of service."

"Is he dead?" the great black eyes asked of Mrs. Trenton.

"Oh, no! The doctors have cleaned and dressed his head. They say he will probably live."

Mercy had not known she would be half so glad.

"Mother thought I could make myself useful to you, and I am going to stay and nurse him," she said peremptorily.

"Why didn't Mary come? She was dreadfully anxious to be here lately."

Mrs. Trenton was also proud of Mary, and loved her, but Mrs. Trenton was a woman and could not refrain from expressing her anger. She coupled this accident with Daniel's rejection, for she instinctively felt that Mary had rejected him.

The black-eyed beauty said nothing. She installed herself as Daniel's nurse. That evening Harmon brought over a trunkful of her things.

"It will be necessary, Miss Holebroke, to humor your patient in almost all his whims. He will be out of his senses most of the time. Let him imagine what he may please. Just so he do not rise or be not fretted by opposition, all will be going well." So said the doctor.

There he lay, a handsome young fellow, just at the threshold of early manhood. He had escaped the vices of young men. Perhaps his misfortunes had brought it about. Mercy sat and admired his white face. She brushed back his flaxen hair and thought of his father and of the colossal inheritance which it had been supposed would come to the son. She had read of his marvelous escape from death at Canal street, for it had filled the Eastern press. His workmates came up to see how he was getting along and to bring his salary, for the foreman was a kind friend.

"I'd be willing to be sick myself if I could get that pretty girl to nurse me," the news-carriers told their comrades while waiting for the first proof of markets that night.

The young man's case was much more serious than had been prognozed. He lingered between life and death for months. The pretty girl grew white with watching. Mrs. Trenton would beg her to go home and let Mary come over, but the suggestion pained Mercy.

"Anyway," she would say, "you know how busy Mary is. She has been sewing ever since Daniel was hurt. She thinks I ought to come and help her."

For Mary was deep in the mysteries of muslin and Hamburg edging. The sound of the tucker was heard in the land.

And when the sewing machine was not rattling away the Alderman and his *fiancée*, were shopping or superintending the arrangement of the mansion on Ohio street. There was much to do, and the weeks went fast.

"I ought to go and see Daniel," the affianced bride would say, "but I haven't had a moment of time."

She was not going to marry Daniel. What was Hecuba to him, or he to Hecuba? Now, could she go, after all? Mercy was there; that was enough.

She was glad to hurry the nuptials.

The Alderman was certain he was on the right track. He would soon stop building wooden houses on leased ground, join a North Side church, and become ultra-respectable. It suited him. Prosperity has a respectable look of itself.

"Mate," he would say, "call me 'Rafe.' That, I understand, is the proper thing on Ralph. Wyndham's actors all say 'Rafe.'"

And the young lady would box his ears for his nonsense. Neither one was given to kissing.

"It's too silly," said the gray-eyed maid.

"Yes, it isn't business," the landlord would say, as he figured. He was greatly pleased with Mary, or he would not have married her. He had the pick of his ward, and he had no *entrée* anywhere else—and wanted none.

The American woman, if left to her own devices, washes on Monday, irons on Tuesday, bakes on Wednesday, and marries on Thursday.

"If it were done, 'twere well 'twere done quickly"—that is, early in the week, and it is plain to be seen that Thursday is the earliest available date in the week, unless womanly methods are to be disturbed, and what wise man would do that?

The wedding of Ralph Errington and Mary Holebroke was set for Thursday evening at 8 o'clock, Oct. 28, 1869.

Errington was to have a magnificent wedding, too. It would have suited him and pleased DeKoven street to have been married at St. Mary's, by the Coadjutor Bishop of the Catholic Church. But Mary was a Protestant. Perhaps the thing would have as much tone at his house—so he admitted. The other eighteen ring Aldermen set out to help their marrying friend. The tickets of invitation were issued with care. All the chiefs of corporations, all their brilliant solicitors, all the great merchants and contractors would be on hand. That would make the affair a success in the papers. And some of the magnates, who had once worried over getting in the swim themselves, would bring their wives. And Mary would supply the good-looking young folks, for, after all, what is a houseful of big-wigs if there be no pretty girls for the great advocates to amuse?

The gas company put up a fine display of lights. The caterer made an arcade 100 feet long to the sidewalk. The decorators put the last touch on the house, and fixed the last tuberose in the wedding-bell. An army of servants and a housekeeper had taken the "new look" off things. It was a magnificent establishment—the best of its day—and it was situated in the heart of the shadiest residence quarter. For trees are a blessing. Houses can be built. Trees must grow slowly. The North Side bragged that it had trees like an old town in the East.

"I never want to see this dusty Clinton street again," thought the bride.

"Mercy might have been one of my bridesmaids if she had not been so bent on nursing Dan," the bride said. This would have pleased Errington, but at Mary's expense. Mary was a good-looking girl herself. She easily chose a bevy of girls who at least were no prettier.

But then all bridesmaids are pretty.

Mr. Errington had been mean with nothing. He had not, it is true, touched the contractors with a light hand. Yet, it being a festal occasion, and the Alderman giving proof that he was spending money profusely, all parties turned in with a willing hand. Mary with difficulty persuaded her prodigal lover from asking the ineffable Theodore Thomas for figures on music.

On Thursday, Oct. 28, 1869, the haze of Indian summer rested on peaceful Chicago. The whole summer had been calm, equable, halcyon. The sick man lay at Mrs. Trenton's house, and gazed out on the glorious air, where every mote was gilded with refined gold. Mercy sat beside him. "Oh! Daniel," she breathed, "I hope you may get well."

He started, and looked at her. The October air recalled his scattered senses. It was on these afternoons that he had whistled the tunes for Mary.

"And may I whistle for you?" he asked, his face wreathed with smiles, like the face of some flaxen-haired boy, begging favors of a fond father.

"Indeed you may," came from the beautiful lips, and out of the eyes twenty fathoms deep.

There was silence again. The great, cool sun went down.

"Come to supper, Mercy," Mrs. Trenton called. "We must be at Mary's early. Too bad you're not going."

"I do not like crushes. They have moved heaven and earth to have the affair a grand one. Let those enjoy it who wish to."

Mrs. Trenton thought Mercy odder than Mary.

"Well," she declared, "if my sister were making such a catch, I would be there. I'd believe you were jealous, if I had not heard Errington admit that you wouldn't look at him. He said he liked you for it."

"Do you think Daniel is doing as well as he might do?" asked Mercy. She had forgotten the wedding already.

"The doctor says so," said Mrs. Trenton cheerfully.

"He is out of his head, and yet the doctor would be apt to think him rational."

"Well, you know the doctor charged us to humor all his notions, and avoid crossing him."

"Yes," said Mercy. "But tell the servants to stay in."

"I declare," Mrs. Trenton said to her spouse, "I believe Mercy would have liked to see us stay at home, too. Edson Trenton," she said sharply, as she saw her husband bent on scanning the *Evening Post*, "there's something in Mercy's actions that makes me suspect she loves that boy."

"Well, she's a hummer. I wish I weren't married myself." And therein the disturbed reader had his revenge.

For on the street cars wives cannot pinch and bite their offending lords and masters.

The throng, in wedding garments, entered the arcade. The immense parlors were full at 7. At 7:30 not an invited guest was absent. At 7:45 the celebrated preacher arrived and spent ten minutes shaking hands with the people nearest him. The best man showed the minister the license and put a hundred dollar bill in his hand, which the minister turned over to his wife with loud laments, for he needed it to make his fishing expense good. At precisely 8 o'clock the ushers cleared the way for the wedding procession, and that march began which had been so carefully rehearsed under Mary's direction the night before.

It is the ambition of every woman, they say, to have a wedding, with a white veil and orange blossoms.

And Mary certainly looked her best. The orange blossoms were a small part. Her dress had been designed in Paris, and made by the best artists in Chicago. It was simple in cut but elegant in its effect. The stuff was a rich creamy satin, which spread into a very long train. At the edge was old point lace. Around the neck was a high ruff of real lace, from the neck to the floor was a plaiting of plush that barely shaded from the creamy satin into a deeper tone. One would think that the plush were the satin in a cross light, or under shadow. Beneath the veil shone a couple of trails of simple vari-colored rosebuds with long stems. The rope of roses was brooched to the neck with a diamond, traveled to the waist diagonally, and there sought the trail, a rosebud of different hue peeping forth at each span of distance.

The effect of this rich dress and its appropriate trappings of diamond-buckled slippers and many-buttoned gloves was electric, so far as the women were concerned. The men said she was pretty. The women said more. They vowed she was well dressed. "Where did she get so much taste?" asked the leader of the *haut ton*, who had come under protest. Mary, this *grande dame* mentally resolved, should become one of her own set—until she had married her daughter, at least.

The bridesmaids were equally fortunate in their attire. The groom and best men were all they should be—that is, nothing. For the wedding is the one place where women comes forth and fills the whole bill. And why the women make men go there at all puzzles the oldest married wheelhorse in existence.

The bride marched slowly forward on the arm of the bridegroom. The bridesmaids and groomsmen in pairs—one, two, three, four, five—followed, bearing flowers that scented the vast parlors anew. The head of the procession reached the marriage bell. The men went to the left, the maidens to the right. The long file of twelve people faced the great assemblage, which craned its miscellaneous neck and peered.

The popular preacher stepped in front of the chief actors.

This marriage, which all persons enter without much thought, is proclaimed to be the most momentous rite we have. We are born. Surely, there is little ceremony at such times—outside the palace at Madrid. We die, and go we know not where. But we marry, and alter every relation to the world—and all with a solemn word. Can it be too solemn?

On the right a bevy of maidens, all testifying by their presence that they believe in the divine ordinance of marriage. On the left, five young men, who hope they are going to get well out of it. In front, the leader of the *haut ton*, whose place has been kept to her with exceeding difficulty and considerable backbiting.

"These Presbyterian house-weddings are simply atrocious," says a beau five-feet-four in height, at the rear of the parlor.

"Everything is flat on a level floor," grumbles another. "But I suppose the lunch will be fine. Keep near this door. Those people in front calculate on paying their congratulations and then getting right down here. I've seen 'em do it too often. We may not see 'em married, but we'll have a front place in a corner, where no one can spill coffee on us. I thought I smelt coffee then. Coffee has a good odor."

"Let us pray!" said the minister.

Such a command always surprises a parlorful of wedding guests. They were so unprepared for it that their heads bowed reverentially. Man is a religious animal.

"Do you take this woman?" "And do you take this man?" "And now." "And now may the blessing of God the Father." The orator had a voice of extraordinary sweetness and force. The long questions rolled up the gradual steep of their accent, and the "Yes" of the bridegroom struck its discord. Again the ascent began, and the whisper of the bride joined with the last of the interrogation.

"What God hath joined together let no man put asunder. Let us pray."

By the side of Daniel's couch sat Mercy Holebroke, and tears were in her eyes. She was unhappy. She knew that Mary was marching at the head of the company and leaping this moment to a social place for which she would have paid whatever price might have been asked. Mercy was glad she had a sufficient excuse to stay away, and yet she was sad in that she should desire to absent herself from an occasion so splendid. We are social beings. We feel most at ease when we are committing the follies on which all our fellows are bent. Mercy pondered whether she had done right or wrong.

"Mary did not want me there, except for the looks of it," she said, "and not one in fifty will know she ever had a sister."

And then she looked at poor Daniel, and was glad she was with him.

For he was gazing lovingly at her.

"You could not stay away from me; could you, my love?" he said.

"No, Daniel."

"You thought you did not love me. That was right. Oh, how you did seek escape! My own, my own!"

She wet the cloth and put it to his throbbing brow.

"I knew you would come to me, even if it were an eternity. How I have loved you! Have I not, little one—say? Have I not?"

"Yes, Daniel."

"I was sorry I loved you. But now I am glad. You will never be cruel to me again—you will not: will you?"

"No, Daniel."

"I am so weak now it would kill me. I would bear it willingly, but I am too ill."

The tears stood in her great eyes.

"I will be kind to you," she said.

With that he passed again into seeming unconsciousness, and Mercy sobbed. It was a sad evening.

Anon, the patient spoke again.

"Kiss me, my little one," he implored—a strange light in his eye.

"Yes, Daniel," she said, her heart beating.

"Kiss me, my love. I never asked it before. Please come to me, and forgive me all my sins."

She looked all round the room. Her face turned a thousand colors. She gave him the shyest of a maiden's kisses.

"God bless you, forever, my sweet little one," he crooned, and raised his hand to caress her shapely head.

The effort was too much. "It's come! It's come!" he gasped, and pressed both hands to his temples, where the clavus had seemed to enter.

She seized the ice and passed it all over his head and face. As she wiped the water away she thought the hue of death was there. She thought his face grew cold, she bethought herself of the hot bottles at his feet. She was everywhere at once.

Then she fell upon that ice-cold face in a passion of grief and kissed it in a hundred places.

She thought she felt his heart beating. "Maybe he is not yet dead," she gasped, and wondered that she had not called the servants. One went for the doctor at her behest. The other took her place as watcher. She seized her outer garments, and was out at the park looking for a car.

"Let me off at Ohio street," she said, and waited an eon while the car tinkled down Clark street, the main artery of the North Side.

She hurried from Clark street toward the lake. She crossed Dearborn, State, Cass, Rush. The streets were jammed with carriages. The drivers descanted on her good looks. She sought the side gate. She entered the kitchen.

The guests had just filed out to the refreshment tables.

"Find Mrs. Trenton and Harmon and Mrs. Holebroke!" commanded Mercy.

There was a commotion in the supper-room. Mrs. Trenton was seen making her way toward the rear apartments.

"Daniel's dying! Can't they come?"

Another commotion among the guests, and others pushing their way toward the servants' bailiwick.

The rounders are ensconced in an absolutely impregnable corner. Everything is within reach,

"These macaroons are devilish clever. A good macaroon must bend, you know. Didn't get a good one last winter!"

"Say, don't stand too near that castle of ice cream. The whole campanile of the Florence Duomo fell on my coat last Tuesday night. I must quit drinking coffee."

"Yes, coffee is a vile drug. I don't sleep any more at all. Did you put those two small bottles down there. Keep your heel against them. We must quit drinking champagne, too —after to-night."

"Wright is doing some good catering this fall—for so early in the season. I say, old man, what's going on over there?"

"I guess something's up. [To the next guest.] What's the matter? It isn't a writ of replevin on the supper, I hope. Oh! Yes. Ah!"

"Start the music," said Mary, with a set face.

The strains of the favorite waltz floated down the grand staircase. The rounder could not hear the remark of his fellow-guest:

"How's that?"

"There's death in the family."

"Well, we must all die some time. I suppose I'll die if I fool with so much of that patent cake. But just save me one more piece. That will do. So her cousin's dead. Why, Errington told me she was without relatives—an orphan he was educating. Don't eat those sandwiches. They're potted meats."

The music waxed in time and tone. The rounders made merry and prepared for the ball. Mr. and Mrs. Trenton, Harmon, Mrs. Holebroke and Mercy hurried toward Fullerton avenue in carriages.

Nothing could buoy the spirits of the hundred women.

"What an evil omen!" whispered the bridesmaids one to another.

The gay bride looked once more at the party as they set

out. One might have believed the cat was in her again. One might have suspected that she wanted to go with them.

Yet it would have been only a suspicion at best.

---

## CHAPTER XIII.

### THE ELIXIR OF LOVE.

Do we live logically? Does one event follow another in due order, and because of the event preceding it? Are none of our emotions thrown away?

For instance, you are at your desk, bent on great deeds. Your pen and paper are locked in a drawer. The key is not in your pocket. It is then ten miles away, in the suburbs! Shocking dilemma! Panic of annoyance! It is wise to look in your vest-pocket. The key is there! The work is possible. One minute of the vilest apprehensions and disappointments. Was it logical—useful? Had it genesis? Did it also spawn into eternity?

Now Daniel, though he had appeared in those unpracticed though beautiful eyes of Mercy, to approach *rigor mortis*, was not to die. The little group coming from the wedding gathered by the bedside, and thankfully saw that the doctor had already restored him.

"It was a collapse," said the doctor. "I presume it is the turning point for the better."

Harmon joyfully carried back the news to Ohio street; Mary was glad. But it counted little with the wedding guests. It would seem vulgar to force one's family affairs on their attention, and the bridesmaids' superstitions having been aroused, could never be laid.

But Mercy wondered why it had all happened. It was a

hard question. Its like bothers us all. She sought her pillow, happy and yet ill at ease. There was a small statue in
Daniel's room. Its face made her blush with maidenly
shame. She wished she had not come to nurse Daniel. She
wished she had not gone down to Ohio street. She wished
she had attended the nuptials as a guest. Yet when she
thought of the ashes that had seemed to gather on Daniel's face,
she knelt in her white robe, pressed her throbbing brow into
the coverlet, and thanked God Daniel had lived. And then,
as she blushed once more, she thought:

"I would be thankful that anybody recovered—'even the
least of these'"—and slept—for women sleep far better than
men.

The wedding trip of Mr. and Mrs. Errington must be a
short one, as Mr. Errington's business pressed. Mary intended to go to Europe. That was why she had married—
so she supposed. But her husband could not start until the
Council adjourned for the summer. Besides, he was just
now starting a company which was to erect smelting works,
make Babbit metal, and assay ore that could now be brought
over the new railways.

While the dance went on Mrs. Errington retired, doffed
the magnificent robe of marriage and reappeared, the quiet,
go-ahead lady of the house, ready, in traveling dress, for a
ride to New Orleans. She would rather that the trip had
been deferred, for she disliked to go away with Daniel dying.
She received the news of his restoration, with the hopes of
his doctor, just as she was leaving the mansion. A half hour
before it would have been sufficient to know he lived. Now
she compared her course with Mercy's, and wished she might
stay.

"I dislike going," she said to Errington, "because there
are many things about that big house that need attention.
I want you to let me bring over as many of my mission boys
and girls as we can use."

" All right, sis," he smiled. " I like to see you interested in the house. That's what I married you for."

They were a practical pair—gray-eyed, both of them. Both wore gray suits. Neither carried much baggage or weight.

And yet, with all her practicality, how much had my lady of caprice ever studied the wishes of others ? How long would dear Ralph pass as a companion ? The thing bored him anyway. He had done it because respectability had become his god. He was now a man of affairs, who found it difficult at all times to recollect Errington, the boodle Alderman, exalted as a man of extraordinary social parts. Mercy, who endured him because he was to be her brother, he almost worshipped—respectfully. The man who would have insulted Mercy would have heard from Errington. Mary had married him because she did not believe that life on an unpaved street was respectable or practicable—for her. She had not learned what poor Errington knew—that the improvements should be put on the character, not on the house. So, by the time the pair had reached New Orleans, Mary was as well bored as her husband. She had there a letter from Mercy. Daniel continued to improve. The wife wanted to shorten the trip.

" What ails me ? " she wondered, petulantly.

And in the house at Fullerton avenue Daniel was gradually restored to sound mind.

" Ah ! Mercy," he said one afternoon, " is that you ? Where am I ?"

" At Mrs. Trenton's, Daniel."

"Haven't I been sick a long time ? "

" A very long time, Daniel."

"Oh, I remember. I was thrown from a buggy. Was the buggy broken ? "

" Not seriously ; but your head was."

"Ah ! yes, I thought death had come. Mercy, how hard it is to die, isn't it ? "

"It is for you," she said.  She was nervous and excited.
She could have wished he had remained her patient forever.

. "Mercy, where is your sister ? "

"In New Orleans."

"In New Orleans !"   He looked at her in blank astonishment.   "Oh !" he said, without emotion, "she must be married."

Mercy said not a word.

"She's married, isn't she ? " he asked.

"Yes, Daniel, she's married—to Errington."

He lay there and thought.

"Well, Mercy," he said, "I believed at one time that to
see Mary marry another man would kill me.  It doesn't—
does it ? "   He smiled.

Mercy looked at the statue, and her cheeks mantled with
shame.

"I shall always like her, because she is your only sister,
Mercy.   But I shall not love her.   She need not fear that.
My love for Mary was based on some misapprehensions of her
character."

His face was mortally sad—as sad as death.   But he spoke
the truth.

"I told her I should not want to meet her any more, but
I shall not be unwilling.   I am glad she married Errington.
I would hate to see harm come to her, because, Mercy—be-
cause I loved her, once."

"I hope she will be happy," said the girl, simply.

"She was always very thoughtless of others.   I have tried
to avoid walking even on sandflies, because I thought Mary
did not think quite enough on such things—not sandflies,
but human feelings.   Oh ! Mercy, you have been so different.
I shall be your brother all your life !  God bless you, Mercy !"

It pained the girl to the heart.   Her bosom rose and fell
tumultuously ; but he was blind.   He did not look closely
at women.   He was a trifle shy of them, at best.   He now

' This is a little cap the boys want you to wear '   Page 59.

regarded them as doubly dangerous to the welfare of men. He could remember only Helen of Troy and Lady Macbeth.

He loved Mercy like a sister. What other term of endearment could she expect from him? She secretly wiped her tears away, and made glad that he was convalescing.

"Mary will be back next week, and writes that she shall expect us all at her house," the maid said, a few days afterward.

"I will go," he said. "I am glad Mary invites me. I'll show her I'm cured." He spoke with a feeling of humiliation for his folly of the past year. "For thou knowest that we are but as grass," he chanted to himself. He gazed on the beautiful girl who bustled around preparatory to leaving for home.

"You owe your life to Mercy Holebroke, young man," said Mrs. Trenton, in a menacing tone. "She has been here half the time."

"I owe her a big nurse's bill, then," he laughed. And as he watched her the vision of all her loveliness came to him for the first time.

"My," he thought, "how lucky I was I did not fall in love with her! *She* would have been sorry for me. *She* would have been good. And the memory of it would have killed me. What eyes! What a neck! What superb braids of hair! What a complexion! I wonder if I ever looked at her before."

Familiarity with her charge had put the girl off all constraint in his presence. She stood at the glass and arrayed herself. A handsome woman looks particularly well when her arms are up and her whole mind is on some hair pin that has proved entirely recreant.

Daniel was watching her like a hawk. "Ah, I am warned in time. She is most beautiful—in form and spirit. For her, men are fated to lose their sleep, to curse the breath that gave them life, to become the gibe of acquaintances and

the foolish almoners of hard-earned wages.   But a little more
and I, poor butterfly, would have had my wings burned off
once again.   Even now my heart goes toward her.   Why
does God make women such as she is and fools such as I
am ? "

He shut his eyes obdurately.   The beautiful woman looked
at him fondly.   He was so glad she was going, for he felt
the weakness of his flesh.   His chastened spirit was still
strong.

"Good-by, Daniel," she said, and her own womanly pride
compelled her to be brief, for it was in the air that he cared
nothing for any woman on earth.

"You are well named," he said.   "You have been an
angel of mercy to me."

And yet he longed to tell her what he had said to Mary—
that handsome women were not careful enough of men's sus-
ceptibilities.

"For, had I not suffered the tortures of the lost," he observed philosophically, "I should have gone head over heels
in love with Mercy."   He congratulated himself on his
escape.

He returned to his place at the proof-reader's desk

"Don't you let me hear of any of you smart Alecks crackin'
any jokes onto him ! " the foreman warned the sharp-tongued
wits.   "Dan, any time you want to stay out till 11 o'clock
just do it, that is till you're real well.   The boys are all
anxious to see you catch on strong again."

So Daniel found it convenient, at Mrs. Trenton's urgent
suggestion, to go over and get Mercy the night of Mary's return to the Ohio street mansion.

"I came to get your mother and you," said Daniel.

" I will wait for Harmon," said the old lady.

"That is bad for me," thought Daniel, who had calculated
on paying the greater part of his civilities to the mother.

But Mercy had little to say.   It delighted Daniel.   Really he was getting his senses. Not every woman could turn his head now. He was in a seventh heaven of self-respect when they arrived at Ohio street. The bride met them at the door. She kissed Mercy, of course. She came near kissing Daniel. She was so pleased to think he was sensible.

"Daniel," she said, going straight to the point, "you and I could never have agreed."

"I am all cured, Mrs. Errington—Mary," he said, for it sounded too tragic.

"Just the man I wanted to see, Dan," said Errington. "Come in here—to—this—library—library—that's it. You see, this grand act is newer to me than it is to you. Leave the women to chat, and give me a half hour or so."

The Alderman was in extremely good humor. Everything had prospered with him, and he wanted the whole family to prosper. He reckoned Daniel as a member of the household. The more in the family the more respectable.

"Dan," he said, "my business is getting too big for me to handle. I'm starting a smelting company, besides. Now, you ain't in very good health, and you ain't getting rich."

"I'm earning a pretty good salary," said Daniel, contentedly.

"Ya-a-s, but what is it? Now, Dan, I'm going to offer you something good. Don't you play the independent racket. I know you won't. You've got pretty fair sense."

Daniel winced. He felt as if he had as little sense as any man he had ever heard of.

"I want you as a sort of lieutenant, to collect my rents and keep my moneys. I shall need you in a thousand ways, and as I am going to Europe in April, to be gone a year, I shall expect you to take full charge in my absence. It's a big thing for you, Dan. Of course, you know you'll not be worth much before New Year's. I'll give you fifty a week till then. And next year, Dan, I'll give you a check for $5,000. Will you do it, Dan? How about that?"

It looked to Daniel as if he ought not to take a place under Mary's husband. Yet, when he thought of it, what was Mary to him now—or what was any other woman? He owed $300 at least on account of his illness. He wanted to make a present to Mercy.

"Dan, I'm a man of business. I know what's good for you. You'll be well off if you come with me. You'll never have the offer again."

Daniel went out of that library a hired man. Mary came forward to meet him.

"Did you make terms?" she asked, and grasped both his hands.

Then she had known! It was strange.

Yes, he had made terms. He went to Mercy and asked her if he had acted wisely.

"Of course you have," she said, overjoyed that his prospects had improved.

Mary was happy again. She was not bored. Why was that? She gazed on Daniel and then on her husband.

"He's a splendid fellow," she said, speaking of Errington, who was busy with some estimates.

"Excuse me, folks," he smiled, "it is going to cost money to keep up this sort of thing, and I have a chance, early in the morning, to take another trick."

He was too familiar—too shoppy. It angered Mary. It angered her, because it humiliated her.

"Daniel would have said that differently," she thought.

And Daniel talked to Mercy until, getting alarmed for his safety, he sought Mrs. Holebroke, while Mary was contented to have him in her sight. She had been anxious to get back to Chicago. She had not known why. Sitting there, in that luxurious apartment, the coil that had promised never to loosen was suddenly sprung in her heart. She found herself in a panic. The room was unsteady, like a star in a telescope. She had lost Daniel. But pshaw! she did not want him!

She was his constant attendant. Had he seen this room? Had he been up-stairs? Had he tried the piano? Wouldn't he whistle "Vuelta Zingara?"

"Certainly," the young man said. He whistled it. She played the chords.

"How flat that sounds!" he thought. "What a fool I was!"

"How remarkable!" she thought. "Why haven't all men music in them?"

"Whistle it again!" begged Mercy, with her big eyes.

And Mary seized the request as an excuse to begin the solemn foreplay. But she stopped as solemnly.

"Once is enough of that!" Daniel had said. For there must be a season for him in which all the music of the past would jar on his sensibilities. "Once is enough!" he repeated, and left Mary with a queer feeling in her heart. She started to catch him and pull him back and make him repeat the aria, but restrained herself barely in time.

"I'll do something foolish," she muttered, and set her face as she had done the night she heard Daniel was dying.

It was a strong, stern character—slow to move. Above it was an impulsive, moving caprice, catching at every passing thing. Caprice had married. Character was to keep the contract sacred. Would character do it?

The young man had never been so happy before. Happiness, for him, meant peace, rest. He gazed upon the future and saw a release from the proof-desk, and thereby escape from the memories that clustered there. Two women loved him, and though he did not consciously suspect it, it is hardly probable that he could have failed to profit mentally in an atmosphere so favorable.

The young wife of the Alderman gazed on Daniel with a rapidly-growing satisfaction. She went over the recital on the drive. "Goodness!" she ejaculated, "how the boy loved me! I hope I am not going to love him that way!"

She pondered on her situation. At every thoguht of Daniel's faithful devotion, which was now as clear as day to her, her heart bounded in gladness. "Nobody else will ever love me that way!" she murmured. "I ought to have known that such a devotion would kindle me at last!"

Her heart sank in an abyss of fear that she had lost him. Then light came to her again. For women are far more hopeful and yet more practical than men.

"He loves me or he would not be here to-night," she thought, and as the she-tiger rises and lashes her great tail when the cub is taken out of her cage, so this gray-eyed wife surged with electric power, and yet was still.

"He loves me. Love is eternal. He can no more escape me now than he could at 257 Clinton street. He thinks he can—that is all. I have him, already."

The refreshments were under discussion. It was hard for the hostess to restrain herself. She desired to show her preference for Daniel.

With much misgiving the young man had taken his seat beside Mercy, and Mercy was happy.

He looked into her eyes once or twice. "I must not do that," he thought. "I wish I could tell her—but I cannot —she is too good."

He was urged to tell her that she ought to be more careful with young men; that they were very foolish and vain; that they thought they could have any woman whom they really loved. If she only knew, Mercy would not be so free with her favors—as Mary had been. If she only knew what depths of torture there were in a disprized love, she was so true and tender that she would never arouse such a tempest until she was ready to calm it with her own love.

"She is too beautiful! I cannot do it. I owe her too much." So the young man quieted the voice of duty to his own sex. To hurt her feelings would be a sad repayment of the great debt he owed her.

The wife saw Daniel and Mercy chatting together, and her face clouded. "Mercy nursed him," she pondered.

"But she's as proud as Lucifer. She has always said she would never take my leavings, and she has often told me he loved me to distraction."

She watched them a quarter of an hour, being particularly vivacious and attentive to her husband's needs—he needing nothing. Then she said to herself:

"It's as plain as day that he cares not a straw for her, at any rate."

And yet, when the she-tiger rose, when that great tail rapidly moved as a warrior's sword comes out of its sheath, one who could have looked down into that gray-eyed woman's soul would have seen danger to man or devil who stood in her way.

Her impulse came upon her.

"Merce," she said, "we're going to take you to Europe with us in April."

"That will be bully," said Errington, who had never heard of this project before.

Mercy looked with deep inquiry into Daniel's eyes. She so longed to see him express his disapprobation of this idea. She had not wanted to leave Daniel at Fullerton avenue. She did not, now, want to go away from him a whole year.

Daniel was full of his new life as a man of affairs. He would have to build the smelting works. He heard with actual delight of this European trip for both his women friends. All the tempters he had ever known or ever should know would be across the wide seas. "I shall not make a fool of myself for a while, anyway," he bragged to himself.

"Go, Mercy," he said, as she peered for advice into his eyes. "I took your judgment to-night; now you take mine."

"You'll go, won't you, Mercy?" said Errington, taking a new interest in the summer's programme of pleasure.

"Yes," said the beautiful girl, proudly; "I shall be glad to go."

And Daniel gazed in rapt admiration upon her.

"Now I am on safe ground," he said, and made himself delightful to two women—to one who loved him madly, and to another who loved him as well as any man may deserve to be loved.

---

## CHAPTER XIV.

### THE SHOE ON THE OTHER FOOT.

The plan of the Smelting Works Company was well worth Alderman Errington's attention. It was to be stocked for $250,000, in 2,500 shares of $100 apiece. It was to involve the expenditure of about $300,000. Only a minority of the stock was to be sold. Midway in the scheme a heavy assessment was to be levied, and as the stock was to be sold only to small holders, a heavy depreciation in the shares was to be forced by their manipulator, and the most of the minority stock was expected to come back to Errington. Building thus began in January. In May little had been done and much had been spent among contractors, who had paid well to get their jobs. It is one of the strangest things in the world that a man will report the loss of an old overcoat to the police, while he will take little note of the manipulations by which the piece of paper in his pocketbook has been reduced in value from $100 to $1. Knowing this peculiarity in men, Ralph Errington cleared $50,000 by having faith in the future of his smelting company after the $100-men had lost faith.

Daniel was at the Ohio street mansion much oftener than he would have wished. He had created a sensation on quitting the proof-room, for all newspaper men dream of leaving the business. His salary was computed at $10,000 a year, and three of his quondam comrades at once went into store-keeping for themselves, where the grand worry of getting rent for their landlord settled down on them and made them gray before their time.

"My wife likes to have me do as much of this planning at home as I can," Errington would say to Daniel. It was extraordinary how much interest the wife took in the smelting works. She learned what metals were to be turned out, what chemicals were to be used, what money was to be made; and, altogether, she was around the library entirely too much.

"She's queer," said Daniel. "I have always misunderstood her."

She hovered over him. She was patient—far more patient than he had been. But as she waited for the return of the love that had burned within him the fires of her passion would sometimes leap overhigh. She had underrated his sense of honor.

"He is blind!" she would say, in rage.

But he was above the crime of loving married women. The thought had never entered his head.

After weeks she saw it. It made her mad with very envy to possess him.

"I had the man's soul once. He would have followed me to perdition then, and love is eternal—it must be."

She would order her carriage, and, reaching the drive over which they had coursed, she would send the coachman back home alone. Then she would strive to remember the spot where the proof-papers had been thrown away.

"Oh! If I could only find a single sheet!" she would lament. "What a fool was I!"

The winter's snows had lain on the ground. A piece of white print paper—what is it?—passing fragile. She found no token of that ride.

"I am happy!" Daniel would say. "Why did not God give me some humility that I might have escaped the scourge?"

The young man's financial situation rapidly eased. He settled with Mrs. Trenton munificently—far beyond that good lady's wishes.

"I want to get Mercy a present for her birthday," he said. So together Daniel and Mrs. Trenton went shopping. On State street they met Mary. They told her their mission. The gray-eyed wife was jealous of Mrs. Trenton.

"Why did you not ask me to go with you to get Mercy's present?" she scolded the next day in the library.

Daniel began to be thankful he had not married Mary. She was morose, and seemed unamiable. Her "magnetism" counted for less every day.

Errington knew Daniel had a present for Mercy. It was hidden in the library, and Mercy was over at the mansion this afternoon.

"Come in, Mercy," the Alderman said; "Dan's got something for you."

"Why do you want to tease her?" Mary said spitefully, as though she thought her husband made too much of his sister-in-law. She was secretly glad of his admiration for Mercy.

Mercy came in. The women were to start for New York the next week. Daniel was safe. He thought too much of Mercy—he saw her beauty too well—with an eye far too practiced—to want her near him much longer.

"Mercy," he said, "you know I am not rich, but I wanted to show you my appreciation of your goodness and mercy to me last fall. It is a nice, useful present—that I know, for I have seen you fuss with your hair a great many times."

The girl blushed—but with pleasure.

The young man had bought for her a triple looking-glass, then a high-priced Parisian novelty. The edges of the three plates were bevelled, the backs were elegantly decorated, and the girl, putting her fine head between the two side glasses, could see every part of her coiffure at the same time. A Russia leather case, with handle, made the glass portable and convenient.

She was delighted, and was enough of a woman to at once see if her hair were arranged at its best.

Daniel laughed. A man descries the natural traits of the fair sex with an odd satisfaction. "God made them so," says the man, and gives his approval.

"Mercy," he said, "there aren't many girls who need a Parisian mirror as badly as you do."

He watched her womanly glee with a pleased air. He thought he had merely touched the feminine chord in her nature.

The wife saw him. She could not understand his thoughts, and she could not restrain her impulse. For a moment she was rash.

"You made *me* no present!" she complained.

He turned upon her in surprise.

"Did you aid Mercy when I was sick?" he inquired, innocently.

She was confused. It was well Mercy was so happy that she could not see or hear.

It was well Ralph Errington had those minor shareholders where they must let go and give him their $50,000. He could see such chances to make money. He could not see that his wife was in love with another man.

As for Daniel, he did not believe that women ever loved at all. He was safe. They could not harm him further.

"Better that I suffered," he soliloquized; "wisdom comes at a great price."

He took Mercy home. "I am very happy," he said, "and I feel I owe my life to you, my sister."

Why could she not accept his brother's love? Why could

she only blush, and be happy and miserable by turns? Why could she not warn him that Mary was too free with him? Oh! she could not! She could not!

"Daniel," she said, "I would rather not go to Europe."

"Pshaw!" he said, "you only fear the voyage. It will do you good, Mercy. I do not think you look quite as fresh as you once did."

Now, why should he say that cruel thing to the beautiful woman who loved him?

She said: "I will go if you think it will make me look any better."

"That is a good sister," he said, and marveled that he kept his head so well. "Oh!" he cried, in triumph, "I have suffered, but I am strong. I wonder why Mercy doesn't get married, too? I suppose she must be engaged," and he peered at her forefingers. They were bare. "An awful pretty hand and foot!" he admitted.

The wife debated her journey to Europe with increasing anxiety. "I need time," she said, and I shall have Mercy with me. The danger lies with Mercy, though Daniel doesn't know it, I think. He loves me or he would love her. When he shall cease to feel my influence he will begin to feel hers."

And it was true that Daniel was afraid of Mary. He remembered the terror she had caused him. She did not know that this very terror was an eternal barrier between them now.

"I wish Daniel could go along with us," she said to her husband.

An idea struck Errington. It pleased him.

"Mate," he answered, "do you think Dan could gallivant you women through Europe a year without creating a talk here? If I thought so, by George, I'd get out of going myself."

"There are two of us—Mercy and I," she said, suggestively.

" That settles it!" he said, well rid of a duty that had an-noyed him. " I'll send Mr. Dan. He'll probably be tickled to death."

Daniel came in. "Dan, old boy," said the Alderman, " we've settled it that you are to take the women to Europe next week, in my place."

Now, what a foolish thing that would be for a young man who was already as near loving Mercy as was Daniel. He pictured himself as a lover once/ more—as a man to whom business and usefulness were secondary things—and his soul revolted.

The wife did not dare to ask him to go. Yet she would have given years of her life to have fallen at his feet and told him she could not live a year from him.

"Mr. Errington," he said firmly, not knowing what might come of it, "it is not business, and I am not going to Europe."

He supposed Mary would revenge herself on him, and that he would have to go back to proof-reading. He felt sure he should fall in love with Mercy, and this he knew too well—or thought he knew—would be another life in death.

And yet, he wished he were stronger. He would have so enjoyed a year with Mercy. She pleased him so well. " I wish women could love me," he said.

He rather resented Mary's dictatorial attitude toward her husband. It would have caused Mary a night of misery had she heard Daniel say : "I wish Mary would not try to be my boss. I'm working for Errington." Yet, how could he get angry ? Everything was contrived for his comfort.

If we, like Mucius Scævola, put an arm in the brazier, our hand is burned away. Nothing will restore it. If we cast away a soul, the soul is lost to us. If love be offered and we refuse it, ought we not to look well to our own hearts to see what may be there in response?

One morning Mary searched in the old book-stores for the

volume—Daniel's present—which she had given away. She had learned it was finally sold in a lot of books, and it was now her hope that she might recover it.

That same day a German girl arrived in Chicago from Chemnitz. She was on her way to Japan, where her lover would marry her. Between France and Great Britain, with their 90,000,000 beating hearts, through the United States with their 60,000,000, this maiden must travel ere she found one heart that beat in unison with hers. Mary had read about the fraulein.

To the beatings of such a rare heart had Mary turned a deaf ear before her own heart had asserted its empire.

" It is worse than Mucius Scævola," she thought ; " I could do that. But I cannot give up Daniel. And then the only peace she had came in the thought that love was immortal.

Mary was a great lady on Jefferson and De Koven streets. She had milk from Mrs. O'Leary. Her coachman lived on Forquer street. The mission was just south of Polk, on Jefferson. She patronized this thick population, and the people were often at her house—servants, messengers, gardeners. They looked upon Mary as their good goddess.

" Dan, you'll have to take Mate to the mission, Sundays," Errington had said, and Mary had clung desperately to this custom and right. She lived in anticipation of it. She disguised her affection for Daniel. She lay as still as ever poor mouse lay, for absence from him was torture. And gray-eyed women of Mary's cast prefer that other people should endure the torture.

She rode with Daniel toward the Foster mission that chilly April Sunday with feelings most solemn and wretched. She must at last go from her handsome and happy companion, and she could hardly bear the thought. She wondered what black fate had put the Dead Sea fruit of European travel before her maidenly eyes when Daniel Trentworthy lived only by her smiles. She saw her good looks and her vivacity pass for nothing on him, and then she saw them passing away in her gorgeous mirrors. The north wind came down as they crossed the West Side bridge, and she shivered to the marrow.

A washerwoman looked into the beautiful carriage and envied its mistress.

"I never was better in my life!" declared the secretary of the Alderman. He felt a solemn influence, and he wished to shake it off. He was happy, and was bound to stay that way. "Enough of the dark valley!" he shuddered.

At the mission he saw Big Bill, and gave that worthy a dollar. That restored the secretary's good spirits.

A moment later the superintendent fell dead. He was well beloved. It was a dreadful thing. It put an end to the session. It cut Mary's afternoon short.

Now was the winter of Mary Errington's discontent. The haughty woman of six months ago was almost despairing. The sudden ride back against the benumbing north wind gave her the feeling of death. She wept.

"I know it was dreadful," said Daniel, with compassion. "He was a great believer in you, Mary."

She could have cried forever to hear him speaking soft and low to her.

"Oh, Daniel," she sobbed, "I dread to go to Europe."

"So does Mercy," he said, and wondered what Europe had to do with it.

"Women are very queer creatures," he observed, philosophically. He had heard Harmon say it. He had heard the foreman say it. He had heard Errington swear it by the great horn spoon.

He was beginning to believe it himself!

## CHAPTER XV.

### ANTIMONY.

"I BELIEVE Dan inherits all his father's financial ability," said Errington to Mary. "I'm glad I can leave my business in his hands."

It cheered her to hear Daniel praised. It was all the satisfaction she had. She could not yet be his wife. She was his mother.

No coaxing would take him to New York to see the party leave.

"It's business. The boy's business. Dan, I'm going to take you in as a partner," said Errington, approvingly. And then he whispered: "When you and Mercy come to terms. Eh! you rascal, you! I'd like to be in your shoes."

"Good-by, Mercy," Daniel said. "God bless you, my dear sister. I'm sorry to think you'll be away from me a year."

"But it is big luck for me," he admitted, as he was tempted to look down in her beseeching eyes.

"My! Mercy Holebroke is a beautiful woman!" He was just getting back to his eyes and his senses.

And was not that a hard position for a maiden who wanted to cry, and who must wait till her turn came to bid good-by to her mother?

So Mercy blushed and turned pale, and held back her tears.

"Good-by, Mary," he said, "I've heard you say often that you would pluck out your heart for a year in Europe."

If love were immortal, as this wife thought, she questioned that this young man, a volcano of affection, could leave her without a pang.

Volcanoes sometimes become extinct.

"Don't let the grass grow around the smeltin' works, Dan, me boy," was the injunction of the Alderman, as the train pulled out.

So Daniel was free! It pained him a little, as he saw the tears in Harmon's eyes and heard the moans of the mother heart. It pained him a little. Mercy was a girl after his own ideal.

But the gray-eyed woman! He was growing uneasy over her. She had made him too solemn last Sunday in the carriage! He had had all the misery he wanted, and he associated all misery with women. He never saw men in tears until they had been in love, or married. "Errington gets along," said Daniel, "but I could not."

He had looked forward to this hour. He had wished it had come when he rode with Mary last Sunday. He took a car and rode to Mrs. Trenton's house. That lady had just arrived also from the depot.

"Daniel," she insisted, "you are a heard-hearted young man, or else you are as blind as a bat."

He looked quizzically at the good woman.

"You ought to know Mercy worships the ground on which you walk."

This, of all things, was the most ludicrous speech he had ever heard Mrs. Trenton make.

"So did Mary," he said tauntingly, "when you thought she could so enjoy a buggy ride."

Her face shaded. "Tell me, Daniel, about that ride."

"A burned child dreads the fire," he said, irrelevantly, for he could not keep his thoughts from Mercy.

"Will you have some strawberries, Daniel?"

"No, I will never ask Mercy to be my wife nor any other woman."

"Strawberries, Daniel?"

"Although I am making lots of money this year, I wish some of my old comrades who are settled had it instead of me."

Mrs. Trenton let him alone. He had not thought to look at the locomotive or its engineer. Would the train go through safely?

9

He took the long ride in the street-car which he had made with heart so turbulent when the gray-eyed maid was along, and which he and Mercy had taken so often and so peacefully. He reached the modest house at Clinton street. He beheld the loneliness of that mother heart, and pitied her. He could not put away the feeling that a kindred feeling was making him wondrous kind. He was not so glad that Mercy was gone.

"Gracious!" he cried, smiting his breast, "she did not go a moment too soon. He went to bed and dreamed what a good girl Mercy was, and she began to have black eyes instead of gray. When he awoke, he remembered this. "If Mercy is losing the gray eyes when I dream, then I'm falling in love with her surely." He admitted it with self-reproach.

The smelting works went forward with a rush. The newspapers gave the institution free advertising galore. The chimney rose to a height that put it on the level of the shot tower and the water-tower as a sight of the city. The cupolas, and blasts, and cranes, and moulding-rooms, and treasure-house, and ore-bins, and side-tracks, were on a magnificent scale. Antimony had been found as an ore in Colorado, silver and lead were coming in from Utah and Wisconsin. It was deemed possible to make all the Babbitt metal, type metal, white metal, gun metal, bell metal and amalgams that would be used in the West. A brass and bronze foundry was a part of the scheme. The stock was unpurchasable.

It may be that the great money-maker, now absent in Europe, had over-reached himself. It may be that it was unwise for him to attempt respectability with his record open behind him. The stockholders who had sold their stock set up a loud complaint, and what was more to the point, laid plans for revenge. When a man occupies a political position, personal revenge can nearly always be gratified. Especially was this easy with Alderman Errington's enemies. He had a year to serve in the Council, but he had moved out of his ward. He was a silk stocking. The old blower and striker had become a prominent citizen. It made Jack and Bill, and Mike and Larry angry to think of "Ralphy" Errington as a silk-stocking. They set out to down him.

Daniel's first letter to his principal detailed the efforts that were making in the old ward to break down the Alderman's following. "Let them go it, Dan. Tell them I'm out of ward politics. But I will not resign under fire." This was Errington's reply.

But it annoyed the husband to be traveling in Europe while he had so many interests at stake in Chicago. He sometimes doubted the advisability of being respectable. Still respectable he was. He was proud of his wife. He walked up and down the boulevards and by the shops of Paris, with Mercy on his right arm and Mary on his left, and he failed to see anybody else who looked "as well off in women," as he put it. He was astonished to find that Paris could make a fire ordinance work, and saw many things that repaid him for his journey. Chicago, of course, was the biggest, most wonderful, and best built town on earth—yet there were people, and houses, and streets in London—so he admitted. He would have moved to London, except that respectability came far too high. He blessed his own institutions. "We have but one grade of nobility," thought the tourist. And in his mind's eye he saw the packages of greenbacks he had taken out of the briber's fruit-basket.

"It makes no difference how they became Dukes—they got there. It makes no difference how I got my money. I've got it. And I've got Chicago."

He thought of his 400 tenants. He thought of his great mansion, his library of 10,000 volumes, all picked out by Daniel, for the wife had suffered not a book that Daniel had not chosen. He thought of the great smelting-works. He looked sidewise at his beautiful sister-in-law, and when people addressed her as Madame Errington he was by no means insulted.

When Mary arrived in Europe she heard a great deal of a case of poisoning by a Scotch doctor who wanted to get rid of his wife. The doctor had made an insidious use of antimony, in various preparations, and it was the talk of the day that never did mineral poison do its work and leave less trace of its presence. The wife died so gradually, and had believed so implicitly in the fidelity of her murderous husband, that the evidence leading to conviction had nearly all been circumstantial, extraneous to the deed itself. Mary read that a post-mortem examination had failed to reveal the metal. The doctor was to be hanged. All the maudlins in the civilized world were weeping for him. She wondered if he were leashed to a woman for whom he had no love, while another love lay dormant—while another lived without whom life was a nightmare. She laid down the newspapers with a profound feeling of pity for the doctor and the matter passed out of her mind, and well it might, for it was the first time in Europe that her thoughts had once diverted from the handsome young man in Chicago whose miserable slave she now was. She took note of places and lions only to write about them and send the long letters to Daniel. He was interested in the travels of the party, and read her descriptions with care. He answered her epistles with letters of thanks and reread the doings of the party to the folks at home.

And Mercy—what should she write? If she made the letter long, it would look forward. If short, she feared Daniel might grow still colder. She treasured even his brother's love. She ended by being her honest self. She told him she was lonesome, and homesick—that she sighed for home, though she knew the trip was enlarging her view of things. "Chicago is not the only place in the world," she wrote. "It is a city that has little and claims much. Yet it is the only place in the world that I sigh to see."

Daniel went about his work with a glad heart. "You are so good to me, my sister," he answered, "that the time goes

by like a summer's day. Write to me often. Do not forget
me."

One day one of the nineteen ringsters came to Daniel's
office and ordered that young man to lock his door.

"You're Errington's smooth young man," said the caller,
"and you are in with all his play. You worked this smelting
works panic."

Daniel protested that he knew absolutely nothing about
Mr. Errington's private financial affairs.

"It won't do, young man. Errington has gone to Europe
to avoid service, as the lawyers say. Now, you cable to your
man that the eighteen say he got $10,000 on the deal with
the Sub-Aqueous Amusement Company, and that the eighteen
has got to have $5,000 apiece, before Aug. 1. Tell him D. K.
and B. say so."

With that the "hard man" representing the eighteen left
without as much as good-by, and care at last sat on Daniel's
troubled brow.

He cabled to Errington that an Alderman, representing
eighteen, wanted $90,000. He did not know what to say,
except that such a demand had been made.

Errington, Mary and Mercy were at a Swiss hotel. Mary
had passed a peculiarly wretched day. She had lived over a
thousand times those hours at Clinton street when Daniel
would tremble with pleasure if she but addressed him a word
at supper. She thought with amazement of the days and
hours that she had denied the boy all sight of herself. She recalled his alacrity when she would ask him to go over to the
mission, and she coupled those happy walks down the narrow
Jefferson street toward Polk with that awful ride in the carriage the day the superintendent died. How she had tortur-
ed the boy with her declarations that she would marry no man
who could not keep a carriage, and go to Europe every other
year. "I think people ought to travel *some* in their own
country!" the girl would toss her head and say, as they passed

into the still narrower way at Harrison street. Errington had not come on the scene then.

"Errington!" she hissed between her teeth, and looked at him as though he had taken her cub away. She had moments of almost uncontrollable fury. She was not a woman to be balked, and yet she was hardly three months on a tour farther and farther away from Daniel. Why had she done so much to preserve appearances? What were appearances when the situation grew every day more insupportable? Mercy was getting letters from Daniel, and was not reading them to her sister. That fact alone made the wife's breath short.

There sat this politician, old enough to be her father. How she resented his age now! How she despised a man who would marry a woman who did not love him!

He held a dispatch in his hand and gazed at it with clouded face.

"Mary," he said, hesitatingly, for he expected a genuine storm, "I'm afraid I'll have to post off home. Daniel advises me to come. Business is going wrong—and this thing takes money, you know."

An unexpected joy came to the gray woman's heart. It was Daniel's message for Mary to come. It must be.

"I'm so glad!" cried Mercy. "I'm homesick already. I'll go back with you."

"Of course, I do not want to be away from you, Ralph," the wife said obediently.

Errington waited for no change of opinion. He hurried to the landlord and countermanded all previous arrangements.

Daniel was at the depot to receive the tourists. He had bad news for them.

"Harmon is very sick, and your mother could not leave him."

"What is the matter?" asked both the sisters in alarm.

"Lead colic."

"What is that?"

" It is a disease that attacks some typesetters. The type gives off a dust, and there is antimony in the metal to keep it hard and free from rust. I suppose you know antimony is a dangerous poison."

" Yes, I have heard so," answered the gray-eyed wife, looking on Daniel, and gloating over the fact that she had rescued him from a printing office. How good-looking he was ! How jealous she was growing of Mercy !

---

## CHAPTER XVI.

### DIATHESIS.

Now Alderman Errington was not a man to be blackmailed by a fellow-boodler. He called those ringsters together and read the law to them.

" You duffers," he said, " can't expect to go blowing your money against wine and women and then come back on me. Do with your boodle as I did, and you will not need to whine. And remember this : ' Whenever you ones get ready to go down the road, I'll make the best fight of you all to get clear. If I go down for three years, you will go down for ten.' "

To go down the road is the simple term of the thieves for the trip to a penitentiary.

The ringsters shivered. Their dream of bleeding Errington was o'er. Worst of all, he would make no more deals.

" You'll have to get in some other go-between," he concluded. " I'm going to vote steadily agin the combination."

" What have they got on you ?" asked Daniel.

" Dan, dear boy, they are a pack of bloodhounds. They've got nothing—nothing. I've got it on them. But say, my boy, I've done a good deal for you ; now haven't I ? Well, you stand by me—say, will you ? "

" Of course I will. Don't you ever believe I'll go back on a benefactor. I don't care what you've done. I'll always be true to you."

" Yes, Dan; that's you, I know it. Now you take care of the women folks and let me fix them fellers over here on Jefferson. I think we can start the blasts in a week. Dan, there's millions in that scheme."

He went off with a will. He was a born money-maker. " Ha!" he thought, " this is pleasanter than picking out your trunks at an English station. This is a heap more sensible than looking at a church that lost its boom in the year of our Lord 1200."

The ores began to arrive, the hot blast began to roar, the fumes of vaporized metals began to blast the surroundings, the citizens complained about their eyes, and the great oculists took specks of metal from the iris at $25 a speck.

" I ought to have a rake on those eye-doctors," thought the great smelter. A rake is a gambler's tithe or toll, which he takes as payment for furnishing the arrangements. The word *rake*, alas! has been heard in Chicago far oftener than the word *tithe*.

And Mary was much at Harmon's side. She conned the encyclopedias. She bought works on poison. She became an adept in diagnosis. Harmon mended, and went back to work. Mary's antidotes were magical; her prophylactics were worth Harmon's carrying. Often had she tried to wean Harmon from his trade. No, he liked it. She had feared it would injure her position in society, but it did not. He would come to her house to take supper, and she would hear a low hiccough. A cup of strong tea would be at hand in an instant. "Drink this," she would say, and Harmon would feel relief. She was very skillful.

" We're turning out a heap of type metal and stereotyping stuff Harm.," Errington would say at such times.

" There's a great deal of poisonous metal in the air at the

works," the wife would remark. "I was there yesterday. My dear, I am so afraid it will hurt your health."

She had not long my-deared her husband.

She was growing thoughtful and tender. It did not appeal to Ralph Errington's nature.

"Fudge!" he retorted.

"My dear," she said, "you show its effects already. You'll yet be as sick as Harmon—and he is foolish to stand over a type case."

"Oh, what are you giving us, Mate?"

But my-lady's mind was on the subject. "I don't want you to go there," she said.

"Well, I'll go, just the same," he answered. He smiled at the idea of not going to the Great Occidental Alloy Works. "That's too good," he declared. "She's getting to be a granny. But I'll attend to my own business. She always was strong-minded, and now she's got her head turned doctoring up Harm."

He entered the works. The flavors of all the metals greeted his nostrils with the odor of 500 per cent on his investment. His face was pallid in the white light of burning antimony, but his money-getter's spirit rose to supernal heights. "Oh!" he said, "that smells like business!"

They were burning out zinc. "What makes the fume?" he asked of the boss.

"We're clearing off the antimony."

"Did you ever know it to hurt anybody?"

"Sometimes a man can't stand it. But it about all goes up."

The family physician was questioned by Mary about Harmon's case.

"Do printers get sick very often?"

"Not down sick, like your brother. There are perhaps 500 typesetters in Chicago. I presume Harmon is the only one suffering from acute symptoms of antimonial poisoning.

But printers are gradually poisoned very often. A workman who ordinarily does not take enough fresh air to outweigh the effects of the poison has a very peculiar diathesis. It would not take much more to kill him. He does not, on the average, attain to an old age."

Mary visited the works. She inquired casually which was the antimonial ore. There it lay in heaps, fresh from Colorado—hard, gray chunks, the rock holding crystals of the metal. She gazed on it as one fascinated. Where did they put the ore after smelting it—that ore, for instance? She pointed to the antimony.

The boss showed the pigs of lead-looking metal.

"Oh!" she exclaimed; she supposed that the alloymakers used a sort of powder or butter of antimony.

No, the pigs were what they used. Again, they might not have any antimony by itself for months.

"I am so afraid of my husband losing his health here," she said to the boss. "Remember, if ever anything should happen to him I should never forgive you people who got him interested in these works."

"I never heard of but one bad case, ma'am," said the boss. "I knew a man who got it so bad that nothing ever saved him. He was sick a year."

"Smart wife, Errington's," the boss said to a helper.

"It is very strange," she muttered as she went homeward, "that a type-setter should get sick and a smelter should escape. The doctor says it's all a matter of diathesis. I will study that word."

"Mary," Daniel said one Sunday in September, "I guess you had better have one of these men about the house go over to the mission with you. Ralph has some enemies over there who will take advantage of anything to hurt him or you. I would not like to hear you talked about."

She was deprived of her only right. What did she care if all DeKoven and Jefferson and Taylor streets talked and wagged their tongues?

Of course, Daniel, I will do whatever you think best."

"Well, I was uneasy all last winter, and now Ralph is going to have trouble. Hasn't he told you ? "

Have trouble! She had married a man because he was rich, not because he was to have trouble. She married him for better, not for worse. (

" He has told me nothing."

The fire bells rang a general alarm. The entire populace poured southward toward the bridges. Great clouds of smoke rolled toward the zenith.

"There is a great fire, Daniel. Will you not take me to it ? "

She was triumphant. "He shall love me!" she said. She took his arm and walked in the crowd. She nestled close to him with every surging of the mass of anxious beings. He was so handsome and so strong! His arm would go out so sturdily as the crush came in crossing the bridge. She gloried in her good fortune. She was thankful that the mission was out of the question. Never before had she enjoyed the opportunity of clinging to him as her awakened heart prompted her to do. They got out of the mass after crossing the bridge. She had always detested crowds. She loved this one. Oh ! for a bridge like the one over the Potomac, over the Scottish frith—a never-ending passage, where people might push her and attempt to trample her, and where Daniel should say : " I guess you will have to cling tight to me, Mary !" Then, " Keep off this lady, you ! Be more careful next time !" with a lunge that would send the clown forward smartly.

What a god a man becomes to the woman who hopes to secure his love !

" I tell you," the foreman of the proof-room had observed to Daniel, " these women that are hard to catch—that are slow to warm up—they'll lick the right man's boots ! That's what they'll do,"

It was the great Drake Block that was on fire. Its mansard roof—the pride of the city—was all aflame. It stood between Washington and Madison streets, on the east side of Wabash avenue, and was even a more conspicuous building than Field & Leiter's new retail establishment.

The wife and the private secretary had reached the little plot of ground called Dearborn square. There, for hours, they watched the slow destruction of nearly three millions of property.

Some of the citizens asked why a tinder-trap was allowed on top of five stories of stone front. But Chicago at large was so smitten with Mansard's contrivance that it was said if Chicago must burn because of Mansard roofs, "Then let her burn!"

The fire was very deliberate. It was beyond reach, and could take its own time. It was a delightful afternoon—not a cloud in the sky, not a breeze astir. Spectators fell to discussing their mutual affairs.

"Will you be down to-morrow, George?" one would ask the other.

So the wife, watching her opportunity, found it here. The young man was, of course, interested in the doings of the firemen.

"I have had some of that!" he said, significantly.

"Do you remember how we practiced together, Daniel, in those days? I wish they would come again."

"I was a ninnyhammer in those days, Mary. I must have caused you much annoyance. But you brought good luck to both of us."

He was thinking of Mercy. He looked into Mary's eyes. They were black now—so he thought. Whatever traits the sisters had that were alike were here credited to Mercy's account. He looked as though he were admiring Mary, but he was trying to see Mercy. Mary, the gray-eyed maiden, had died to him that cruel afternoon in the spider—that afternoon which had so nearly killed him, body and mind—which had so clearly set its mark between the past and present, between continuous disaster and uninterrupted peace.

"I wonder if I am not already in love with Mercy past getting out," he thought as he gazed in Mary's face.

It was the only happy moment she had found since the coil of love had sprung in her heart. She dared not to speak ; she dared not to move. She hoped he might gaze on forever. "The building will burn for hours," she calculated greedily. He still loves me. I will have him."

"Let us go home," he said.

Her moment was over. She was so loath to go that she made excuse after excuse. But Daniel was accusing himself of thoughtlessness in that he had not gone over for Mercy. He hoped there might yet be time.

"Come on," he said, "let us hurry. Here is a car. No, I cannot walk. I have an important engagement."

The wife, balked, was yet happy beyond her hopes. "He is so upright that though I saw his love, I could not move," she said, and then she set her gray face.

There was but one person in her way. Ralph Errington was where he might be poisoned with antimony.

---

## CHAPTER XVII.

### IN LOVE.

THE fall and winter of 1870-71 passed. Daniel Trentworthy had $5,000 of his own money. He bought a handsome little brick house and lot on West Washington street, which then was enjoying the prosperity that always follows the paving of a street in a town that is below grade.

The chief owner of the alloy works was on hand night and day. The output of the metals that enter into commercial use was immense. His face assumed a transparent look. He lost interest in everything save the furnaces.

His wife protested with increasing urgency that he was killing himself.

"Pshaw!" he said, "I will outlive Harmon. See how hard it is to kill him! He gets $5 a day. I get a thousand —some days."

In February there came a warm, damp air, and smoke fell to the ground. The Alderman came to his home at night with a brassy taste in his mouth. "I must get a gold spoon," he said. "Silver tastes bitter to me nowadays. One evening late in the month he could eat little supper. He had severe palpitation of the heart. Further on he was seized with violent illness. There was a great uproar at the house. Doctors came in the greatest haste.

"It is the smelting works!" the wife said.

"It is cholera morbus," the doctors said. One doctor thought it might be sporadic cholera. "There are cramps," he said. "It is the diathesis of a cholera patient."

The wife was not satisfied. She must have the best advice. The greatest man in the city came as a special favor at his own fee. The wife gave him her reasons for believing it might be mercury or antimony in his system.

"It is antimony," the great man said. "He will not die, or he would already be dead." They gave the patient quinine and opium and applied leeches to his throat and stomach.

It was a fearful attack. Ralph Errington issued from it, in appearance, a decrepit old man.

"Keep away from the smelting works!" cried the doctors. The great specialist was gone now.

But how could a poor dollar-getter, to whom time was

money, and money was power—how could he stay away from
his gold mine? As well try to keep a miser from counting
his treasure. He haunted the works and everybody declared
he was a wretched fool.

"It makes me sick," said the boss, to see a man who will
not take a lesson when experience teaches it. He comes
around here like a ghost, and it hurts the business, because it
scares our men. Now, Errington's one man in five hundred.
He's the second man of the kind I never heard of, or heard
tell of, and he'd die rather than give up that he can't stand
the dust and fumes."

It was not alone the antimony that was breaking the
successful Chicagoan. The way of the transgressor is hard.
He was out of politics, and the new Council was not willing
to dicker with the sub-aqueous corporation. The agent
indignantly referred to previous Councils and produced his
proofs. The summer of 1871 opened with rumors of corruption at some time within the statutory limitations, and a grand
jury was asked to look the matter up. Errington had paid a
great price for his respectability. He had a high regard for
all the people with whom he had gained a good social standing through his wife's folks. He could not bear exposure,
and so cast himself on Daniel's advice.

Daniel talked to Mercy about it. The pretty girl lived on
in hope. Her patient of the long ago was still her brother.
It was such an age, she thought, and yet it was only a year
and a half—scarcely longer than a heart stays hurt. Both
Daniel and Mercy were attached to Errington. They could
not bear to see him ruined. And with his approaching
troubles came these awful attacks of illness.

How did the gray-eyed wife bear up under all this load of
trouble? Not only did she have her own husband in charge,
but she nursed Harmon, whose case grew equally serious,
though less acute in form. He had come to Ohio street. She
alone could administer relief. When doctors had failed to

quiet the suffering of either or both her patients, some gall, or tea, or application would save the suffering one. Belief in her skill was growing.

"I have been repaid a thousand times for my studies," she would say.

Mary had married for a trip in Europe and a house where great parties might be given. Her poor old mother lamented the distance now, as she came on her visits of mercy.

"Never a party has she had," the mother would murmur. And then she would look at the faces of the two sick men and grow uneasy beyond expression.

"I think they are getting better, mother," the gray-eyed woman would say.

She would have given her mansion if Harmon's case would have yielded to her remedies.

"I am afraid they will both die," the stricken mother would lament. What were her hop-bags now; and all her simples, when leeches and the strongest drugs were the only remedies to which the sick ones would respond.

"Isn't the Christian's case a strange one?" the printers would say. "And he has a brother-in-law down the same way."

"Yes, but it's Errington, who got up the smelting works. They make the Babbitt metal there, and type metal, and all that."

It was poison. Poison is partially defined as a substance which, in passing through the tissues of the body, sets up inflammation. Inflammation of the alimentary canal, when acute, attacks the life savagely, as it were a case of cholera. Then, if the patient withstand these attacks he must subsist on a small allowance of the fuel which is furnished from the capillaries that suck from the alimentary canal. With the entire passage in a heated state the patient will grow weak from lack of blood, and the administration of invigorants will only arouse the dormant inflammation. Through a constitution predisposed to "lead colic," and through twenty years absorption of metallic dust, Harmon Holbroke, the Christian, was now hopelessly ill.

Mary Errington bent every energy to his care. "If he only had a constitution," she would reason, "I could restore him."

But the Christian had no constitution. Year after year he had gone five nights a week to that typesetter's room, where the floor had not been washed since 1848; where layers of dirt, chiefly tobacco, were four inches deep around the posts of the case-racks; where the thermometer, burning at 110 of a hot summer night, under a hundred gas jets, drove men to strip almost naked that the people might have the latest news of battle or reconstruction. There he had dug his wan fingers into a ball of pink chalk designed for a lady's face, and striven to handle the turtle type that stuck together with ink as though they were magnetic. A horrible air! A place filled with experiences that affright the new-comer. There—that his mother might not want, that Mercy might stay East, that Mary might graduate from High School—had the Christian toiled.

There are many unknown heroes.

"The Christian doesn't drink," the foreman had said, "but he means all right, just the same. He's a mighty sight better to his family than some of our fastest men who drink the most with the boys."

A "fast" workman was highly considered on a morning paper in those days—especially if he drank well.

"I don't know but you were right, Mary," the sick brother said one day. "You can take care of mother and Mercy, You know I opposed your marriage at first. But money is a useful thing when one loses health."

It maddened the gray woman to think that the brother to whom she owed so much should sink so steadily.

And when Daniel would come into that house of misery,

10

where the superstitious servants held council every night whether or not the curse would fall on all, Mary would meet him with such tenderness that the young man pitied her from his heart.

"Mary has a deep nature," he said to Mercy. "She is greatly improved by her misfortunes."

The pretty sister was over at Ohio street early that morning. "Ah! I'm glad you've come," cried Daniel. "I can take you to see the German procession."

Mercy was happy, and the gray woman saw it. She interposed no remark. There was none to be made. The unmarried sister had been much neglected of late. For a year she had been a recluse. For a month she had often been alone in the Clinton street house.

What seasons of dryness fall upon our lives! There are times when the dust blows upon our souls, month after month. There are seasons when every friend loses interest in us, when every once pleasing memory grows stale and unprofitable.

Poor Mercy, on that unpaved street, with trouble falling thick upon her family, with her noble brother no longer standing as a pillar of support, with the young man she loved making no sign, but taking all for granted that she could forever be his sister and not cry out, the strain that was on her heart—poor Mercy, it was a season of unquenchable thirst, of weariness without sleep, of falling eyelids without rest for the eye.

In this Sahara of the spirit rose up this little oasis of the German celebration. She went with Daniel. And she was happy. And Daniel was happy.

The Germans had "sent ten thousand Frenchmen down below—praise God, from whom all blessings flow"—such was the bitter jest of the time, for the times were bloody with civil war here and Commune there. The Kaiser had put on the imperial crown in a French palace. But the great Kaiser and his greater chancellor did not feel prouder than

Daniel as he left Mary's house with Mercy in his care for the day.

She looked into his handsome face and recalled the hour he had been hers—hers to fondle and kiss. And then she thought of the statue.

"Did you know that man ?" Daniel asked.

"No, I never saw him."

"You turned almost scarlet."

"Did I ?" and she was already pale with fear. Oh! she was a guilty piece ! She pitied poor Errington.

"He never was as bad as I !" she confessed ruefully to herself.

Daniel gazed at her, full of admiration. He stepped high. He cast a menacing eye at all men who looked too long at the beauty by his side. He thought that she might have known that even passers-by disturbed him. He was head over heels in love once more. And when he announced the fact to himself he was not filled with consternation, as he thought he should have been.

They were still standing at the iron gateway on Ohio street. The promenaders were passing. It was a holiday, and the North Side was the centre of the festivities.

"I think we had better go on down to Wabash avenue," he said, for he wanted to walk with her.

"I have a house," he thought, with a strange exaltation. "I could keep her. I wonder if she will ever forget what a fool I made of myself over Mary ?"

He looked in Mercy's face. There was no hope. The maiden considered that she had been much wickeder than her brother-in-law. She was doing penance with prudery.

It was too late. He dared not give her a sign of his thoughts.

The gray woman stood at the open window above the staircase. Her heart had hardened anew that morning, as she saw Harmon sinking in strength.

Her heart was stony now, as she saw these young unmarried people depart. She turned to her duties. She shrank not. She had two patients to nurse, who, everybody knew, were suffering from mineral poisons, gradually absorbed into their. systems.

" Bad cases !" said the doctors.

———

## CHAPTER XVIII.

### SOMETHING ON DANIEL'S MIND.

WHY does a man fall in love ? Undoubtedly it is a provision of nature, at times even more arbitrary than the instinct of self-preservation.

Why had not Mary fallen in love with Daniel while the influence operated on her ? Not because she had not felt that influence, but because another and transient desire was just then paramount.

Darwin speaks of the dilemma of a migratory bird, forced to choose between the desire to fly away, and the desire to stay with her fledglings. The time come, the mother-bird finds that the impulse to fly is uncontrollable, and succumbs to it. Arrived in Africa or South America, she is no longer the slave of that instinct. Then her mother-love again holds sway, and she may die of lonesomeness, while the fledglings may die of neglect. I am not arguing that the hypothesis is based on possibilities. Darwin must do his own arguing. But it suits for my figure. Mary, flown to Ohio street, wanted Europe and society no more. She wanted Daniel. She could not, or would not—there is no difference—live without him. Pitiable victim of such omnipotent desires !

Again, why does a man fall in love ? Why are the eyes

hoodwinked until ugliness becomes perfection—until Bottom becomes king of the forest? Possibly it is a relic of barbarism. Possibly nature meant that when a man fell in love he was to fight and win, or to die and rid the race of his bad prowess. Possibly Daniel's desire to seize Mary was correct in natural law, and, in general operation, would improve our breed of man, which is running desperately low. But civilization interfering—the maiden being secure from her true lover's chase—in what an unnatural plight does the disprized lover suddenly find himself! His suicide often promptly attests this. Perhaps his death would have resulted as often under the old tribal regime, when men fought for their women. But at the least, does it not affirm the solemnity of love? Will men and women ever stop reading love tales; will he or she who may be at any time the victim of despotic, of mystic natural forces—will he or she refuse the study of the strongest emotions we have? Hardly.

And what has civilization done for man, after balking his prowess and dwarfing his breed? It has left him to the snares of self-destruction. Yet, if he escape them, he may outlast the film which nature put on his eyeballs, and may see clearly once more. It is the very persistence of love! For were a proud man's idol married, as Mary was, he could only worship her from afar, even if the chicken's lid still lay on his eye. But that veil drops off. Some day he looks at his whilom mistress, and lo! she is only a woman. She must be compared with other women, a harsh thing to do, any woman will admit! So, then, escaped from bottomless terrors, the man's selfishness has play. He is undoubtedly hard to shoot with Love's second dart. The prettiest woman in Christendom may smile on him and seek to enmesh him with her queenly favors. He will not put himself upon her attention. He has no lordly conceit. He is for a given time a drone in the hive of generating life. He has not entirely lost faith in the desirableness of women to men, but he has gotten the idea that he cannot have the woman he may want, and no amount of sweet insinuation, no amount of gentle favor, from the queenliest and best will arouse him from this torpor. But, if the queen be patient with her poor subject, the time will come when Nature will move him once more, be he ever so stubborn. The veil will fall upon his eyes once more, and he will look around for the peer of her whom he lost through the conventions of civilization.

To such a second stage was Daniel come. And Mercy had been true, and had grown even more beautiful, for since the German procession she had hope. But your lover with his second veil is a wise animal. There be silver foxes you cannot entrap. He is a silver fox. Though it take him years, the second maid shall never know he loves her until she first makes bare her heart. Thus the proud beauty, scorning the prayers of all her lovers, must make love to Daniel, or lose him. It is a hard thing for a maid to do. She doubts if she has retained her innocence and purity. What would her mother say?

With the inconsistency of common sense, the hard-headed mother would say it all depended on whom the man might be.

This was Mercy's situation during those dry months in the late summer of 1871, when Daniel and Mercy, in going and coming from the Clinton street house, were together much of the time.

Daniel was certainly cold in his outward bearing toward Mercy. The gray woman of sorrows looked at him and said that, whether or not Mercy would marry him if she could, he did not love Mercy. Love was eternal. She, the gray woman, was winning. The gloom that grew over everything affected her not. Her mind was on a great project. She was not one to fail.

The patients were both sinking rapidly. The family were all at the Ohio street house every day. The doctors said a damper air would aid in giving the sick men strength, and fell back on the unparalleled drought as a cause for the non-efficacy of their medicines. Grass and foliage were badly burned. A shrub, watered properly from a hydrant, would give off its moisture within an hour to the fevered atmosphere, and be seemingly dryer than when watered. There often comes upon Chicago a straight south wind which blows with peculiar steadiness, night and day. The true south wind sucks moisture like a sponge. All through this memorable summer there had been protracted seasons of south wind. The spring and early summer had been very dry. A good rain fell the 3d of July, and people felt that the backbone of the drought was broken. But this was only the beginning of the parching which the city endured. Starting in dry where ordinarily it is wet, the dog-days passed without rain, as they often do, but the equinoctial brought no clouds. The gales came, truly enough, but they were thirsty themselves. The shingles of wooden houses lolled like mastiff's tongues. Two and one-half inches of rain was all the drink that Nature gave the region from July 3 to October 9. The equinoctial gale came barren as Sara before Abraham was promised seed. It was difficult to stand up in the streets. The wind blew in all directions. The passage of a main current through a street would be so rapid that the wind would rush in from all cross-streets, as fences and sheds are sucked towards a tornado.

On Friday, the 6th of October, 1871, Daniel left the house at Ohio street at noon. The patients were both very low, but as they had been sick so long, it was thought they would eventually overcome the disease. Mary was sure Harmon would be out soon. She almost clung to Daniel as she accompanied him to the door. To touch him was all she lived for now.

"How the wind blows!" she shivered as she opened the door but an inch. "Oh! Daniel! stay in this afternoon, and help me! I am so weary—so weary!"

She looked for pity in his face.   He was profoundly sorry
for her.

"Mary," he said, and tears rose in his eyes, "I once
thought you were heartless.   Forgive me! will you?   I am
sorry I wronged you."

"I forgive you freely," she answered, and restrained herself from throwing her arms about his neck.   She was certain he loved her, and that her fears were as nought in fact.

"Stay with me, Daniel," she pleaded.

"No, Mary," he replied.   "I know your load is heavy.
But so is mine.   I have been at work night and day to save
the honor of this house.   I now have an engagement that
must not be broken."

She shivered.   He went out, and a gust swept through the
house.   The light, hard cough of her gentle brother answered
to the draught.

It was a day as cold and ugly as ever was seen in Chicago's
Octobers.   The streets were clean, as the dust was all in the
air.   Daniel's appointment was at the Palmer House, on
State street, at the northwest corner of Quincy street, and,
though he rode to the Clark street bridge, his walk to the
hotel covered and filled him with dirt and sand.   The wind
howled so one's voice could not be heard on the street.   The
man had not arrived at the hotel, and, as this was not strange
under the circumstances, Daniel took advantage of a bath to
"bring himself back to life," as he thought, for he was very
cold and much exhausted.   The Palmer House was the nar-
rowest structure for its height that had been built in the
city.   Two sides of it were on iron pillars, and yet it was
eight stories high, the three upper floors being in a handsome wooden mansard roof.   This hotel was the pride of the
city.   Daniel, fresh from the bath, lounged in its magnificent
waiting-rooms, and was in excellent condition to treat with
the ex-disbursing agent of the Sub-Aqueous Company.

This worthy had not thriven since the days of the California pears. Some of the eighteen Aldermen had "leaked." He had thus gotten a bad name. His "corner" on the Board of Trade had collapsed, and now the Citizens' Committee was hot on his track to make him give the particulars of his Aldermanic adventures to the grand jury, which was to meet the next Monday.

"If you do not," they threatened, "we have enough on you, old man, to send you down."

These things he was to relate to Daniel. He lived in one of Errington's little houses on Jackson street, between Canal and Clinton.

"Now, I ought to git out of this city as fast as I can git," he explained, "but I want means, and I want my family safe. If my wife owned the house, she could do enough dressmaking to get along."

"When can you start?" asked Daniel.

"To-morrow is Saturday. I'll go to-morrow night if you'll fix this. Remember, I'm sorry for Errington. I know he's lost his health, and I guess they'll all try to bleed him. But you see where the prosecution will have me if I stay."

Society is organized of law-abiding citizens, who punish law-breakers. Each of these citizens wants every law-breaker punished, except it be a friend or relative. Daniel wished all bribe-takers might suffer the penalty of their crimes, but he was willing to go a good way to save the husband of that sad-faced woman he had once loved. Errington was his patron. It would be perfidious and ungrateful not to attempt to keep him out of the toils.

It must be remembered that the brother who abandons the wretch who has been grasped within the hand of the law is not considered so good a citizen as he who goes to the end of fraternal affection in opposing the procedure of justice.

Equal and exact justice always punishes somebody else's brother. When it comes near one's home it is Juggernaut.

It was the opinion of Daniel that the affair of the Cali-

fornia pears was the only operation in which Errington
could be cornered. If Errington could show a sale of property from the agent to him, then he could show that the
money the squealing boodlers saw him take was due him on
the property. Daniel proceeded to arrange the matter. The
ex-agent was to take the property on a sale ante-dated. The
agent was to get out of town, and Daniel was to furnish the
money. He quieted the alarm of the agent, spent the afternoon in his company, and returned to Ohio street for supper.

The servants whispered together and looked at Daniel as
he ate. The wind whistled and howled, and the coke fires
in the grates roared and crackled merrily. The cook kept
everything locked closely. Two or three people watched him
prepare the food.

" There's been so much poison around, and antidotes," the
second girls said apologetically, " that we has to be very ·
careful."

"It is strange how servants will fall into a panic !" Daniel thought, as he and Mercy ate a hurried repast, each
desiring to be upstairs with the patients, who were reported
to be worse.

The blast tugged and pounded on the mansion. A brick
fell from a chimney with a crash. The three servants who
had been in a group set up a scream.

" If I were Mary, I would dismiss every man and woman
in this house ! " he muttered.

He took Mercy's arm and led her up the grand staircase.
" Mercy," he asked, " how long have the servants carried on
this way ? "

"I've noticed it for weeks. But since this fearful windstorm
came up— it's a week, isn't it ? it seems so—they have been
much worse. I suppose it's because Ralph and Mary are both
away from table so much."

" Those dining-room girls looked at you and me very
strangely."

Mercy blushed, but Daniel did not blush.

The girl was uneasy. She turned and entered Harmon's chamber.

Now, what thing was in Daniel's mind so weighty that he could not see sweet Mercy's blush?

His face grew livid, and he entered the chamber of the gray woman's husband. She was watching—silently, patiently.

---

## CHAPTER XIX.

### THE COMING EVENT.

As Daniel entered the sick-chamber, the wife was giving her husband his evening's potions. He soon grew worse.

"Oh! Mary," cried the young man, "it's the medicine that hurts him. Can't they do something besides give him pain?"

It was hard for Daniel to see his unfortunate patron in such a plight.

She worked cheerfully, like a trained nurse. Too much sympathy would only deplete her resources, and she needed all her endurance.

"He takes his opium now," she said, mixing the draught, "and that removes all the serious effects of the emulsions."

The patient, relying entirely on her, obeyed her every notion. His strange face—strange at best—fair, frightened, a look coming largely from red eyelashes and gray hair, once red, which could not be parted, gave forth to Daniel the idea of a man hunted. Hitherto, Daniel had ascribed this look to the fear of approaching prosecution, while the ex-Alderman lay utterly unable to use his great wits in "fixing things." But, now that Daniel came to turn over

another idea, he was astonished to see that the look of the
hunted animal came to Errington out of his desire to shake
off the poison that he felt was in him. "It is awful stuff,
Dan," he moaned. "I can feel it whenever it takes hold."

"Oh, no, you cannot, dear," smiled Mary.

"She thinks I can't, but I can," he said. "The moment I
take the medicine it seems to fight the poison, and I reckon
I'll die yet while they are fighting together."

Daniel's teeth chattered. He tried to cheer the ex-Alderman by telling of the deal he had made over on Jackson
street. It was a good idea, Errington admitted, but it would
look scaly at the Recorder's office, if the grand jury ever
went that far. "Men like me," he said, "don't hold out a
deed two years. But it's precious little real estate I've held,
after all." It cheered him, on the whole, and took his mind
from the antimony.

Daniel went into Harmon's room. The gentle Christian
could barely smile.

"Does he take much medicine?" Daniel asked of Mercy.

"Very little."

"Does he have acute attacks?"

"Oh! no. He's beyond that," she whispered.

"Did Mary give him drinks of opiates?"

"No, not that I ever saw. The doctors have all the time
given Ralph far more medicine, and worse doses, I guess,
than Harmon has had to take."

"Does Mary watch Harmon as closely as she watches
Ralph?"

"Oh! yes, indeed. She cries over brother a great deal."
Mercy was herself weeping.

Daniel returned to the husband's chamber. The patient
was in a stupor. The gray woman stepped forward and
grasped Daniel's hands. "Oh! Daniel, it's such a comfort
to me to have you here."

But as Daniel looked at her in the new light, he grew pale

with fear. The baleful surmise that had come upon him would not away.

"You have been very cruel to me," she cooed, "far more thoughtless than I ever was with you."

"I have tried to aid you all I could, but it is only within a week that you would accept aid. You might have had a dozen skilled nurses," he answered, but his teeth chattered.

She would not be put off.

"I have been very patient. You said, once, that you had been patient. But you were not. It is I who was patient—am patient."

She thought she was, but she was not. The young man turned his head toward the couch of the exhausted sufferer. The frightened look was on the singular face, even in its stupor.

The gray woman looked also. Daniel's brain reeled. He thought he saw a look of mortal hatred in the gray eyes. He thought he saw the great cat, opening its mouth, yet making no noise, setting its jaws and traversing its bars, the very apparition of suppressed fury.

He had for weeks dwelt, as it were, under the shadow of the penitentiary. Its gates had seemed open for Errington. To save him had become the dream, waking and sleeping, of the private secretary. Such a view of the majesty of the law is valuable to any poor unit of society, be he the grandest of citizens. To-day he may sneer: "I am the law!" To-morrow his enemy may be the law. Or, the next week, equal and exact justice may become the order of the day.

If to the young man who loved the beautiful Mercy, and who now dared to hope she might yet learn to love him—if to this young man there loomed the power of the law in the ever-present vision of four walls with sentry boxes, what must be his sensations when the vision of the gibbet rose above that reddish-gray man's pillow.

Emotions of gratitude to Errington were sufficient, but the

vengeance of the law was paramount. The gray woman's words were lower and sweeter, but Daniel heard them not.

"Mary," he said, "I think he is worse. I am going for the doctor."

She would have dissuaded him. His fears were groundless. Had not all the doctors failed, and had not she brought relief? So she interrogated him. But she smiled and let him go.

He sought the cook. He questioned all the servants. They were panic-stricken, but they attributed the sickness to a curse that had come on that house. They knew nothing and suspected nothing. And yet their foolish imaginings, misunderstood by Daniel, had brought forth the night's events. The cook locked up his victuals because there had been theft. Poisons and antidotes were his excuse.

Daniel's fortitude returned. He cheered the servants by saying he expected to get better treatment for the master. He returned upstairs. The house was cold and the gale howled. The wind was at the height of forty miles an hour.

As he returned to that great staircase his limbs again trembled and his jaw would fall. There came upon him a desire to enter that dreadful room once more. There succeeded a thankful feeling that Mercy was near. Then, almost with collapse, there appeared the second thought of his dear Mercy and her continual presence in that house. He thought no more of Mary's room. He was at Mercy's door without further sentient feeling. He saw her face. He grasped her hand. He examined her face critically. Thank God! There was no antimonial diathesis there! Harmon slept. Daniel led the girl to a farther corner of the room. He had never supposed he would speak his love to her—not for years—not until he thought she had learned to depend on him—not until habit had come to the aid of such an unlovable lover. But danger made an orator of him.

"Mercy, Mercy," he implored, "believe in me!"

"Why, Daniel, what has happened?"

" Believe in me ! " he prayed. " Believe in me ! "

She spoke not a word. She sat in front of him and held his two hands in hers, and then she kissed his two hands and wept. She was in fear. She was a young girl. The gale threatened the exposed house. Death threatened her dear ones. That one who was dearest of all talked riddles. She sobbed.

Her tears brought back his wits. What language in a woman ever said as much as her grief ?

" Ah ! " he cried, " you do love me ! Then you will believe in me. Mercy, we are all in danger. The devil is in Mary's heart. I saw it ! I saw it ! I cannot say why I believe it, yet I saw it."

The girl was sobbing as she had been at a funeral. The emotions of the pair fluctuated between love and terror— between deep sorrow and great happiness.

" Promise me, Mercy, that you will eat no more in this house. When you drink, drink directly from the hydrant, and secrete your cup. Do not, as you value your life and mine, depart from this."

" Is it Ralph's enemies who are going to kill us all ? " she asked trembling.

" Yes, it is Ralph Errington's worst enemy. It is Mary. Forgive me, that I say it so openly, for I love you so, Mercy, I want you to be warned."

" She never did it, Daniel ! " the girl sobbed loyally. Some one had done it, but it could not be Mary. Oh ! she did not doubt that Ralph was poisoned, but some one else did it. That is good woman's logic. It is the way God made woman, else, having reason and justice in her soul, she could never be true to false and shifting man.

Yet, when she thought she had displeased or doubted Daniel, she threw her arms about his neck. She remembered the touch of his face, exactly as it had seemed when the statue looked at her. She poured her pent-up affection upon him, and promised him, oh! how faithfully, that she would obey him forever, if he would only love her and be hers, so that nobody else could claim him.

What man would not compromise on such a basis? Somebody else was poisoning Ralph, but she would see that nobody, not even her own sister, should poison her.

Harmon awoke, and their demeanor changed with the circumstances.

"I will return and sit up to-night," Daniel said, and went out into the gale. He sought an old doctor who was held in high esteem in the Fire Department years before. Daniel told him, there were two patients at Errington's house who were undoubtedly the victims of antimonial poison, one having inhaled the dust of a type-case and the other the fumes of the alloy works. Their symptoms were different, but their condition was hopeless at present. Would not a change to a hospital do them good? The doctor thought that if they were chronic sufferers the change would be desirable. Take the patients to Mercy Hospital, where treatment could be had and paid for on any scale of expense. The Elm street hospital would be nearer, however.

Would not the doctor go to Ohio street with Daniel?

He thought it too late. It was after 11 o'clock, and the night was terrible. Doctors are never alarmed about chronic cases, or is it that they distrust the saving power of a prescription that, in all probability, will be changed the next day? But doctors have a grand pride of profession. If Daniel requested it, the physician would go. They re-entered the hallway, at Ohio street, and waited below.

Mrs. Errington sent down word that she had retired, and that the patient was still asleep and getting needed rest. The doctor was inclined to be indignant that Daniel should have placed him in an embarrassing position—for when a man is dying under one doctor's hands it is unprofessional for any other doctor to be around.

But Daniel still had the right to see Harmon, and Mercy
was more than glad to again greet the physician who had so
impressed upon her the necessity of humoring Daniel in his
delirium.

The aged curer of disease looked at Harmon with the
sphinx-like face of an eminent practitioner. They could not
tell what the decision would be.

"The man is worn out with hard work," the doctor said.
"He has the diathesis of a slow mineral poison, but it could
not well be said that the poison would kill him. He is tired
—too tired to—get well soon."

Mercy threw herself at the foot of the bed and buried her
face in the coverlet. The doctor took his leave. Daniel
returned. Harmon had awakened.

"Oh, Harmon! My blessed, gentle brother, why did you
work so hard for us? Why did we let you do it?"

"I have been well repaid for living," he said; "only don't
forget mother when I'm gone." He sank once more to sleep.
The consciences of such self-abnegating men are like white
lamb's wool—ay! are white as no fuller can white!

The mother had been persuaded to take a night's rest at
home. Daniel led Mercy to her chamber. She promised to
lock her door, and proclaimed her sister's goodness and her
own lack of heart in kissing the man she loved, while such
an unhappiness rankled in her soul. She was in a ferment
of feeling. The equilibrium came when hope told her that
Harmon would get well after all.

Doors opened and shut all over the house. Daniel sat by
Harmon's bed and read of murders in the palace. At times
the watcher would start wildly, having imagined that he saw
a gray woman striving at the lock of Mercy's door. And
then a thousand strengths would come to this young man,
and he would rage, thinking to penetrate to Mary's couch,
and tearing the secret from her, cast her forth upon the
blast, a Fury who might ride well-saddled on a night like this.

11

Such, reader, was the crisis in that great house as it rocked and creaked under the shadow of a catastrophe which was to make mankind turn pale.

For the great city itself was marked with the diathesis of destruction.

----

## CHAPTER XX.

### THE SATURDAY NIGHT FIRE.

In the morning Daniel awoke Mercy early, and together they took breakfast at a restaurant. Thence they proceeded to Clinton street, where Daniel was given his old chamber and lay down to sleep. The mother set out for Mary's. Daniel had much to do. He could not afford to go to Fullerton avenue. He arose at 12 o'clock. He was to spend the afternoon with the agent.

"Mercy," he said, as they debated the strange state of their affairs, "I can see now that it has been your presence and friendship all along that have held me fast to the path of honor and duty. There were pitfalls about me that I did not see; I see them now, and I know that you alone have preserved me."

He left that humble home speaking bravely, but wondering where matters were going to terminate. Could he bring Errington through without indictment by the grand jury that would begin its sessions Monday? Could he prevail on Errington to go to a hospital? And, even if Errington would go, would not Mary go with him? What was his duty as a citizen anxious to keep free of the foulest crime that had ever come straight home to him? And what grounds had he for suspecting Mary? None. Yet she had been too loving last night. So he thought—but did he not think so, too, when she played " Vuelta Zingara " because she knew he liked the air, and yet had been engaged to merry Errington all along for four months ? Thus he excused the gray woman—for thus the assassination went further from his garments.

He made the arrangement with the ex-agent. It was late in the afternoon when they finished the interview. The wind was not so fierce, and the temperature had risen many degrees. Daniel was anxious to get to the North Side, as Harmon was known to be very low, and he could not bear to seem unthoughtful of the self-forgetting friend of his youth —the only link between his boyhood and his present life. But go he must to Mercy Hospital. He took a "hack." They would give the patient a good room, looking out on Calumet avenue, but would not be ready until Monday. Daniel was to meet the ex-agent at the corner of Clark and Adams streets, and see him off at the Canal street depot.

The man was there. It was 10 o'clock. " I have thought of a document that you want," he said. " When I closed the deal for the Sub-Aqueous Company the nineteen crooked Aldermen fixed up a paper to the effect that they were all equally participants, and would all stand by each other. Errington tried hard to get quit of 'em, but they made him sign it, along with the rest. Then they had a row over the custody of the paper. So I says : ' Gentlemen, I'm in this pretty deep myself ; I'll just keep it for you.' I solved it effectually, and took it to my friend, the County Clerk. ' Here is my widowed sister's will,' says I, ' keep it in your safe for me.' So he put it away. It's in the Clerk's office. It ought to be destroyed. Here, I'll write you an order for it. Got a pencil ? Yes. There—that'll get it."

They started for the depot. As they approached the corner of Adams and Wells street flames belched out of a grocery, and with the instincts of Chicagoans, who dearly loved a fire at that time, the men, with five hundred others, ranged

themselves across the street, and the patrolmen came up
with a rush and speedily put out the blaze. The two men
started for the depot again.

As they turned it seemed as if the whole western heavens
were ablaze. The sky that a moment before had been black
was now the background of more sparks than Chicago had
ever before seen.

A planing mill at the corner of Canal and West Van Buren
streets, just over the South Branch, exactly four blocks south
of the point where Daniel had hung on the wires, had broken
into full blaze, and burned with a briskness that was entirely new to sight-seers. When Daniel was a boy, coopers'
shavings were considered the very best of kindlings, because
of the vigor of the fire they made. The planing mill, sitting
in the midst of a lumber yard a block in size, burned as if it
were filled with coopers' shavings—as if it had a blower over
it in some fabulous grate set into the dark night. People
gathered on the east side of the river and bespoke a hard
task for the firemen. The block was all on fire within twenty
minutes. What was strange was that the lumber burned as
furiously as the planing mill. Much feeling had grown up
against wooden planing mills, and the crowds were glad to
see this one go. Millions of feet of lumber, several coal yards
and two blocks of tenement houses were threatened. The
fire gained in fury and noise.

And now a spectacle that was novel, and has never been
repeated, was offered to the startled city. A golden storm
covered the town as far northward as Lincoln Park. What
made so many sparks ? And what made them last so long ?
Everybody asked this. These sparks could only be compared in persistence with the mineral filings that burn so long
in the sky after a first-class rocket has exploded. The slate
roof of the Fort Wayne freight depot, a structure a block
long, was covered with bright coals for hours.

"Trentworthy," said the ex-agent, excitedly, "What do you think now? My house has got to go! Ain't that hard? Ain't that hard?"

And so the two men ran around to Madison street, pushed their way westward to Clinton street and reached the endangered home of the man who had hoped his troubles were over. Like heroes they worked to get out the furniture. There was not a great deal to save, yet it is notable how long a pipe will stick in a wall, and how hot a stove will be if a party of men be anxious to get the things out of a house.

And Daniel did not forget Mercy's home. Careful observation from that quarter soon assured him that the house was safe. It was a block to the leeward of the oldest line of fire. Nothing was disturbed in the house. No one was there but a badly-frightened servant.

The great fire spread backward to Clinton. It burned northward to Adams. It swept eastward, two blocks wide, to the river. As the blocks next the river were far more than three hundred feet deep, the total extent of the burned area was called six blocks. The loss was $1,000,000. The salient feature was the unparalleled flight of sparks. The dramatic portion was the salvation of a large elevator that, standing by the river in the course of the fire, was in imminent peril several times.

Men stood and pondered over the peculiarities of this conflagration. "It might have gone farther," they said, with a queer feeling that it is said a gamester has when what he terms an invincible hand proves to be second-best.

It was, then, possible that Chicago could burn! There was a merry crackle about that fire that no one could understand, because the desiccating power of the week's blast had not been considered. There were men who claimed they had foreseen it all, but their remarks were not considered important enough to be reported until the next week.

The firemen performed prodigies of valor. While Daniel

and his burned-out acquaintance stood by their furniture, on Jackson, beyond Clinton street, they saw a fireman enter a little wooden house that seemed all ablaze. He put a ladder up inside, and then disappeared in the smoke. He knocked a hole in the shakes, or shingles, with his pipe, and when he emerged above might have been taken for a martyr at the stake. He was surrounded by flame, and hemmed at the waist by lolling shingles that, like all Chicago, thirsted for water or fire, which ever might come first. But, a moment afterward, the great stream fairly knocked the ridgepole from that roof. The whole fire was out instanter. In all his experience Daniel had never seen an act so deliberately brave.

"If that engine had failed him, he'd a-been a goner," said the agent. And even while he spoke, the men came running away from that very engine, carrying two dead laddies, and the house that had been saved was on fire once more. This was the second engine that had been lost.

And now the editors set to work to bring out an account of this conflagration that should startle the region, as Chicago had always startled it. The headlines reached to the bottom of columns thirty-six inches long. Page after page of the great sheets were filled with everything that everybody could write about it—"and about it," as Byron might say. There was no possibility of supplying the demand for papers. "One of the severest sufferers by this appalling conflagration," said the press, "is ex-Alderman Errington, who owned many of the cottages and tenements in the blocks west of Canal street."

Yes, it was a bad night for Ralph Errington. And in many ways. For, as Daniel stood at the pile of household goods, a detective tapped the ex-agent on the shoulder. "I have been looking for you," he said, "don't leave the city, as they will want you at the jury-room next week. You will not be touched if you do not try to skip."

"Get the paper, Dan," said the ex-agent," "and I don't

think I'll have to give up anything to the grand jury.

So the game was up. They must face the grand jury. This fire disaster would cost Errington $20,000. Daniel hurried over to the mansion. They had heard the bad news. Mary did not complain at his long absence.

"Ralph is better," she said. "Harmon is lower, I think."

The private secretary watched her. He thought she was sorry that things were not the other way. He went to Errington's bedside. The man had not had an acute attack in twenty-four hours. He was much encouraged. The bad news that Daniel brought could not distress him. "I think," he said, "you had better try to see the chief clerk of tho Clerk's office to-morrow. He lives on West Taylor street somewhere, and the O'Leary boys can tell you just the house. Mary has them around here a great deal, you know. Get a carriage and offer to take a friend or two. Stop at the Court House and have him get you the document. Buy everything for the boys; that will be all right. I have had my money back on them houses. I'm awful glad I hain't had any pains for a day. I wonder if Mary hasn't killed out the poison. Dan, did you ever see such weather? I never knew tho wind to blow like this before—never in my life."

"Mr. Errington," Daniel said, after the sick man had finished his say, "Mary has had a great deal to do lately. She looks very much worn."

"Yes, Mary is a good wife."

"And Harmon, let me tell you—now don't get nervous— is very low. My doctor was here last night, after you went to sleep, and says Harmon is dying from past overwork as much as from poison. Such a man as you, he says, must re- cover, if he keep away from the cause of the poisoning. Now I thought, inasmuch as Harmon cannot be moved, and inas- much as being here would not help your spirits, that maybe you would not mind going down to Mercy Hospital for a week or so, to see if it didn't help you, right off."

Daniel made brave to look firmly at Mary. She sat speech-less. The proposition came upon her like a stroke of light-ning.

The sick man was hurt. "Oh! Dan," he said, "That's hard. That's hard, Dan. Oh! I didn't expect that."

The gray woman would triumph and not say a word. But she had endured a bad moment.

"I want to tell you that my doctor says you would get well at Mercy Hospital, and that I have been there to-night. They would give you a room that cost $30 a week or more."

"Why didn't your doctor come in and see me last night?"

"Because I was not willing to disturb you, dear," said the gray woman.

The project took a different turn in the man's mind. He wanted to live. He thought he was going downward of late —as he was. He grasped at this straw of hope. It was not to be put out of his own house—it was to go out.

"This house has cost me a heap of trouble, Dan," he said.

And the wife was forced, for fear of Daniel, whose slave she was, to let the sick man plan his departure Monday.

"You scare me with your harshness to me," she com-plained, in a low voice, as Daniel started for Harmon's room.

Daniel had loved her once. He could never be cruel to her. Besides, his suspicions might be without basis. He spoke pleasantly to her. He urged the idea of the hospital. She did not oppose it.

He bade her good night, and was almost sure she clung to him.

"Is that the way women do when they are used to a man, or do they do it because they love him?" That was what Daniel asked. He could not tell. Mary had misled him once. He must not be too conceited.

Nevertheless, when he looked at Mercy he had no doubts. He did not want her to die, and his heart labored at the thought of it. He repeated his warnings, and Mercy promised the greatest circumspection.

Daniel watched away an easier night, and the gray woman returned to her rich boudoir.

"Monday," she murmured, and set her face.

---

## CHAPTER XXI.

### AT EIGHT FORTY-FIVE P. M.

The big wind, which had been the one topic of general conversation,.previous to the Saturday night fire, now rose to a hurricane which threatened great damage. The vast crowds that hurried, for Sunday sight-seeing, to the waste place south of Adams street, did so at the risk of impairing their eyesight, for the ashes and soot and sand eddied and poured forth in quantities that would surpass the credulity of the hearer of this tale. The people came miles and stayed to look but five minutes. There it was. A flat place in the heart of the West Side, without a ruin remaining.

In the central part were the two abandoned engines, blackened and twisted. It was not a pleasant sight, even if one could have gazed at it without endangering the eyes.

The scientists, or some of them, discourse on the overwhelming percentage of water in all things terrestrial. Was the equilibrium destroyed in that five-month drought, and that wind of a week that would suck the hydrant water off a lilac bush in an hour, leaving it dryer than it was before?

Was there a peculiar electrical force in the air—an explosive tendency? Was the air itself so dry that it was inflammable?

Was it not the time of all times when Chicago should be

on the watch, with fifty fire engines, that incipient fire should perish in its weakness?

And if there extended to the southwest two solid miles of wooden houses, with fences built high to emphasize neighborhood hatreds, and barns clustering thickly to complete the solid wooden connection, then should not the inhabitants be on the outer walls, water in hand, to quench the idlest flame?

Should not the wind come off some well-built quarter, where the fireman, in case of conflagration, could make at least a passing stand?

But Chicago had only eleven engines when it set out to fight the Saturday conflagration.

It lost two of those, and several of the others were partially disabled.

The department having stood before that fire—the men having fought within ten feet of an intense, infernal heat that had made Daniel and the ex-agent writhe a hundred feet away—these firemen were *hors du combat.* The man who had been in the battle all night and far into Sunday, could not fight again Sunday night.

The hurricane that blew over this drought-dried city came over a country that had seen no rain. The air that was cold on Friday seemed superheated on Sunday. It was very hot —a sirocco. It came from DeKoven street. It passed into the lake at the water works. It thus blew south of southwest.

Did ever city show such a predisposition for destruction? Was there ever a diathesis so striking?

If the prophets ever combine so many bad antecedents again, they may foretell great events. They may arise and prognose balefully.

Daniel and Mercy repeated the course of the preceding day. The mother stayed closely by Harmon, and Mercy and her lover returned to the Clinton street house, where they

found the servant in a high state of disquiet, notwithstand-
ing the presence and assurance of Daniel on the previous
night. The largest fire ever known in Chicago, and only a
block away, was apt to terrify the only occupant of a house.

They were by far too close to the center of interest. Clinton street was thronged as it had never been before.

"Mercy," Daniel said, "I am sorry I have so much to do
to-day, for Harmon's state is critical. I feel I ought to be
there this afternoon. I will go to sleep here, again. I sent
word to Mrs. Trenton not to expect me home until the folks
were better, and she will not worry. You had better go back
to Mary's as soon as you can, and help your mother. I hope
to arrive there about dark. We will go out for supper. Isn't
it dreadful ? "

He was weary and his spirits were low. Death was over
them. And, when one loses a self-forgetting friend, what a
loss is that ? Though Daniel's personal affairs, owing to the
liberality of Errington, were highly satisfactory, still, his
two friends were in the dark valley. Could he afford to lose
them ? Thus, setting sympathy aside, he was very uneasy.
The weather had sucked the courage well out of men. He
looked from the Clinton street house northward. It was all
ashes—now in gusts, now a steady storm of the desert. He
thought of camels, with their ugly, patient attitudes. "I
wish I had one," he muttered, and went to bed.

It was a dreadful day ; every living witness testifies. The
wind gauges record it. The barometer has it chronicled.
Thus bad began.

When Daniel awoke it was one o'clock. He was late. He
cautioned the girl about the necessity of care, gave her fifty
cents if she would stay in and keep the house locked against
all comers, and sought the O'Leary's cottage at 137 DeKoven
street. The children told him where the chief clerk's house
was, back on West Taylor. He knocked at the door. The
head of the house had gone to the concert at Turner Hall, on

the North Side, at Chicago avenue. Then Daniel visited the ex-agent. Daniel's desire was to go to Mercy, and yet he felt that Errington's affairs were of very great importance. The ex-agent also thought it a matter of the highest urgency that they should obtain and destroy that inculpatory document.

The feeling of unrest came strong on Daniel. He spoke of it to the ex-agent. "It's the dry wind," said that experienced person—"and the crooked work. You are not used to fretting."

Back Daniel went to West Taylor street. The ex-agent was already in a part of another cottage, and was cheering up. He had money, and did not lack wit. "I will go with you," he said. "When you catch the chief clerk call for me."

The master of the house on Taylor street had not returned at six o'clock. At that hour the tobacco smoke was getting very black in Turner Hall, and Hans Balatka was preparing for the closing march.

Daniel went to Clinton street for supper. "I'm glad you stayed in," he smiled to the servant, and thought it was the only thing that had gone right in the day.

At eight o'clock, having waited as long as he could, he walked rapidly down the street to Taylor. He had been told the chief clerk was always at home Sunday nights at 8:15 or earlier. He pulled the bell. Yes, the master had come. Would Daniel step in? There was company. Would Daniel step up-stairs, where the chief clerk was washing the dust off his face, neck, and ears?

Daniel knew this gentleman. "Glad to see you, Dan," he said. "Take a seat by that window. Yes, I know about that will. It's in the outer vault, where we keep all such special deposits for friends. The watchman can get it. I'll just write a note to him in a minute."

It was 8:20. Daniel gazed out on the alley that ran between DeKoven and Taylor. The wind blew through the window casings.

The householder washed and splashed. "Ah!" he said, "that feels good. I'd like a bath all over, but my people are all here, and I'm late now. Good music and very good beer this afternoon. I'll go in the front room and write the note to the janitor."

"Dan's in a hurry for that will," he soliloquized as he read the ex-agent's authority to give the document to Daniel.

It was 8:30, and Daniel sat gazing on a point that must for ages, and for countless millions of people, have a dramatic situation that cannot be revealed in phrases.

But Daniel was thinking of Harmon.

The chief clerk was laboring at the note, for we are all literary creatures. We love a smooth sentence. It was an oppressive air, there was no music, and there was no beer.

Meanwhile, at Ohio street there was another acute attack:

"Mary! oh! Mary! I'm taken again!" cried the husband of the gray woman.

"It's nothing, dear," she said. "It will pass away."

But it did not pass away. Was it not terrifying—this once strong man, his hair starting in all directions, his red eyelashes, his pale skin, his frightened look—the cramping of the legs, the utter badness of his taste, the nausea, the heartburn, the fire all over? How gladly he seizes the bowl of emetic! How gladly he would die now!

And then, weak and without force or spirit he lies back, almost at collapse, almost at death from shock. One more acute attack, one more effort of nature to throw off the irritating substances that are eating him, and the shock will kill him—as if he had been beaten with a club.

"Mamie," he moaned, far down the valley, "don't let me go away from you. Don't let them take me to the hospital."

He was too weak to remember who wished him to go. It must be an enemy.

The gray woman reassured him. She wet his cold forehead with a sponge dipped in alcohol.

"You have been a faithful wife, Mamie. You have watched me all the time. Forgive me, Mamie, that I was so stubborn about the smelting works. I didn't believe, until the foreman said he would quit if I didn't stay out of there. Every time I went I had one of those attacks."

"But this," he moaned, looking up at his keeper as a hopeless dog looks in its last moments, "this, Mamie, was the worst attack I have ever had. Can't you help me, Mamie? Forgive me, dear. I love you. I will be a better man. Can't you help me, Mamie?"

She sat stoically beside that couch of foreshadowed death.

"Please give me the opium, Mamie; that helped me so much the other night."

He knew its taste. She could not refuse the draught that would again put him in a torpor. She rose to get it. Watch her, reader. Does she move reluctantly?

"Mary, come!"

It is the white face and great black eyes of Mercy.

The two women dash from the room. The sick man looks for his opiate. The room is empty. He sees the vial on the stand. It is but three feet away. He is sinking, and the fires within him are setting up brightly once more. He tries to shriek. He tries to reach. He tries to understand. He can do nothing, but falls back into hopeless despair.

The fires begin. He is willing to be burned. But he is not willing that his Mamie should be gone. He would cry out in his utter solitude, but to cry would require forces that are now denied to him.

And now, in the other sick room:

"Harmon, dear, can't you speak once more?" It is the mother's voice. The two sisters are on their knees beside the bed. The mother alone has the supreme privilege of the moment.

"I am not suf—," he said. "I th—I will get well."

"Oh! Harmon," they sobbed. "Oh! Harmon!"

It is misery itself to see the living as they receive the dead. For this reason doctors grow proof against emotions. The doctor was on the other side. He held Harmon's pulse at the upper arm.

It was now hard for the patient to breathe. But the departing spirit had much to say. It must crowd it all into one unfinished speech.

"I—have—had—a—very—happy—life. I—"

So have all who forget themselves and live for their fellow men.

The dead was come. He who had lain, a precious burden to those loving hearts, how lay he now? Horrible! But not horrible to God! Ay, and praise that God—not horrible to those for whom that tenant had lived, and left his frail and yet beloved house behind.

The cathedral gong in the great parlor struck the third quarter after 8 o'clock P. M.

The gray women re-entered the other chamber.

---

## CHAPTER XXII.

### PATRICK O'LEARY'S BARN.

WE may cast our eyes backward to the early days, forty years before this night of oncoming ruin, and see the trees waving over the stream at the foot of West Taylor street. We may behold Patrick O'Leary and his wife on the little cabbage patch up the way. Old streets—some of these that are back thoroughfares of the later day! We may see him safe in his cottage, beyond the reach of the landlord in Mayo. He waxes better off and builds an addition to the house, so that the neighbors call it a double cottage in trying to remember it.

And now in these later years he needs a shed, at the alley, for the real-estate speculators must invade his cabbage-patch, and fight his title, even to the ground under the very house that he lives in! Musha! Yes, he must keep the horse further away from the cottage, for the fresh air is being cut off. The village is growing, and Halsted street is no longer at the far west.

He casts his eye across the scattering town. There is but one brick building within sight—the Lake House. He hitches his express wagon and meanders with the road from the trees at Taylor along the bayou to Wolf Point, where he may cross on the draw-bridge. The schooners leave lumber there, at Wells and Market, on South Water street. We may see him whipping the inglorious steed homeward over a bad road with the fagots for a city's pyre. Load after load, it toils over the greasy clay. Let no man stop the portage! It is the chariot of grim Destiny.

Set those posts firm! Ah, it is expensive, this keeping the horse and cow so fine. So good a shebeen had never the O'Learys on the old sod. Throth now!

And at the heads of the posts nail scantling, and two feet from the ground. Thus, as we should build a stockade, we have an inclosure fronting the alley, twenty feet; backing from the alley, sixteen feet. The gate shall open to the alley, from a pathway five feet wide. The shed and the pathway shall fill the width of the lot.

Seven feet to the top of the lower floor; ten-foot si boards along the alley, fourteen-foot side-boards al the inside; a roof that shall slant from the top of the fourteen-foot sideboards to the top of the ten-foot side boards at the alley; a floor above that partly covers the ground area; sideboards all around, that are nailed in perpendicular position; cleats over the joints of sides and roof; an eight-foot gate; an eight-foot board fence running forty feet to the rear of the cottage on both sides.

Here the demon slept for decades. The alley waxed in Irish splendor. Would you look upon its counterfeit presentment? Go presently to Jefferson street, between Taylor and DeKoven, and gaze westward at the coupon, the stub, of this momentous lane—at that part which, escaping the events of the October night, remains to recall the very essence of that other part which gave to the world one of its conspicuous events.

The barns increase and magnify until the great improvement of Patrick O'Leary becomes a shed in name. " A miserable shed," say the neighbors, after years of ill-concealed ill-wishings. Along the alley, as often as a barn, might rise a house, known for a house by its white mosquito-netting at the windows, but adding all the time to the area of wood for the suckling moments of the monster that was to be born in the O'Leary stable.

And presently, as the proud householder shuts himself in the eight-foot stockade, between his double cottage and his barn, he gazes forth upon the uprising at Jefferson street, between the alley and DeKoven street, of a row of brick stores, with living-rooms above—five stores, with lots that come toward the O'Leary cottage 75 feet, where a row of sheds must add to the fire litter. At the alley, a two-story barn. Between the Jefferson street lots and the O'Leary cottage one large frame house and Mrs. Annie Murray's cottage. Behind each of these, large sheds like that one upon which we must ever look with awe. South of the O'Leary's the cottage of James E. Dalton; south of that still, Walter Forbes, William Lee, Morris Conover, three in a bed, a two-story cottage; back of it a pretentious barn. Across the alley, sheds, sheds; the barn of the chief clerk, a paint shop exactly opposite the large barn of the three men in a cottage.

Walk up and down that alley once more. Step across Jefferson street into the ante-fire alley. Gaze upon its salient points. You may have some satisfaction of that craving faculty of the lover of great events, to see it as it was—as it can not be again.

What would we not give to look upon Blackfriars' play-house! Not that it held Shakespeare, but that it fixed the walk and look of Hamlet, the mocking laugh of Lear, the balcony of Juliet, the knocking on Macbeth's gates, the pillow of Desdemona. Take now, dear reader, that woodcut of old London bridge, where the houses go across the Thames, where the human heads stick forth on pikes to make all men loyal subjects of the good Queen; is it not blessed that this woodcut, preserved by chance from the corrosion of years, has also by the veriest chance held over for our mortal vision a view of that roundish play house, that Blackfriars, where, humble as a stableman, the king of human minds put forth his sceptre as graciously as Ahasuerus reached out to Esther the beautiful! Are not you, am not I, glad to come even that near to William Shakespeare? So would we gaze on this manger of October. So would we to-day welcome that chance picture, which, in fixing the object of something thought to be notable, should have handed to another age the apparition of something superbly illustrious.

It is gone. We may only go along the alley and say: " It was here. Here it stood. Set here the monument. Here slept Ate, the fury, for thirty years. One hundred and twenty-five feet east from Jefferson, on the south side of this alley, now so proper with good buildings; 175 feet in a straight line from the northeast corner of DeKoven and Jefferson streets, at No. 137 of the latter street—there it stood, and bided."

" On the north and east lines of e. ½ lot 12, block 38, school

section addition to Chicago," says your maker of abstracts.
Take to the County Treasurer that description if you should
come to pay taxes on that lot, prolific of more than man can
tell.

Into that shed, along with the monster, along with the
biding Ate, go the increasing herd of milch cows—one, two,
three—six, some say; a goat, a calf, the horse, the wagon.
The house itself is so large that Patrick McLaughlin may
have the front end; "for what is style, so long as you have
the money?" ask the father and mother as they lock the
barn this night and count their brood. Monsters springing
autocthynous out of the soil of this heaven-cursed e. ½ of
lot 12; let the father look in the eye of his oldest boy and
foresee that lump of a lad ten years anon with his red knife
of murder over wife and sister! Lift him, Patrick O'Leary,
and put him in your manger—with Ate!

But if the father see not this, let him put his brood to
bed, for milk-people rise very early. Let him ask: Did the
load of timothy hay get well stored in the mow yester afternoon? Aye, it was well laid. There is not a straw lacking
in the train. And the beasts are well bedded with planing-
mill shavings.

And that tenant, Patrick McLaughlin, he keeps no milk
to sell. The weariness of 3 o'clock A. M. does not stare him.
He will not to bed with the O'Leary brood—and Ate out in
the manger. He, with his fiddle, will welcome a greenhorn.

Who was that greenhorn? Let him rise and say, "It was
I who journeyed to that spot for *that* welcome!"

Thus settles the darkness. People not thick upon the
streets—too much wind for that!—a howling blast, awful to
think of! Look with the eye of the ages upon that scene!
The O'Learys almost asleep— it is hard to rise at 3 o'clock
A. M.! The McLaughlins preparing for the greenhorn.
Mary O'Rorke looking eastward out of the Dalton cottage,
sure to see a light reflected, unable to see the stable where

Ate stirs and is to wake. William Lee, closing the blinds of his rearward west window. Richard Riley, at No. 130 West Twelfth street, in the act of raising his north window, to step out on his porch.

In the Court House cupola, a mile away, Matthias Schaffer, looking dimly on all the city.

Mary O'Rorke, William Lee and Richard Riley, their eyes peering into darkness, unconsciously ready to fix the first movement of Ate outside her lair! Matthias Schaffer, ready to see it, if he look that way!

The monster wakes after her long sleep. Now is her moment, or never. "To night! to-night!" she whispers, for she would wake no one—mankind hates her so. This genie is down in the bottle, now. Be still, Mary O'Rorke, and William Lee, be still one moment more!

Ate is but a spark, like one of the golden motes last night that floated to Lincoln Park. Ate is a golden mote that leaps across a chasm from wisp to wisp. Ah! that joint of grass was almost fatal to Ate! Will she leap that place? She leaps! It is a full fiftieth of an inch along a wisp of timothy, but it is a wide span for Ate. It infuriates her. She seizes two straws, unseen of men. "Ha!" she whispers, "I have them all!" She crackles. Hear it, oh, Patrick O'Leary, and enchain that dreadful demon again! Look north of northward, Patrick O'Leary, and though you might sleep on in safety after unleashing Ate, take pity on those twenty-one hundred acres, on those hundred thousand fugitives, on those seventeen thousand houses, on those three hundred ghosts that are else to wander hither complainingly within the span of the dreadful day that is to come! Hear you not that light crackle, sleepy man? Wake! wake! your demon grows ambitious. The gale is shouting to her. She peers out. Up past a broken cleat there darts a steel-like tongue. The roof heaves and moves like the deck of a schooner. It is Ate, grown strong beneath, after tasting of the gale. She tugs again, and laughs so loudly that three witnesses look upon her first merriment, yet not with sufficient horror.

Those who have trustworthy watches say that the world gave chase at a quarter before nine.

This *danse macabre*, this rise of Ate, the fury of Homer's Gorgon, seen by William Lee, as he closed his westward blind, was that night, at a quarter before nine, simply a shed furiously on fire. What had William Lee thought had he known that countless millions would look with his eyes upon that lurid unchaining? Had he not then cried out that he had seen Ate herself, or Medusa undamming Phlegethon, hell's river of fire? Surely he had run to the city, to let them lay waste millions and avert the event.

You look straight upward to a tower with golden ship for weather-vane. You say: "It is not high;" and yet, mark you, a sparrow flying down is long in reaching earth. Then, from afar, you cast your longing eye and see but mist above the town. There is no tower. You say in triumph: "'Tis not high!" But even as you murmur, upward on your startled gaze bursts forth that self-same, only tower—and mart, and dome, and spire sit squat beneath.

Thus William Lee gazed simply on a shed on fire. But generations, crowding afar to the theatre of history, will behold, at that humble alley, a genie that grows collossal as recede the ages.

## CHAPTER XXIII.

### THE GAS-HOLDER.

At 8:30 P. M. Daniel sat looking at the darkness of the alley. "Here, Dan," said the chief clerk, "see if this is all right," and Daniel rose, passed to the front end of the house, and scanned the order for the needed paper. "It is a little unusual, and you may have some difficulty in getting into the office, but if you see the watchman and give him this, you are all right. Don't be in a hurry, Dan, I haven't seen you much of late."

So Daniel tarried a few minutes, perforce. He was greatly under obligations, and he desired to show it. The men conversed rapidly for a quarter of an hour. They together stepped into the hall.

The back end of the house was on fire.

At once the large company of people who were present began the removal of goods. They had seen so much of it the night before that they were becoming expert.

"Dan, you might help my neighbor there; he is all alone. I guess I have more than my share," said the good-hearted clerk.

And Daniel went at work with a will, and soon had everything out of the next cottage, and had it across Jefferson. He had not stopped to look at the owner. But Daniel knew all about fire. He had worked with a view to saving everything. It was the action of a skilled brain and a good right arm. The householder stood by his effects and grasped Daniel's hand as the cottage went down under the blow-pipe flame.

"You've forgotten me," he said, "and I didn't deserve so

well at your hands. But I know you and Harmon Holebroke
—both. I want to say you can command me—d'ye hear?
My name is William Fullmer."

It was the Hogmouth!

Daniel was glad to be at peace with all the world. "Harmon," he said, "is lying very low at Errington's house. I'm
afraid he can't live many days. He might die to-morrow."

"I don't want him to die till I see him. He was the best
man in the office. I always knew it, but it seemed to make
me mad. I'll go and see him to-night. Are you going
over?"

"Not just yet," answered Daniel, who beheld the fire already
leaping Forquer, Ewing and Polk streets. It had divided
into two columns of blow-pipe flames. One was between
Jefferson and Clinton, and the other between Clinton and
Canal, nearer the river.

The department were late on the ground. When the hose-
cart reached the plug at the corner of Jefferson and DeKoven
streets it had run eleven blocks. Matthias Schaffer, turning, in his vigil, to the southwest quarter, saw the fire, but
located it a mile too far away, and sounded box 342, for
Halsted and Twenty-second streets. The blow-pipe had
been in full operation fifteen minutes before the firemen were
well at work, and wherever an engine got in front of the
head of the column the machine could with difficulty be
saved.

It is tolerably well established that no alarm was ever
struck for the Chicago fire. Matthias Schaffer, discovering
that box 342 was too far away, concluded that the engines
would see the fire as they went past. The still alarm to the
hose cart, eleven blocks away, was received seventeen minutes before the Court House bell struck.

Engine after engine arrived and got into trouble without
staying the progress of the fire. The west side of Jefferson
street was preserved, as much by the hurricane as anything

else. The mission at Polk made a great fire, and the high school at Clinton and Mather, the watch factory, and Bateham's planing mills and lumber yards offered an impregnable advantage to the flames.

It was here that the Fire Marshal understood that he could not stop the fire west of the river.

It was an appalling thought, and its dreadful import became more apparent when the planing mill began sending great brands upon the gale. The conflagration was now so extensive as to act upon the currents of air, and spectators to the leeward were in danger of being sucked into the flames. Women, especially, were glad to struggle southward against the wind, which made a noise that drowned the roar of the disaster.

But Matthias Schaffer, on the Court–house, did not underestimate the present character of his approaching foe. The great bell rang out repeatedly, and finally, as he saw the column rise up for a moment, as the currents of the tempest changed, he began the constant tolling of his charge, that no man should sleep while the monster approached.

One of the most frightening aspects of this red pillar of fire, as seen from the Court-house, was its frequent inclination eastward. It might well be compared with a waterspout at sea or a tornado's funnel on land. The base gyrated as if it were held by some power upward in the dark sky. Sometimes, to the eye of the observer, it would turn blacker than night, and then the change to brightness would confuse the eye. As if resting in its bending down, it would again lie flat upon the houses, and when it rose once more the conflagration would prove to have moved northward a half-dozen blocks. The smoke and cinders now rattled against the cupola on high, and Matthias Schaffer was a brave man to stay up there in the tempest.

But Daniel, on Jefferson street, could not see this total vision. He could only surmise that Mrs Holebroke's house was at the left of the line of progress. He hurried thitherward up Jefferson street. On his right the buildings grew somewhat sparser. He ran through the alley from Jefferson to Clinton —an alley that might be called Tyler street, now Congress, and reached the house. The servant, with her satchel, sat on the steps. She was about to flee, for the air was dense with smoke.

But Chicagoans, by a week's practice, were coming to believe that sand and smoke could be endured. Together Daniel and the servant began removing the household effects into the open space at the corner of Jefferson and Harrison. A man caught hold of the piano with Daniel. It was Fullmer. "One good turn deserves another," he said jocularly. They emptied the house and stood in the open place watching the advance of the flames. Then Daniel bethought himself of the countless cups of jellies and jars of preserves that Mrs. Holebroke and Mercy had boasted of having in the cellar or basement. He left Fullmer and returned to the house. Across the alley a great wooden house was burning, but the wind was blowing for a few moments furiously from the west. The home of Mercy was only lazily catching fire.

"Foolish as it may seem." Daniel said, "I believe I can save this house. It's been a good house to me." And setting to work, with a garden hose at the hydrant, he easily put out the fire on the sideboards. The roof did not catch at all. The house was saved.

It must be understood that 257 South Clark street stood on the west of the line of the fire, and on the west of the burnt squares of Saturday night, now lying northward only three blocks. Thus, by the pivot of this house, the fire swooped to the right, and its northward flight on the West Side was headed off at Van Buren street by four blocks of ashes.

This the Fire Department of Chicago did: It controlled the fire of Saturday night. It protected Jefferson street on the west until the gale whipped the conflagration over to the east side of Clinton. Through these two circumstances there was a probable salvage to the city of what may be estimated at three hundred squares, more or less thickly built upon.

Daniel was already weary, but the conflagration, he felt, was now nearing its end. He reassured the servant, and hired boys and men to carry back the goods to the house. His heart was full of thanks. He took it as a good omen. The preserves had preserved not only the house, but perhaps a large portion of the West Side.

More planing mills were now on fire, over toward the river. A hide tannery was also sending so much bark into the air as to arrest the attention of the West Siders.

One hundred and fifty acres were on fire. If one had desired such an exhibition, what fuel would have been more to the purpose than these dry cottages, board fences, sheds, tan yards, planing mills, shaving heaps, factories, lumber yards and wood depots?

The tannery was especially effective in its explosions of brands. Six great wains, filled with shavings for cow litters, stood in a row and gave off their entire contents to the upper air—a dreadfully significant offering to the genius of destruction.

What would this gale demand of this unparalleled fire? What would this hurricane lash these 150 acres of fury into doing? It was a fearful thought—almost beyond thinking, for man must have practical limits within which to control his ideas. There, ahead, in the ashes of Saturday night, stood the Nelson elevator. Truly, it is before this fire, but why does it turn red-hot at such a distance? It is the power of Ate, before which nothing is to stand. It is not fire. It is chemistry. It is not conflagration. It is hot blast. It is the Bessemer process of reducing cities. An elevator, hundreds of feet away, turns into a living coal 150 feet high. It is iron and grain. It cannot blaze. But it may glow like purest jasper and glitter, seen of all men.

But still, this elevator, before the blowpipe, is the only point in the direct fury of the hot blast. Surely, the river will stop the sideward progress. The 150 acres are all afire. The westward and northward lines on the West Side are defined, and will be Jefferson and Adams in the main.

"Great God!" say men who see the living coal 150 feet high and bulky, "I'm glad nothing is near that elevator!"

And men who had already been ruined, joked about hot grain, which had that summer made some noise on the Board of Trade.

In just two hours 150 acres of inflammable material had succumbed. Men looked into the sky and saw such sights as they had not hoped to see. The whirlwind would wrap a million sparks into a ball and dash it into the sucking depths of some maëlstrom.

"How about those brands?" one man would say.

"Worse than that last night," another would answer.

And then, as the Court-house bell tolled and tolled, there rose a raft of fire—perhaps a roof, perhaps a nucleus of brands braided by the whirlwind—seen by T. Z. Cowles, seen by Gustavus Percy English—seen by ten thousand other blackened faces.

This great bat of fire sailed as a bird of prey, with eye intent on destruction. It did not ride in the blast: that might have dashed it to pieces. It rotated, it fluttered, it caught the forward air currents, and departed as a balloon begins its voyage. The tan-yard sent ten million out-runners in its van. The planing mills saluted with salvos of brands as the red barge passed overhead.

It crossed the river at Jackson street, nearing Adams. It was finishing its voyage. The sustaining current was diverted, and the flat raft shot edgewise to the earth as a card, thrown by a skillful hand, cleaves the air that might oppose it.

The hurricane caught that vampire, and sent it with out-spread wings against the side of a wretched wooden house next to the gas-holder, next to the tar works. The whole side was a furious blaze in a moment.

Thus began the second chapter of the great fire.

Now, out on the blackness loomed the gas-holder, a monster basin, inverted over water, with the South Side's store of light for nights not lit by Sodom's fate. A gas-holder, with 1,500,000 cubic feet of gas, highly explosive.

Could it blow up?

A gas-holder in Cincinnati, holding this same 1,500,000 feet, had exploded, with effects that had been seen and felt for ten miles. All men from Cincinnati cried out. All eyes were fastened on the vast red bulk, hanging in a frame, its pulleys and weights doing little service now, the fullness of gas holding the mountain-like cup of iron at its highest poise.

The bell tolled more rapidly. "Drive everybody out of Adams street!" yelled the great-hearts of that night.

And now the burning of a city began to unfold its terrors to feeble men as they looked skyward at the reservoir of added destruction that stood well within the surrounding fires.

Spectators afar off turned their heads in fear and clapped their hands upon their ears. Men near by ran for their lives.

And Ate, high on monster's wing, looked upon the city and made noise as no hurricane and no conflagration had yet cried out.

# CHAPTER XXIV.

## TRANSFIGURATION.

MORE disastrous than dim eclipse was the scene in the great streets of the South Side, where million-dollar structures stood in colossal rows. The citizen to whom the knowledge had come that the fire was crossing at East Adams, might hurry out into the street. He would meet scarcely a soul—as though all had fled but him.

One may not be so bold as to imagine the light in which Moses stood as God passed by on Sinai's top; one may, with the same reverence, refuse to conceive the light of the epiphany which fell upon the beloved of men outside the holy city. And no one who did not behold it can, in his mind, illustrate the arch of nocturnal heaven as it was lit that night by the torch of the destroying angel. The universe was white, so that no star could shine. The hurricane blew a fleecy vapor through the sky, like a great auroral tumult, until one might see twenty miles into Lake Michigan. Cocks crew more than thrice that night, and beasts arose, doubtless marveling more than men—for men had not yet believed their own senses.

And when a man moved toward that gale, he must guard his eyes, for pebbles as large as small marbles were upborne in the blasts, and each intersection of streets brought new currents and added fury.

As Daniel came down Madison street ahead of the fire, and as ten thousand people fled fearing the gas-holder, a man entered the gasworks, pulled a valve, and opened a sixteen-inch vent-hole in the vast reservoir. A blue flame shot into the zenith, and for a second burned perpendicularly among the auroral clouds, in defiance of the viewless Niagara that was sweeping over the city. Then gradually the great gas flame bent down, as Matthias Schaffer had seen the red pillar bend at 10 o'clock. As the gale pressed it it lengthened, reaching over the roofs of all the houses on Wells street— across Monroe, Madison, to Washington, a tongue of flame 1,500 feet long. This blaze, narrow at first, would grow wide in its bed of lolling shingles and tar roofs. Rising, this whip of Até would miss its roofs and lash a street full of abandoned women, just turned from their orgies or their sleep, carrying feather beds and fleeing before the only catastrophe that could make such a lot worse.

This flight of the head column of fire from the gas-holder across the wooden roofs of Wells street to the Chamber of Commerce, on Washington, was the most terrifying spectacle in the whole event. The passage was made before the eyes, as fast as the eye could follow the current of Phlegethon.

Daniel had bethought him of the newspaper office where he had once worked, where he had heard a fire reporter say that night that they were preparing a great exposure for the grand jury. Daniel had believed, after leaving the West Side, that it would be well to make some explanations to his friend the city editor in question, go to the Court-house and thence to the Ohio street mansion.

It was absolutely impossible for living witnesses to consider the destruction of Chicago in its entirety. They attended to the idea of the hour, not to the affair of the century. Thus Daniel, with the gas Phlegethon flowing from Adams to Washington on Fifth avenue, turned not from his purpose, but climbed the four iron stairways of the daily newspaper office in which as proof-reader he had spent so many unhappy nights. At the top he found men who were just grasping the affair in toto. The insurance was being dropped and the burned streets rather were going on record. As the fire reporters would reach the great local room the circle would set to work to guess whom the new-comer might be. Men were so black that they could not be recognized. " I am English," " I am Cowles," " I am Walker," " I am Meacham," would be necessary.

" My God ! did you see English ? " the city editor would say as he recalled the fiery-eyed black man whose clothes were tattered with smoking holes, and whose every movement betrayed the weariness that was left him after the sucking of that remorseless gale. He had been all around that fire ! He could not speak aloud. His voice sounded a story below, down the iron and the tile corridors. The entire loss of the voice was a phenomenon of the night.

" All sit here and write whatever comes into your heads ! " commanded the editor, and the only man who had seen fell upon the floor and was fast asleep.

But what had been, had been. There was enough to come and for all to see. The city editor was in a fire-proof building. Its walls were of stone ; its beams were of iron; its ceilings were of corrugated iron ; its stairways were of iron. He was safe. His paper would have the only account of the greatest event since the London fire. So he swore. And would willingly have given his life for such a triumph. But his men were bewildered. They ran around the room in a circle. They sat down and wrote pages of interjections. They shook each other by the hand and said the fire would go past on LaSalle street and Wells.

But back south it was coming in three columns and crawling eastward. Daniel saw that whether the building were fire-proof or not it would be surrounded with fire. He had seen the grain elevator turn to a living coal without giving out a flame. He warned the city editor to save the library and files and carry them south of Twelfth street.

But how could a city editor who had seen nothing except the red wheel windows of the Chamber of Commerce believe that a blowpipe force was loose on the city that could smelt solid squares of stone buildings as though they were ore pounded in charcoal?

"It took the Drake Block nine hours to burn, a year ago," he said. "We must not lose our heads."

He wished Matthias Schaffer would quit ringing that old bell. It frighted the isle. And in truth Matthias Schaffer was just then fixing the striking apparatus preparatory to escape.

"Wake! wake!" cried the brazen tongue, ever faithful to the city. For thousands were still asleep in the third, fourth, fifth, and even sixth stories of the doomed buildings that stood closely in the way of the first column of fire.

The little group in that lofty place of vantage, gaze loyally on the dome of the Court-house. It is the voice of the city to-night—the only thing that answers Ate back. It seems painted on the inky outer regions, where peace reigns but doom is writ. The side-lights increase. The group take to trotting about the room, for the nerves of men are too fine for spectacular events that make centuries ask questions.

The wind, sixty miles an hour; the van of the conflagration a legion of Siberian wolves, noncarnate, invisible, insensate with fury that they must lag behind the tempest and tear asunder all they have overtaken.

"Now," cries a brave one, "Farwell Hall is on fire!" That is this side of LaSalle street, but two blocks due west. On Forquer street that would have meant fire in the local room in five minutes. There is, then, somewhat of difference.

Like an explosion, the next block northward gives up its roofs to the flames. The blow-pipe is now on the Court-house. Will it turn a living coal?

It is the climax of the advance. It is the heart of the city. It is the centre of all radii. In the presence of such an expectation it was observed and testified that all men held their breaths, fixed their eyes upon the splendid dome, and could hear no comrade's question.

Wise and intelligent men—ready to use God's senses as God would have them! .But only as He would have them for once in 5,000 of His years!

Did you ever divide the time sharply between It Was and It Is? On the 7th of August, 1869, you stood at a great telescope, watch in hand, and knew that at ten minutes after 4 o'clock you would see the moon touch the sun. Yes, some power was answering your expectations. There! was the first contact.

You know justice will be done at 12 o'clock. You wait for this same Court-house bell. Your second-hand approaches the vertex of its dial. It is there! Deep! goes the bell! The murderer drops to his doom.

There is something in that completion of expectation that will ever startle the soul. The mother knows her child is to die. He dies! Hear her shriek of surprise now at the event! Solemn, solemn—like this gazing for the living coal!

The blow-pipe turns to smoke. A veil of blackness fills the air. They shall not behold after all!

"Look! look! you'll never see it again!" cries a voice hoarse with excitement.

Does the whirlwind throw the hideous mist aside or are these three domes, the two lesser and the one greater, turned to sapphire and jasper, and seen through the inky vast and middle of the night?

With Aurora waving her banners of white vapors in the daylight-sky of midnight; with Ate pouring outer darkness below; with Phlegethon sweeping in like Niagara—there shines the fascinating vision! Angels might not tremble more in gazing on the great white throne.

But how long may. men stand awe stricken? Witnesses said a minute, some ten seconds, surely not two minutes. Sublimely beautiful it is—the skeleton of this dome on inky sky with the light of transfiguration for all the zenith. Each stanchion of exquisite pearl; each nail and screw of blow-pipe colors, for jewels; the hurricane clearing it of the smallest corruscation.

It is too beautiful to see. Its half-remembered vision may fascinate the mind of puny man for decade after decade.

Crash! It is over! The cupola is down. The bell out on the roof is down, ringing as it goes—clanging into far-off times.

We hear it yet. It had pealed for Fort Donelson, for Vicksburg, for Gettysburg, for Appomattox. It had tolled for Lincoln, and at each clamor of its tongue men who looked now, hoping to hear all, turned then and wept, hoping to hear not at all. It had rung all day for the great railway. It had tolled as long for the three firemen who went to their death when Daniel leaped out of the vortex.

It fell, and as it fell it gave four great smothered clangs, such as no man's right arm could have brought forth from its concentric echoes. It gave four great cries—that it had seen and had recognized Ate—that destruction had come upon the city, whether for her many sins, or simply out of her inconceivable misfortune.

It gave, with brazen tongue, aye, with its whole sonorous house of sound, the reading of the scroll that now unfolded before those who would hear and those who would see.

The proudest and most ambitious city of the western earth must become as ashes and cry in her grief to the world. The world never heard such cry before. What could it do but turn pale, as men did now when they heard the last and loudest peal, and knew that Chicago had no voice, and saw the pavements burning in gridiron form, and hurricanes of blow-pipe flame piercing alleys filled with smoke, that at once set up fire; wide sheets of flame flapping in the upper air like jib-sails of some aerial Great Eastern; fire flies of black tar paper spreading slow wing and bursting into incandescence; cornices of zinc purging amber, silver, gold, crimson, emerald; arabesquerie of blow-pipe energy playing upon the façade of stone building, until the gases within might grow to burst the edifice.

Underneath, in the gulf stream of Phlegethon, fire of tar and jeweled pebbles, living with heat.

Overhead, transfiguration, Sinai.

In the upper air, the auroral clouds, the hurricane, the roar of Ate's car, the last clangor of the bell, echoing outward.

Men looked at their watches and wondered—for it was to be seen that the watches went on, and on. By that sign alone it was not doomsday.

It was precisely twenty minutes after 2 o'clock A.M., Oct. 9, in the year of our Lord, 1871.

---

## CHAPTER XXV.

### BIG BILL.

Now, while Phlegethon went by, there were not only men and women to stand aside, with their little ones, but there were other breathing things. There were dogs, and cats, and birds, and beasts, and gamins—newsboys. And one of these was Big Bill.

As cities grow older there is to be noticed a growth of human feeling. A newsboy now-a-days counts for more than he did in '71, small as his total may be.

Exactly how Big Bill came into the world must, like the coming of Ate, forever remain a mystery. Perhaps if the wickedness of men had not prevailed; perhaps if rulers new in office could do what they set out to do, and forever fail to do, then Big Bill would have stayed back inert.

But he came forth, and though those bipeds without feather, who were already alive declared it was monstrous, or at least evil, it was very natural. It was very like a man-child. A visitor from another world, organized on different ideas, would have seen little difference between Big Bill and the new-born scion of the house a mile eastward on Wabash avenue.

Whether he had a week or a month of his mother's milk matters little, for his season at her breast was as short as though she were extremely fashionable. He did two odd things. He refused to die, and he did not set out to grow. At two years he was an "orphan," and lived because the poor, who are often noble, were cheered by his prattle, and reckoned him worth as much as any other pet.

At four he ventured as far northward as the corner of Jefferson and Harrison, and gazed in astonishment at Jefferson street, which there widened to 100 feet. He was considerably less than three feet high, and on this account made the butchers whistle. There was a butcher in that agreeable quarter who weighed 400 pounds and looked short in six feet four inches of stature. He was called Little Bill. This new-comer, being the smallest waif who had ever arrived at the corners in quest of adventures, was called Big Bill. The human mind loves compensations.

Man becomes of age at twenty-one years in America. Horses, dogs, rats and gamins vary between three months and five years. Big Bill started out early. He was standing at the corner of Randolph and Clark streets, in the flood of the main artery of Chicago's life, within a month after he came out of the narrows of Jefferson street and scared the butchers.

Big Bill's education was not neglected. He was forced to learn the difference between the *Evening Post* and the *Evening Journal.* He was presently compelled by some occult process to be able to judge whether a paper were to-

night's or yesternight's—probably by the degree of dampness
of the sheets, though the Jay Goulds of the gamin world
would often dampen old papers with much foresight and financial ability. When twenty boys slept in a hallway it was
a matter of gravity that Big Bill should keep out from under.
If it were very cold, he must, of necessity, sleep on top the
ball of gamins. There is a fine vitality in a heap of newsboys
which keeps them alive in a hallway with the thermometer
at 35 deg. below zero outside. A bickering, kicking, vicious
mass of small humanities, maybe, but wonderfully fit to live,
wonderfully apt to live.

It is easy for a grown man, three feet high, with a screech
like that of Ate—it is easy for him to sell papers. Citizens
carrying candy home to lumpkins six years old, the pride of
their hearts, beheld this stridulous mite of four, this locust of
sound, fighting the battle of life, and the citizen declaring
that it was outrageous, bought a paper and demanded full
change.

It *was* outrageous. The child of the people has a poor
father. The friend of the people gives them a thin decoction
of friendship.

It was outrageous, for this Big Bill had to fight the battle
of life without the advantage of bulk. Whatever his littleness
gained for him his littleness lost for him. To do business
required protection, sponsorship. If he earned 5 cents, 4
cents went for services performed in his behalf. Either muscle
would rob him of all, or protection would tax him four-fifths.
And the tax collector was far more of a ferret than ever
worked on the town assessments.

One day Big Bill looking up saw the *Evening Post* in
large letters on a sign. He recognized the words because
they were in *fac simile* of the heading of the paper. He
grasped the idea at once that all signs meant something.
Coffee was 10 cents, instead of 20, as the tax collector had
said. When knowledge pays that way the signs in a lunch-
counter for newsboys are soon read.

Big Bill went out and looked up Lake and Randolph streets. There were object-lessons by the thousands. A great gun rose up five stories. He went thence. It was a gun-store, of course, " Guns," said the great sign, and he knew only the s. He could not read these signs as he could those in the restaurant, where the other boys could be appealed to, but he knew they meant something.

That was all the scholars knew about the Moabite Stone at first.

Inconceivable fountains of knowledge spread before him. The Alexandrian Library never gave scholar greater thrills of delight. In two more years he could read the letters. He had all such words as had a representation by picture. He was reckoned as most learned among newsboys. But he had to sleep at the top of the heap in cold weather, and was always in danger of the hottest place in July nights. For, be it known, a gamin was a gamin. If he took to himself certain hallways in winter, he would be frozen if turned forth. But having established a squatter's title by virtue of 35 degrees below zero, he must hold it. It might be 100 above in that bedlam on a summer's night. There must be no hiving to new quarters. The policeman was on watch for that. Gamins, like other small life, are unpleasant things to get fastened on buildings or alleys.

But it is not to be imagined that Big Bill had no joy outside his great studies, his Alexandrian library. There was, near the main bayou, on Clark street, a very large bird store. The younger city seemed to need pets more than does the Chicago of to-day. In the show windows of this place were cages of monkeys from Africa and Brazil, parrots of all hues and names, squirrels that toiled like Sisyphus, mocking birds, puppies that slept exactly like gamins, but with less barking, and such reptiles as might catch the eye of the bartender or maker of aquaria.

God made a portion of his creation with wings, being

evidently satisfied that there was already enough overreach-
ing among the remainder. He gave that winged portion his
permit to range the air uncircumscribed by the narrow bounds
of city, state or nation.

What shall be our estimate of man, therefore, if we enter
this vast inclosure and see the space to which he has chosen
to limit that yellow songster of the Canary Islands, whose
little throat, by unfortunate chance, has happened to please
the ear of him whom God made to reach out and grasp and
hold? It is custom to put up the baseball of the season as a
sacred packet, assayed absolutely official : none genuine unless
signed. Perhaps man has given the commercial canary a
cubic cell larger than this official packet, but not four times
larger. It is a space just bigger than a man's clutch.

The prisoner of the state convicted of fearful crimes may
at least march in and out of his cell, but this wee yellow-coat-
ed songster—what bank did he break ? What house did he
set on fire ? What stock did he water ? What railroad did
he wreck? What city did he discriminate against ? Thousands of these little pine packets, reaching to the ceiling, so
high the chirp of the bastile cellman comes down like the
twitter of a swallow from an eave.

What a kindergarten for Big Bill! How he may delight
in the pandemonium of noises that buries some struggler's
cries. And if, with his sharp eyes, Big Bill save some prisoner from suicide, then the keeper will be glad to have Big Bill
about.

How rapidly he comes to know the short chaffinch, the
stub-billed bullfinch, the blackbird with his magnificent
ocellus and clearest of calls, the cross-bill, the fallow-finch,
the redbird, robin, skylark, thrush, bobolink, cuckoo, weaver,
fieldfare, oriole, wheat-ear, lark, mavis, thistle-bird, nightingale, redstart, ortolan, redwing, roller, swallow, swift, titmouse,
linnet, goldfinch, scissortail, wagtail, tropic bird, the stubby
whippoorwill, the warbler, and a dozen kinds of humming-

birds that hint of the innumerable variations of this
species.

The little birds, the songsters, do not make up the riot,
that is heard in a great bird store.  There must be cockatoos,
love birds, macaws, birds of paradise, paroquets, imperial
parrots, dragon birds, fan-tail flycatchers, goat-suckers, golden
pheasants, guineas, bluejays, jackdaws, lories, woodpeckers,
queen's pigeons, bushshrikes, trogons, wrynecks, hoopoes,
yellowhammers, parrots of every length and turn and color
of bill, every mode of train and coiffure, every squint of eye,
style of oratory.

There must be, to give the proper flavor of business, a
certain proportion of the small mammalia—the lemurs and
monkeys; rabbits, ferrets, raccoons and opossums.  There are
rats, but they are not caged.

This region is one continuous, compound, comminuted in-
fraction of the harmonies of sound.  No concert of parrots in
a submerged forest on the flooding Amazon ever gave forth
an output richer in discords.

Big Bill at eight, knew the name of every living thing in
that ark.  In the hurricane of noise he could detect the cry of
a canary in misery on the top shelf.  He had come into the
world a natural child.  He was a born naturalist.

A watchman one night pulled him out of the ball of
dormant gamins in the hall-way and asked him if he wanted
to sleep in the bird store.  Did he ?  Did a duck want to
swim ?  When could he do it ?  From Saturday night till
Monday morning—two nights a week.  He would be locked
in at 8 o'clock.  At 4 o'clock he would be let out.  The
store had once been a house for the sale of furnishing goods.
It had been robbed.  The owner had put iron bars at the rear
door and windows.  He had put iron rolling shutters at the
front windows and an iron gate across the doorway.

Suppose a fire should come while Big Bill was in there ?
Well, the watchman would let him out. Suppose a fire should

start inside ? Well, Big Bill had better attend to that himself, had he not ?

To-night Big Bill lay on his pallet of straw, and the cries
of the nocturnal birds went on as they always did. A new
batch of lifers had arrived the night before, and the hymn to
liberty was as earnest as the sounds of early Christians
worshipping in caves. But there joined to the tumult the
voice as of some great bell-bird enmeshed in the wickers.
The gamin rolled over. "I must save that macaw," he
thought half-waking, and dreamed that the boys were "stuck"
with their papers ; that they had held a council and resolved
on a " rush ; " that they had determined on the assassination
of General Grant ; that they had filled the alley, and made
the grand exit, howling as possessed with a legion of devils,
"Ere's yer extra 'dition—General Grant shot !" The gamin
heard the yells of the rushers and they woke him. The
macaws were indeed screaming. It was daylight, and they
wanted attention. They wanted variation from monotony.
The gamin could not believe that he would sleep past 4
o'clock and miss his papers. That meant disgrace and star-
vation. He had not slept so long. The Court House bell
was ringing.

It was Sinai, transfiguration.

He ran to the door and looked into the heavens. The auroral mists were flapping and careening. He could see into
the heavens, as it were a hot afternoon in July. Danger was
in the air.

" There is a fire around here," he thought, and rattled the
door for the watchman of the block to come. The light
increased. Then darkness for a moment filled the street. The
parrots screamed with delight. The quails gave forth their
" Bob White !" The gamin was scared.

A weird little picture, something like that of Charlotte
Corday, waiting at the bars for the swift hour of beheadal.
A little whitish face, with red eyelashes, with red hair, not

yet gray, that defied parting, pompadour ; a terrified look at best, but a terrified countenance now, indeed.

Rattle, rattle on the door. The watchman gone to Jefferson street to save his own home, and leaving Ate to unlock that cruel iron gate.

But sometimes a scared look may cover a bold heart. It was a big fire or the Court-house bell wouldn't be ringing all the time.

It was in truth a big fire. The whole Alexandrian Library was to be in flames.

The boy seized a board and dashed out the glass in the door. He could climb through, but it would do no good. The iron gates reached to the top of the entrance. He made no further noise, but stopped a moment and mechanically studied the gold letters on the sign across the street. Then he took the long, rolling stepladder and went to the top of the shelves. He took each packet, and with his knife cut out two of the wickers. Then he held the packet at the door and scared the canary forth. It was a slow and toilsome thing to do. The bell said " Run, Big Bill ! " But he could not run. He could let the birds out, and perhaps some of them might be caught afterward. No man went by.

Now the canaries are all gone, and the rarer birds must be freed, for the light is far more vivid and the bell has ceased to ring. This little thing came from Poland. This Western city of Chicago held all the tribes of Christendom. All men must have the birds they saw at home. " I can mount it for you if it should die," the bird-seller would say, and this would close the bargain. This mavis had been expected to cheer some lone Scotch heart. This redbird reminded of warmer suns. · This ortolan was as good as the " Marsellaise." Out they went and fluttered through the bars.

Out went the parrots and strutted wisely down the street. Out went the ferrets, and pounced upon the necks of fleeing rats. Out flew the swift of wing and strutted nought, like simple Poll, looking so wise.

Then when, like captain on some gallant ship, the devoted liberator had put forth the last living thing, when even the puppies crowded through the bars and gamboled toward Ate, he put his face to the window, gazed a moment, and clomb through. He ran up the bars to the top, as the monkeys had done ere they crowded through. Small as he was, it had been forestalled that he should not escape. Burglars had used little catspaws, too. The bars grew warm, the air was filled with fumes. He was nearly unconscious ere he knew his immediate danger. He clambered through the door and sank upon the front end of the heap of little prisons that he had cut open. He knew he was dying, and he thought heaven must be where Jefferson street, reaching Harrison northward, widened to a hundred feet. The smoke and fumes grew denser, and a film gathered on his eyes.

Like a flash the smoke and fumes cleared out of the street. A man came running. He pounded on the gate. " Bill ! Bill ! " he cried, " climb out, and I'll pry the bars for you." He had a rod of iron, and hammered like a blacksmith. " Can't you hear Dan ? It's Dan ! Don't tell me I'm too late ! "

But Dan was too late. Big Bill could see him, but he thought it was a black-faced copper shaking his club at him, and threatening, if he ever made another rush out of the alley, to pull de whole gang and send 'em to de Bridewell for vags.

The man peered in on the scared little face, " I've seen just such a look," he said, with a shiver.

The man pounded on the gate in horror, and aroused only Ate. Down the last block rolled the head of column. The man ran for his life through South Water street toward Dearborn, and the fire leaped the stream direct to the North Side. Ate, peering through the iron bars, breathed upon the dead and his perfect pyre and the dead was as ashes. The blowpipe breath was on the little corpse.-Even the iron bars ran out upon the limy flagstones and set them merrily on fire.

Thus perished a child of the people. Had he come out of the narrows of Jefferson street one generation the sooner, perhaps, with his red eyelashes, red pompadour hair and gray eyes, he might have sold city councils, established smelting works and purchased respectability.

## CHAPTER XXVI.

### ON THE GRAND STAIRCASE.

WHEN Daniel Trentworthy came down from that high room in the daily newspaper office, the latest courier had brought the news that the Grand Pacific Hotel was on fire. This was the counterpart of the structure standing there in 1887. The head of column was cutting a narrow lane of destruction from DeKoven street straight toward the water-works. This lane, at Randolph street, was hardly a block wide. The side progress was slow by comparison. The burning of the Grand Pacific was due to the gradual widening of this lane. At any time after two o'clock Monday morning, if the gale had turned directly eastward, it would have cut off 50,000 people and driven them into the lake. But the main hurricane held steadily to the north of northeast. It was not the forethought of the endangered people who, like Daniel, were bent on seeing the fire while they could, or wholly oblivious to the fate of the city.

Then Daniel, for the first time began to reckon the time at his command. There was the Sherman House already on fire. Guests but a moment ago, as written in their accounts, had looked out of their windows to see the Chamber of Commerce wholly in flames. He could not go to the Pacific Hotel with the hope of getting back to the North Side. He hurried northward:

When he went up-stairs he had thought that all had gone to the fire. Now it was plain that the people had all been asleep. Such a transformation could only be caused by such an emergency. For people were being driven out of their houses or burned in their beds. One hour before Dearborn and Clark streets had been as still as the grave. Now sidewalk and street were one seething, shouting mass, like a crowd before a ticket wagon at a circus that was to be crowded. The desire of the shouters was generally to secure a horse and wagon. But household goods were piled in the streets so that no horse could have passed. Thousands of families dwelt in the upper floors of all the blocks, as elevators, except at the hotels, were almost unknown, and the upper floors could not be rented for offices. The customary spectacle was a woman with one or two Saratoga trunks, begging every passer-by to help her. Foreign women all carried feather-beds. A long file of Swedish immigrants, just in, marched stupidly up Madison street toward Phlegethon. Hysterical women would gather in parties and walk down the streets chanting together "What shall we do! What shall we do!" Following them would pass a drunken phalanx of men, just up from the dives of Jackson street, singing "Johnny, fill up the bowl!"

Plunder and pillage seemed to go on ahead of the column. At its sides there was very little, and that mostly due to drunkenness. In front of Phlegethon whoever broke in and carried off was safe. The owner himself had little objection. Perhaps something might be brought back. He would ask the pillagers to remember him, although it would be difficult to see how they could do so.

At the sides of the lane, however, there was plenty of time

for a removal of goods, if means had been at hand. Two men would mount a barrel:

"I will give $50 for an express wagon that will take four trunks to Twelfth street."

An expressman rattles past, too excited to stop for $50.

"I will give $250 for ten minutes' work!" yells the other bidder.

The expressman stops.

"Come in here, boys," says the jeweler to the rowdies, mostly petty thieves, just let out of the Court-house basement.

He rushes into his store. He hands tray after tray from the safe. The thieves obediently carry them toward the express wagon. As they stand rich-laden around the express wagon, awaiting further orders, there is a terrific rush down the street.

"What's the matter?" screams the expressman.

"They've got the Smith & Nixon building filled with powder to blow it up!"

The Smith & Nixon building is two blocks away, but that expressman is four blocks away.

What could the good thieves do but run also?

Fifteen minutes later the side fires had swept the place clean. From the eastward view but two buildings on the South Side made an imposing spectacle—the Court-house and the Grand Pacific Hotel. The blow-pipe action kept the Court House free of smoke. It burned as no picture ever portrays a fire. The big hotel burned as the conventional picture would have one believe. It was surrounded by small buildings, and was a side fire, without the blow-pipe process. But under the blow-pipe, in the continuous blocks, wall after wall went down so fast, and sent such dense volumes of smoke and cinders into the air that were no tableaux. Five minutes are not enough for a spectacular fire. Instantaneous destruction, as developed at Chicago, was monstrous—like the Pit, hateful, sulphurous, cinderous, choking. It made all men who looked into Phlegethon from its banks look very like imps themselves.

After the Court-house had ceased to shine, a living coal, men had a desire to go away. The smell that Belial, Zamiel, Satan, Mammon leave was proved to be unpleasant to the nostrils of the most confirmed sight-seers.

Two black men drove up to the Second National Bank. One was really a colored expressman. The other was Tinkham, officer of the bank. Together they carried a trunk to the wagon. The expressman was told to drive on slowly, and get to the Milwaukee depot, on the West Side. Tinkham lost sight of the expressman, failed to get a direct route to the depot, reached there after perilous adventures, and found the expressman with the trunk. There were $600,000 in that receptacle, and it was the largest salvage recorded of the night. The money was carried to Milwaukee and deposited in Marshall & Illsley's Bank, and the expressman was paid $1,000.

A man, half naked, dropped from window to window on Dearborn street, at the northeast corner of Madison, in the rear. He made a noble effort to save himself, but was fatally hurt in his last leap to earth. A lady burned to death in the sight of many opposite the Drake block, where Mary and Daniel had stood.

Daniel noticed the continuous shivering of horses. Finally he became convinced it was caused by the presence of sparks and heated particles of mineral. Cats ran up telegraph poles. The noise in the wires at the Western Union building was frightful. The eyes of the rats were noticeable for their brilliancy. Doubtless many of these rodents had run ahead of the fire for long distances. Birds circled at the edge of the flames.

To all who were eastward of the main column the air was very hard to breathe. The dust was malignant. But up to this hour of about 3 o'clock A. M., few people who were awake were burned. Doubtless the loss of life among unknown "roomers" was large, but it was never officially known.

As Daniel hurried northward he thought of Big Bill for the first time. The newsboy had told him of the bird store and Daniel went westward on Lake and down Clark street, in the very teeth of the main fire. He had but a moment after getting there to see the boy's danger and grasp a cross-rod from a heap of street-rail plant. It was too late. A moment more and Daniel, standing there between two blasts of red-hot vapor, would have been a-fire. The bridge was not passable. He fled down South Water to State street and crossed sidewise with the conflagration.

All along South Water street, north and south of the line of fire, men were bringing out barrels of whisky and knocking in the heads. The roysterers would drink out of hats. The gutters of South Water street, therefore, took fire all at once, and the advance of the fire widened greatly as it leaped the main bayou.

At about this hour of 4 o'clock began those ever-memorable movements of two caravans—one south by the avenues, the other west by the Randolph street bridge. Patience, stolidity, fatigue were written on every black face. Great suffering at the eyes was manifest. Children made low complaints. Fugitives were steadied in nerve as they saw the vast crowds of mere sight-seers who seemed to have nothing to lose and no one to save.

Strange comment on our humanity and our subdivision of duty, when thousands needed succor and tens of thousands gaped on with no twinges of duty!

Daniel now hurried toward Ohio street, and, like countless others, accused himself of base forgetfulness of Mercy and his sick friends. Still, was he to blame for failing to compass the whole calamity? Are cities burned so often that young men ought to say: "This is the destruction of a city!" or, "This is only an unparalleled fire!"

He ran now, and worried. Why had he not brought a wagon? Then he laughed, to think he had forgotten that Errington had stables. Yet he did not laugh when he remembered that he had given the ex-agent nearly all his money and the helpers at Clinton street the rest. As he had underestimated the fire before, so now he went to the other extreme. The city was doomed. There would not be a house left. Even the Clinton street home would catch from backfires. Why had he been so thoughtless? Chicago was to perish. Who could believe it would rise again?

Who could look into that blood-red Chicago River, who could listen to the running word that thousands had been smothered in the LaSalle street tunnel, who could look along those red sky lines, those miles of black cornices with crimson behind them: who could look back to DeKoven street, seing that awful lake of fire and sulphurous eddies— who could do this without panic, if, in the light of a De-Koven street fire, he had left anything undone which, in the light of a city's destruction, might have been done? The light thrown by a city is too strong for any man's duty.

The poor expressman, with one horse, would come down into the South Side and faint at the thought of his powerlessness.

Daniel now neared the mansion. Carriages were at the front, and a group of people, with two women weeping, approached, bearing a body on a board.

Daniel could not believe his senses. He ran through the gate. The people did not know him. But he knew them.

"My God! Fullmer, what is that?" He seized Fullmer's shoulder. The printer was superintending the removal.

"It's Harmon's body."

Mercy recognized Daniel's voice. She threw herself on his neck.

14

"Oh!" she wept, "I thought I should die without you."

The old lady needed his comfortings as well. Truly, it was hard. Fullmer had attended to the getting out of the horses. The servants were away at the conflagration, and perhaps already cut off from home.

"Fullmer, how can we ever repay you? God bless you!"

"I'll attend to these folks if you think that you and Mrs. Errington can bring the sick man," answered Fullmer.

"Where shall we go? asked Mercy.

"Go right out State street, to Mrs. Trenton's," answered Daniel, "I will follow you in the next carriage."

Fullmer had shown great ability in managing this affair. Harmon's body had been wrapped in a rug and bound to a common shutter, or window-blind. It was possible to put it endwise beside the driver. Fullmer mounted the box.

Daniel kissed both Mercy and her mother. The great black eyes pleaded to stay with him. Verily, a woman will leave all else that is dear to her and cleave to the stranger whom she loves.

"My own love," she said, "must I lose you, just as I have found you? I knew you would come." She gazed on him as if he were a hero for getting there an hour later than the printer, who had come to make his peace. Daniel winced. He felt ashamed. He wanted to throw himself about Fullmer's neck. He thirsted to do something signally brave.

"Go on, now, Mercy. Be brave as you are good. Drive fast, Fullmer. Take care of them, Fullmer, 631 Fullerton avenue."

And the carriage went around the corner. The brands began dropping from the trees, and the trees shone as though birds wherever any two boughs might start from a main stem had made nests of gold. The horses at the other carriage shivered and were uneasy. They wanted to be off after the other party. They had been hitched oddly, by a strange hand.

Something was wrong. A horse is as nervous as a woman—and very intelligent.

Daniel turned the great brass lever of the door. The ponderous oak panel flew open and nearly threw him down. The gale was at its height. He fought a battle with that door. The gas burned in long blue, sightless lines, and the draperies were torn like the sails of a ship in a squall. Hot with his encounter, with horror, sorrow, shame, and nearly every other emotion, the young man looked up the grand staircase.

Mary stood there. The lights regained their brilliancy. She was attired in a cashmere wrapper of a fashionable color, just then known as ashes of Paris. Its long train was at her side, and covered several of the steps before and below her. Her face, at first lit with expectancy and pleasure, was now clouded with inquiry.

A man had entered the door and had with difficulty closed it after several futile attempts. His face was black, his eyes were red, his clothes were burned full of small holes.

"Who is that?" asked the gray woman, sharply.

The man came on up the stairs. Something in his walk reassured her, and she looked again. Her face began to clear.

"It is I—Daniel," he said.

"Oh! my beloved! I knew you would come! I knew you would come!"

He did not blame her for throwing herself upon him. It was truly a terrible night. He knew now what it was to have been at Pompeii.

She clung to her loved one with a joy she had not lately dared to hope for.

"Be brave, Mary. You're naturally brave. I saw it that night on the bridge."

It would be wise to cheer her, for it was very bad outside over here in the North Division.

" Wasn't I brave, Daniel ? Wasn't I patient ? But he's dead now ! "

Yes, Harmon was dead now. Daniel had forgotten that Mary, too, was Harmon's sister. The gray woman nestled to his breast. She was far too happy to live. She looked shyly up at his face. She was still so afraid of her master, who held her life in his very look. She could not see his true countenance. When one's face is blackened there is only a blank stare.

" I am all yours now," she whispered sweetly. " He's dead ! He's in there ! " She pointed to her own apartments.

If Mary Errington had been adder, aspic, cobra, moccasin, Daniel Trentworthy could not have cast her from him more swiftly.

" Ralph Errington dead, too ? " His voice left him for the moment.

" He's dead, Daniel, and I'm yours. You cannot leave me ! Love is eternal, and I know that you love me ! There's no one between us ! "

---

## CHAPTER XXVII.

" VENGEANCE IS MINE, SAITH THE LORD."

THE gray woman stood crouching and peering into Daniel's countenance. She could not read that blackened face. She was too furious with triumph and hope to receive ocular impressions at best. The young man clutched at the railing with one hand and with the other made gestures of horror. Beyond that slight gray figure he saw the gibbet rise. He saw a man and a woman dangling from it—a poisoner and her paramour—and he saw a pair of great black eyes peering toward the expiation, and wondering if truth and fidelity were indeed dead in the world. His voice would not respond to his will.

"I then consent," his soul cried out. He made a convulsive effort to speak. The word came up his throat and fell, as he was falling, into the grave under the gibbet. "I consent! By silence I consent!" moaned his spirit.

How else could the woman in gray, filled with love and triumph, conceive his silence?

"You'll forgive me, my own," she said, approaching him again. She was anxious to kiss him. In a moment she would be in his arms once more! It gave him supreme effort. His will telegraphed to every station of his body and once more there was response. It was self-preservation. The paralysis of terror was past.

"Monster!" he cried.

"I care not what you call it!" she responded. How well he looked! And how good! She loved him all the better because he had bowed to her whim and renounced her to Errington.

"Monster! Monster!" he repeated, finding that his tongue no longer cleaved to the roof of his mouth.

"Daniel, it was necessary," she said; "I did not know the power of love when I deserted you. Have I not paid well for my folly? Have I not suffered a million tortures where I caused one to you? Take me, Daniel; I am yours. You never can go away from me now. No other woman can get you now."

His voice came back. He had some things to say if he hoped to escape that gibbet!

"Mary—poor Mary!" he began. And then the extent of her crime came on him. He commenced again:

"Mary Errington, I did love you. That is true, even though it should cost me my life to admit it. You could have made me commit murder then. But," he said hoarsely —he gulped it, fearing his voice would forsake him ere he could forswear his crime—"But you cannot make me commit murder now!   You killed Ralph Errington ! "

"Yes, I killed him."

Her snaky eye responded to the graceful swaying of her lithe form, made strangely serpentine by that soft gray fabric, its gray laces, and its long train.

"You killed him, and you ought to be punished for it ! "

My God, how could she be punished ?  She was Mercy's sister.   He cursed the star that had guided him toward this gray poisoner.   "I must be essentially bad," he thought as he sank back in terror of the law.

For the law is more dreadful than Ate.   Let him who has been in front of both Ate and the law bear witness.

Daniel had come to get Errington and Mary both.  Instead of a wife and her sick husband, he approached a poisoner, a corpse, and a gibbet.   A chimney blew off the roof, with a crash that echoed through the great hall.

She was gazing on him with a poisoner's affection.   "I have been punished," she said sweetly.   "You love me, Daniel.   I knew you would be alarmed.  But there is no danger.   He knew what killed him, and blessed me as he died.  'Mamie,' he said, often to-night, 'I lost my life by my stubbornness.'  Call me Mamie, Daniel.   I did it all for you.  No one knows it.  No one can know it.  We are safe ! "

"We are safe ! "  It echoed in his terrified brain, and again the two bodies dangled on the gibbet, and the black eyes asked of God and of man.

"Was I not brave and far-seeing ?  I sent for the greatest physician in this city.   I told him I knew what it was, in spite of three doctors.   I said antimony.   They said cholera morbus.   The physician in consultation said antimony.   It was antimony, dear."

She was a monomaniac, without doubt.   Her occupation was gone.   She put her hand to her side as if to draw a vial from her pocket.  ·

" I hate you ! " he cried. " I am not your paramour. Everybody knows you killed him. Everybody shall know it. Mercy knows it ! "

" Mercy knows it ? "

" Yes, I told her Friday night."

" Why did you tell her, Daniel."

" Because I love her and am going to marry her."

Nothing else would have turned that woman from her hope. Denials of his love would have passed as nothing. But that he should love another woman !—it is the fear of womankind. It is the one crime a man can commit against the woman who loves him to distraction.

" Are you sure you really love Mercy, and are not attracted by her pretty face ? " She hissed her doubt that a second love were love at all.

" I have loved Mercy ever since the day you were married," he said. " Thank God for it ! "

" I wish I could have believed it," she said, significantly.

" I'm thankful you couldn't," he said. " You would have killed her, too."

" I would have killed you sooner," she cried.

" I have been a poor, stupid fool, all the time,"—as he saw the tigress in her.

" Yes, you have been as much to blame as I. I think they will hold us both. Then," she said tenderly once more, " I know your love would come back. Oh ! Daniel, love me ! You did love me ! "

A glass crashed. He had thrown the woman off with each advance. He had not known what to do. Another glass crashed. A smell as of fire pervaded the house.

" The city is burning ! " he said.

" I am glad of it ! " she cried.

He took a few steps down the stairs. He determined to leave her. She turned to hatred.

" Coward ! " she said, " you would forsake me."

"The city is burning," he replied.

Her affection for the dead—her habit—was all there was left to her.

"Help me to save him!" she appealed.

The glasses crashed. The hall·filled with smoke. He could no longer see her.

"It is the body of the crime," he answered. "It is well that it should be destroyed."

"I'll save it, you wretch!" cried the scorned woman. "It shall show your crime as well as mine!"

Her courage was superb. She entered the chamber of death grimly, gladly.

There lay the dead—hair reddish gray, pompadour, scared back; eyelashes red, visible, conspicuous; face pale. One might have thought it were a vision looking through the bars at him who lay on the pyre of bird-packets, except there were leeches at the neck, sucking the dead.

A man, so pushed for time, would have taken the body at once.

She seized a sheet and laid it over the body. A leech clung to her hand, feeling it to be warm. She rolled the body once over in the sheet and dragged her load to the floor.

Another chimney fell, and a flame peered into the room through the grate. The air was hot. It was no longer atmospheric air. One-tenth of it was carbonic acid and sulphuric gases. The medium which she now breathed was a fatal poison.

For one is poisoned truly and chemically when one is suffocated. It is precisely as if the potion were sedulously introduced in one's food. It is as if one carried a vial and fed it to the victim at every opportunity.

So, now, this murderess was each moment swallowing doses of poison. Their action on her vitals was more rapid than had been the action on Errington's body, and it would

"She thought she saw an Ogre standing over her."    Page 217.

be called a different death, but it was one and the same thing. She held her breath, feeling the cutting of the gas. She labored along the floor to the door.

"Help! help!" she screamed, but held to the corpse.

She gathered the Scared Look under her right arm. She clutched at a bronze lucifer. She opened her mouth to breathe. The inspiration was vile with poison. It sickened and hurt her. Her brain reeled. She recalled the last look of terror as her victim had striven to put back the philtre she had drawn from her pocket in plain sight and forced into his throat. She thought she saw an ogre standing above her, and saying: "Open your mouth! It might better be over soon!" She thought she felt a determined clutch upon her breast, a finger forced between her jaws, and she was too weak to even bite that finger.

She let go her precious load. She forgot her victim. She forgot Daniel. She clasped her jaws to hold them shut against the ogre. Oh! how the poison tore her lungs! How burned the fires in her vitals!

"Help! help!" she screamed. How pitiless was this poisoner who told her that she must take the liquid fire!

"Oh! Mamie! Mamie! my God! Mamie!" she murmured, and, murmuring so, opened her lips and drank of the thick and heavy air.

It was Ate holding the chalice to Mary's lips. And yet it was withal a more merciful cup than that out of which Ralph Errington had drunk for a long year. It was the same potation, but there were longer and more potent draughts.

She fell forward. Her lithe body found no resting place until it had reached the foot of the great staircase.

The air became better. The shock aroused her. She did not want to die. Although she burned alive within, there might yet be hope. Besides, it might be a coma. Then she would awake in the midst of true flames. A horrible picture of Servetus at the stake, seen in her youth, came on her view.

The bronze goblin on the newel-post glowered down upon her. She looked up once more for mercy, but the air grew denser. The goblin poured from that same little vial, and prepared to make her open her lips for the last time.

"Help! help!" was her final scream. "Oh, please, Mamie!" she implored, and opened her mouth, and drank the hemlock of penance and lustration.

The back part of the house tumbled down and let the car of Ate by. The back-fires rolled toward the front of the house.

Daniel had left the door open for the escape of Mary. He ran down to the gate. The carriage was gone. Whether it had been driven or had run away, it was time for it to go, and it had gone.

He looked back toward that grand entrance. He saw a gray woman; under her arm there came the Body of the Crime. The smoke rolled away, and he beheld the smallest details—the leeches clinging to her hand.

He heard her scream—"Help! help!" He saw her fall. He saw her body roll slowly, stage by stage, down the staircase. She was probably dead, for well he knew the mortal character of that yellow smoke, and how swiftly it did its corrosive work.

Better that she should die, for justice would then be done. Better the guilty should pass away than that he, the innocent, should perish on the gibbet. He would peer in at her. Better that she perish. Perish she must by God or by man.

"Help! help!" came from the gray form underneath the goblin.

It was Mercy's sister who called. It was a fellow-being. It was a soul he had loved. It was a nature that even now he held in awe. What man, who had been a fireman, could have stayed back? He would save her. She might put him on the gallows, as she surely would. Might God guide him! he prayed, as he made his renunciation of Mercy, and rushed into that yellow smoke, hoping it might also asphyxiate him.

But his was a practiced hand. One is not a fireman for nothing. He grasped that lithe body. He crawled back to the steps, down the steps and into sustaining air, and was not hurt.

"God help me!" he implored, as the gibbet rose before him; "I could not murder her as she murdered Ralph."

He carried her to the side gate and looked into her face.

He had trusted in God and done right, as God gave him to see it. Mary Errington would never betray him as Judas had sold his master. Mary Errington would never proclaim him to be her paramour and coparcener in murder.

Her soul had joined the three hundred that were journeying towards Ate's manger.

———

## CHAPTER XXVIII.

### LOST.

IF the reader has preserved the idea of Daniel's sheet of note-paper as a plan of the city of Chicago, it will be remembered that no effort was made to show the exact course of the north branch of the river. But we have clipped the upper right half of the sheet—the lake shore—say an inch at the top and zero at the mouth of the main river, or north pier. Now, if the straight line, standing for the north branch, be turned so it shall run parallel with that veering lake shore, we shall have both river and shore running twenty degrees west of north.

Phlegethon, the river of blow-pipe fire, began at a stable
on the first mile-ring around the Court-house. Phlegethon
was to reach the lake at this same mile-ring, on the opposite
side. And what was to be its goal?

The water-works of Chicago.

This was the true calamity, namely: A blow-pipe of
flame, of greater power than men had believed to be attain-
able in open-air conflagration, had risen at a stable on the
alley between De Koven and Taylor streets at 8:45 P. M. At
3:20 A. M., or in six hours and thirty-five minutes, it had
cut a narrow pathway in a straight line for a distance of
two miles—by the measurers said to be two miles and 1,252
feet. Engines stationed at the sides of this rapids of flame—
enough engines—could have stopped the rest of the fire.
Nothing could have coped with that direct blow-pipe force,
that blew a building red-hot before a flame need appear.

When Phlegethon had been cut from De Koven street to
the water works, there remained, besides the general northward progress, the fires of retrogression to burn leisurely
backward. There also tarried a detail of the original onset
at the Lake Shore depot, between Van Buren and Polk
streets, on the South Side. Two long freight houses spread
out and protected the whole eastward region until about 8
o'clock in the morning of Monday.

There was now to be no more water, and there remained
untouched the entire North Side of 1,440 acres, and seven-
eighths of the South Side, north of Harrison street. The
true and phenomenal fire was over. In its stead were a thousand furies, any one of them terrible enough.

When, therefore, Daniel came out upon Pine street, to flee
northward, in Mercy's wake, hoping to reach Fullerton
avenue, he must needs find Phlegethon rolling beyond him
and across his path. What he had warned the city editor
would happen, had happened. The city was cut off. Undoubtedly the fire had also come across further southward,

and fully 50,000 people had been caught at the lake shore. So he supposed.

It was with a heart bursting with disappointment that this sturdy young lover, a moment before so fortunate in his escape from betrayal and ignominy, now turned toward the lake shore. He was not alone in that awful hour. Many a heart was sustained by the presence of the host of fellow-sufferers. They looked at this young man, bearing a lady of refinement.

"She's fainted. Papa, help that young man," a little girl would cry.

But Daniel would tell all friendly men to carry all they could of their own. He was strong. It was not yet time for him to be sleepy. His nocturnal hours of watching lately had made him a fit spectator of the besom that swept air and earth.

Then, as they entered the sands, a thief took Mary's hand. Daniel knocked that thief down, and he was kicked by another strong man. There was much glee. Then Daniel took a diamond ring from her finger and started to slip off a plain gold band from the third finger of her left hand.

"Let them steal it. I cannot take it off." The ring remained. What God had joined together no man should put asunder.

He carried that light body and thought of the evil it could have done him. He thought of the nights and days of suffering it had caused him, and for all those hours of grief he loved it none the less. Yet he thought of that dread scene on the grand staircase, and the feeling that it was a poisonous serpent, made him shiver and grow faint-hearted. How fortunate that God had made his most terrible creatures with small knowledge of the havoc they might do! She had loved him. However frightening that love might be, it had come out of her heart. Yes, he would save her poor clay and forgive her sins against him.

What an endless number of unfortunates had been penned
in these hot and whirling sands! The rich and the poor,
the good and the bad, the kind and the cruel, labored along,
judging as to the coolest place, where all was to become un-
endurable, and making countless journeys with precious
heirlooms, with family pets, and with helpless invalids.

A young girl staggered under a heavy load. The roughs
came along and took the best of her belongings—a handsome
clock and its case.

"Is it any wonder Chicago is burning?" she moaned, an
actual believer in the dogma that the modern Sodom was
getting judgment down from Heaven. One who had seen
Phlegethon roll by was justified in such thoughts.

Heavy wagons, driven by half-crazed, liquorous expressmen, came rapidly but silently across the sands, seeking the
points nearest the water. Over the little mounds of goods
these juggernauts would go. The sand would blow rapidly
over a heap of furniture. A child would be seeking shelter
on the windward side.

"Oh! my God! they've killed my boy! They've killed
him!"

Surely enough, a wagon had run over a child almost before
its mother's eyes. Of what use to follow the wretches and
demand of them more care?

Will not the gunners tell you who saved their battery at
Chickamauga, that when Thomas, the Rock, ordered them to
save their guns, after they had protected the retreat of their
army, they drove away under whip, and if the wounded
Union soldier could not crawl from before the juggernaut,
the gunners must shut their eyes and swear all the louder at
the Johnnies?

An old lady lay on her mattress, fatigued beyond care for
the hour. The brands fell faster and larger. The heat grew
insufferable. All the surrounding heaps of goods were moved
along, everyone supposing that all other fugitives were doing

the same thing. Suddenly the flames broke out in the mat-
tross, and the old lady was burned to death in sight of hundreds. It was the dance of death. Perhaps a party had just
left a boarding house a half hour before. So far they had
lost little, and desired to sustain themselves by good spirits.
Such a sight would leave two in a faint, and the rest would
turn around and look at the burning city.

At the distance of half a mile a line of fire a mile long is
broader than the eye can cover. It is an endless sea of flames.
A city on fire, therefore, is like a battle. No one observer
can see the vision unless he be at least ten miles away, on a
high place.

Nobody saw the Chicago fire.

But Daniel saw Lake Michigan, and never shall mortal
gaze on sight more truly appalling. The hour of dawn,
without its phenomena; an unearthly light above and behind; an unending expanse of inky and rolling waters, covered by millions of floating objects—debris of all kinds, taking every imaginable color as their wet surfaces reflected the
changing lights of the conflagration; millions of brands and
sparks falling into the deep waves, each with a low hiss, but
together with the dreariest of sounds. If man may look upon
the true symbol of death and eternity Daniel saw it that
morning. Children viewed these dark waters of Lethe with
horror. They fought a losing day against the sparks that
fell so unremittingly on heads and shoulders.

Another wagon came along. "Here's a man with a body,"
they said, and drew up, hailing Daniel.

"Say, old man, we'll take on that body for $50."

Daniel had not a penny. They drove on. It was useless
for them to talk to a man without currency. A man might
have money in bank. They laughed at that. Money was
what talked there and then.

Daniel did not see how the wagoners could aid him much.
In his opinion, rogues and honest men were all like rats in a

trap. They were surrounded by fire. Far to the south he could see a pier extending into the water. People were out there. Between himself and the pier the sands narrowed, and shanties and lumber piles soon to burn came very close to the water. He felt that he must wait until those shanties burned before he could hope to get past to the pier. There he saw boats coming and going. The sight cheered him. There would, then, be no holocaust, after all, as he had feared. He who had so often scolded at the boats and bridges blessed them well.

The fire pressed toward them. Houses that had, but a moment ago, seemed far away, now burned with long flames that threw their heat to the gale and made the clouds of sand burning hot. What would the nearer fires do that were to come ? People who had gone toward the shanties returned northward, crying that everybody would be burned. Pile after pile of goods caught fire amidst the protestations of the people that it was carelessness, and should be stopped for the general good. Boys on horses, sitting higher than the rest, found the air too close to breathe, and drove slowly out into the water. The fires approached. All must follow the boys on the horses. The children who had cried at the heat and the sparks now moaned piteously as they went out into Lethe.

Then Daniel with his dead, now black and irrecognizable, her fine dress spotted with sooty holes, her gray laces singed and made harsh, put forth into the deep. The heat increased as it was reflected from the water. A woman with three children was at his right, ten feet away. There was the greatest fear of crowding from behind, but all were assured by boys resident there about that the decline was very gradual.

There was no relief to be had until the children were nearly off their feet. The wind was terrific. There was a tendency to scatter, for each feared the next wader would lose presence of mind and cling frantically to a neighbor. The waves were

high although so near the shore. Daniel was in a sitting post-
ure, with the body of Mary across his knees. The waves would
often throw him off his balance, and he found that his burden
was rather an advantage than otherwise. He had no thought
of personal danger, but he did look with amazement into the
future.

He sat patiently, bathing his face and head in the water,
which now had lost its horrid look to him, and wondered
where Mercy was. Where would she go when the fire reached
her? How bitterly he regretted that lost hour in that local
room—that spectacle of the shining dome. The little scared
face at the grated door rose up before him. The lost fortune
of the great landlord came next upon him. His own little
house on Washington street, by this time well on fire; the
death of Harmon, friend of his youth—Daniel wept; the
death of Errington—ah! yes, the colloquy on the staircase;
the escape from the gibbet; the corpse of Mary—

"My!" he whispered, and looked at Chicago in its destruction; "I must quit all that, or I shall be a raving
maniac. It is more than God intended a human being to
see in one day!"

"I'm sorry for that young husband," a good wife said to
her partner in life. "It's dreadful, isn't it?"

"It isn't as dreadful, my dear, as that childbirth down
there," the husband would respond.

Verily every heart knoweth its own bitterness.

"Help! Help! Oh, save my boy! Oh, save my boy!"
There was a commotion in Lethe not made by the gale.

The mother to Daniel's right was holding to two of her
restless sons. The third was drifting out to sea. How fast
the wind blew him, as he blubbered, touched bottom, kicked
viciously, and urged his outward pace.

It was Daniel's place to save that lubber, and Daniel must
be quick. The people to his left had kept as far away as
possible. It is not human nature to court the presence of

15

the dead in the face of danger. There was no one to aid Daniel. He gave a spring, pursued the boy, waded, swam, dove, and finally reached him. The lad was well strangled, but able to get his breath. The host set up a gabble over the event and a man offered to take care of one of the lads. Other mothers became more alarmed than ever, and other lads set out to see how near drowning they could come.

But Daniel, having saved the lubber was raging with anger at the event. The body of Mary could not be found. He searched there hour after hour.

"Oh! see the sun!" cried somebody.

Surely enough, it was 8 o'clock. The sun was two hours high, and no one had known it was morning.

There was no morning in Chicago, Oct. 9, 1871. It did not grow light. It grew rather darker at dawn.

The children complained of hunger and fear. The city burned on—a gray, dusty, occasionally a deep red—on high, black smoke, with some formations like thunder-clouds. A vast repulsive spectacle.

The shanties and lumber-piles disappeared, the heat decreased, the piles of goods turned to ashes and blew away, and the people began to go out on the sands.

Alone, out in Lethe, Daniel searched for the body of her he had loved, of her he had hated, of her he loved now again. He shed bitter tears that she had died. He forgot Mercy, life, Chicago, everything, hoping that he might find the trust that had been put into his hands. To keep that trust he had turned aside from a thousand imploring appeals for aid; to keep a faithful guard he had stood aside and let hundreds of sacred relics perish. He could not save Chicago, but he could save Mary, for her mother, for Mercy—for himself.

Now he had not saved Mary! Great tears ran down his face. There was plenteous pity for him among that band of unfortunates.

"It will come to shore when the wind changes," they cheered him, for they knew he had lost the body in saving the lubber. They had seen his jealous vigil. They had seen his long battle with the sparks in the laces, before the going down into Lethe.

"It will come ashore," they said.

How that word "It" grates on our ears, when first the stranger enters our doors and addresses the term to our own precious dead!

---

## CHAPTER XXIX.

### THE FIRST NIGHT.

How inconceivably lonely did Daniel feel as he came up out of Lethe, and bade good-bye to that light body which he had again learned to love! It was out there somewhere, but not to be seen by mortal eyes. All now was dust and ashes. The glory of the conflagration was gone, never to return, and for that might God be thanked! In place of auroral clouds and Ate's car, there were pestilential smells and pest itself—for was he not on the very Golgotha of the city, the region of the small-pox hospital? Such were the alarms of the fugitives, choking with smoke, weary nigh to death, hungry almost to desperation.

Again he fixed his eye on the pier to the south and determined to reach it. To the northward a brewery's ruins held the flames close to shore, and shut him away from Mercy. He scanned the crowd northward, unconsciously looking for Mercy.

"Heavens!" he shuddered, "how will they be fed?" For manna could not be expected to fall from heaven, and they could not eat ashes. Watching his opportunity in a freak of the gale, he ran around through the narrow place, and was now on his way to the pier. It was a structure of piling and timbers filled with rubble-stone. He got to its end, and was safe, but just as a tug had steamed away with a load of refugees. The man with the trunk at the depot in which were $600,000 had barely enough money to pay his fare.

The strain left Daniel's mind for the moment. Odd and ludicrous scenes came before him. A philosopher sat on the pier. "My son," said he to a boy, "hand me that fiddle. I've got a bigger fire than Nero had." And people clambering over those jagged stones were badgered to dance the sailor's hornpipe, which this musician was playing.

"It's for a record," he said, "Chicago is at the front. Give her a chance, and she will beat Rome."

What was there in men that rather tempted them to hope the fire would clear up every house and outdo history ?

They did not seem to know that history already stood with no example to offer to Chicago.

There rose at Daniel's left an enormous elevator. Its duplicate had just burned in mountains of thick smoke, which had kept him to the northward. It seemed that this one was to stand. He would wait an hour and see. An hour passed and he went ashore and sought the pier next the river. There he found a sailor in a yawl. Daniel told that sailor he was out of money, and the sailor took him across the narrow water without cost. It was the only man Daniel had met who was not playing the Chicago fire for all it was worth.

Four steamers stood a mile out in the lake awaiting events.

Daniel clambered on the outer breakwater, and soon was south of the slips, elevator, and depot walls of the Michigan Central and the Illinois Central Railroads.

Here, spread before his eyes, was doubtless one of the

saddest spectacles the sun, now of a droughty brightness had ever shone upon. At that day what is now Lake Front Park was partly water. It was called the Basin. There were but two tracks for the railroads, and they ran on trestles, twenty feet inside the breakwater. But there was still a very wide space between the building line of Michigan avenue and the water, and that wide space was a mile long.

Into this place of refuge had gone nearly every ousted householder who had been at the east of Phlegethon on the South Side. It must be remembered that the fire started as far south as Twelfth street, lacking a block. If it came over as it was expected to do, it would burn all to the west of the Lake Front Park. But it was the apparent judgment of the host that it would be idle to attempt to secure a safer place. To go south was to run the risk of being driven into the lake where there was little shore. The dust blew in steady streams, and it was the general method of the day for parties hailing from the same quarter to pile a number of trunks in a line, three trunks in height, and strive to form a cover with woolen blankets on the northeast side of the trunks, which would protect the weaker members of the party from the rigors of the sandy, smoky sirocco. At the extreme northern end of the open space, where the side-fires, pouncing on the second Drake block, had burned it in twenty minutes, many of these heaps of goods had been burned. Two charred bodies lay on a set of bent and twisted spiral bed springs.

There was a great but silent panic in this park. A change of the wind to the eastward meant death for nearly everybody, and at the time of the fire in the northern end, every one supposed this change must have come.

Daniel came upon the city editor, guarding a row of trunks and a number of members of his household.

"Dan," said the editor, "both my house and the office were safe this morning at 8 o'clock. The fire burned ex-

actly around west and north of the office.  It was as I said.
We could have printed the whole edition."

" How is it now ? " asked Daniel, looking toward Madison street.

" House and office both gone ! " said the editor.  " How
that sand blows ! " and he crawled under his blanket.

All that morning had gone the innumerable caravan down
Michigan avenue.  Whence came so many two-horse trucks ?
None were going north.  The sun shone down clearly through
all the smoke, which bore out to sea rapidly in a thick vapor.
Down that wide street, teams four abreast, passed the sack
of the city.  Here would be a long slanting-bodied wagon with
high stakes on every side.  Piled like a load of furniture, or
even hay, would be rolls of the costliest fabrics.  Crimson,
yellow, green and blue silks would flash back the sun, and
whole pieces of royal purple velvet would tumble loosely off
the top, to be instantly trampled under foot by the next
teams.  This unexampled caravan was carrying the salvage
of the great dry goods houses of Farwell & Co. and Field &
Leiter.

Along this gorgeous way would come an express wagon
with three or four young men and their trunks.  Such
a vehicle would strive to go past the big wagons.  Men
dragging buggies in which were trunks would oppose in-
superable barriers to rapid transit by horses.  The expressman would travel on two wheels for a block, whipping his
horse madly all the while.  Finally, over he would go, and a
half dozen trunks would tumble around the heads of the
men-oxen.  Nothing ever stopped that caravan  It went on
and on, over wrecks, over everything, silent, orderly, swiftly,
beautiful.  It grew shorter as its base of communications
burned southward, but it did not stop.  A city's riches are
not to be carried away in a day, by wheel, over one turnpike.

No one who saw it will ever forget the feeling of awe which
it inspired.  As silently as Joseph and the blessed Mary

went down into Egypt to escape Herod, so now Chicago put forth into the desert to hide from Ate.

Neither will any refugee, who, with his all, was penned in that park beside Michigan avenue for an afternoon, forget the asperities of that chapter of waiting and watching. The wide avenue had been paved years before with soft limestone macadam. This limestone had worn off, powdered, and the long drought and the tremendous heat of the fire at the north end had made this powder about two inches thick, had it been on the ground. It was not on the ground. It was in the air —every particle of it. It was necessary, if one peered above the row of trunks, to bandage one's eyes, and many were the wretches who ran backward and forward from the water, fairly maddened with the burning effects of that white dust.

The churches were now burning along Wabash avenue, and, as there was no water, there was no reason why the fire should not work southward, especially as the wind was getting to the west. There were noises, as of cannon, and Daniel crossed at Congress street, and found General Sheridan on hand in that region and devoting his resources to the destruction of the blocks of the houses that promised to leave the longest gaps before the lazily-retrogressing flames. The large Methodist Church at the northwest corner of Harrison street and Wasbash avenue was thus prepared for sacrifice, when it was seen that it would oppose the conflagration better by its side walls. This it did. Several other large sacred edifices, near together, had done much to tire out the fire, to delay its retogression, and thus to diminish its fury.

What a blessed sight it was to see a fire smouldering, and the next house not on fire! "Thank God for churches!" cried Daniel, as he saw the vigil in the park ending, and people moving back into the houses south of Congress and Harrison streets.

It was growing dusk. The awful Event was again lighting up. The city editor came back, as express wagons were plentier now. He was to stay with a relative near by, who had so far escaped.

What a night was before Chicago! The first night after the event of centuries! Close, is it not reader? Well, those Chicagoans knew it. They knew they had lived through the spectacle of all history thus far. They were its unwilling witnesses. It is said that to be great is to be lonesome. It is equally lonesome to be within one day of a great event, be it Shiloh or Chicago.

All Daniel knew was that the peninsula of houses east of State street and south of Congress had been left. Around them, before them, with winds again blowing to northeast, was the fire reawakening in a splendor, oh! how hateful! They had seen Ate; they had lived through a thick, hot, exasperating sirocco of smoke, knowing that walls were trembling, knowing that it needed only night to make the volumes of smoke red with threatenings. They now were weary; their brains were full. Into a cup was flowing an ocean.

Chicago was dead. Her corse lay on this weird plain. He must love her well who did not already nose her. He must have love for her dust who did not now turn pale with faintness.

Were the working devils of the spectacle running about over there, lighting up all these *piece de resistance* to make men's hearts break utterly? Was it not enough to know that Chicago *was?* Must there be a peep-show of it? Is not that over there a glorious statue of George Washington? Yes, it took the Pacific Hotel to furnish that one piece of this night's bric-a-brac. What splendid jewels are set upon the circle of the horizon! Yes, those are mountains of hard coal. Let them seethe. That furthest one—it must be three miles away. There lie the twelve thousand hearthstones on which that coal was to have burned. Out here, and over there, and far to the north, are the hundred thousand that Ate chased away.

Who would have believed Chicago had so many tall chimneys? Why should they stand there balancing against the gale while great thick walls worshipped prone before Ate? Weird, weird, full of awful shadows! Fuller of realities that stagger the very imagination of Daniel Trentworthy, who stands there in the presence of the Event—ay, with the Event not yet done, not yet ready for that tremendous page which History was making white to receive it!

A squad of citizens marched up, and asked the city editor's advice. They told him they understood the West Side was not yet burned, but that it was the intention of incendiaries to burn the rest of the town that night. Patrols were forming all over. There was no gas. Daniel, hearing this news, had hoped to get to the West Side and around to the North Side. He was consumed with fears that Mercy would perish. Again he blamed himself for not making the detour earlier in the day.

When he had supposed the whole city was on fire!

But Daniel was only one of tens of thousands who were thus perplexed on the 9th of October.

The citizens knew Daniel through the city editor. They knew Daniel was not a thief. That was sufficient. They impressed him into the service. They told him he would get shot if he went to the West Side, which statement was not improbable.

"You're hungry?" they inquired.

"Not very," he said. "I had my dinner—" he stopped to think—"yesterday noon."

So they gave him his supper on the second day. He ate little. One's palate gets rusty when a city burns.

It was experienced that the greatest of spectacles deprived men of appetite.

Behold, then, Mercy's Daniel, at the southern verge of the embers, with night come on the second day, impressed as a watchman who was to deal summarily with all who desired to heighten the Event.

It was deemed best that each of the patrols at Wabash and Congress should serve two hours and sleep four. The parlors of a house which had been emptied in moving were given to the squad and mattresses laid for them. Daniel was on a narrow pinnacle of saved property. The fire was next door to him northward, and westward the edge was then six half-blocks away, and there extended southward again five long blocks. The ruins were at that hour far too hot to enter. Men also had a special terror of fire. It was shown that the more they saw of it the worse they thought of it. At 10:30 o'clock it came Daniel's turn to sleep.

He lay upon a good spring mattress. He feared he would dream of Mary. If he did he hoped he might see her as she once had been, sitting at the piano, her laugh rippling through the house. He thought how wretched would be his plight if he had really been a party to Errington's assassination, and devoutly said his prayers. "Keep Mercy! keep Mercy!" he implored, and fell asleep.

Could Mercy have seen, how she would have pitied the overtasked brain that, but a moment later, sprang from that mattress to avoid the blue tongues of flame that were darting around the room and encompassing the house. Men had seen the blue tongue that day until it had worn out their cerebellum. Daniel shook himself, seized his carbine and, went outside. It was raining. He felt safer. His nerves quieted. A guard stood sleeping against the patent fence. The wind was blowing worse than ever. What if it had changed its course with that guard asleep! Daniel could sleep no more.

He wondered if that squad over at Harrison and Third avenue were not more careful. There had been a high sand pile there—ten feet high and thirty feet long—Sunday morning. Now it was all gone. Example of the power and persistence of the fire-gale!

Yes, that squad over there were vigilant, but he judged

by their singing that they had been drinking. He saw a great commotion. He heard a young fellow pleading. Daniel woke several of the sleepers and ran around to Harrison street and over beyond State.

He met a line of guns, but the men soon recognized him as a citizen guard.

"We caught a fire-bug. He was setting this house on fire. See? Here's the oil and here's his match."

Daniel must believe. It was true. "Where is he now?" Daniel asked.

"We sent him up to see if the Post-Office was burnt. We were anxious to know, as we expected a letter."

They laughed, and one set up the popular song, "O write me a letter from home!"

In front of them were the walls of a huge brick house. Within, the fire burned vividly. One of the drunken patrols sauntered over there and peered through a window.

"Don't go near there, cully," they said to Daniel, who had followed the man; "you'll get burned, sure. There! your cap'n's callin' you. Run along. Good-by. If we need you, we'll call you."

There was no law. It was a good night, to be sure, for setting fire to houses. But it was a bad night to be caught doing it.

-----

## CHAPTER XXX.

### NOBLE PEOPLE ON NOBLE STREET.

WHEN Fullmer arrived at the Ohio street mansion that Sunday night he found he was too late to see Harmon Holebroke alive. He brought Mrs. Holebroke and Mercy the welcome news that, up to the hour he had left the West Side, the Clinton street house was safe, and probably would not burn. Yet, in the depth of their grief, they paid a secondary heed to the matter. To Mercy's inquiry about Daniel he could say that Daniel was on his way to the house, and this cheered the maiden. The death of a truly good man is a bitter loss to his dear ones, on account of the scarcity of good men. As Mercy looked into a future that had no Harmon in it, the realm was indeed dark and forbidding.

Another great fire was burning. What terrible fires we were having! she thought, wonderingly. And what an awful gale had blown since Friday morning! It really seemed to get worse.

Mr. Fullmer said the fire had caught on the South Side, and would probably burn all the wooden houses in "Conley's patch," around the Armory and gas works. She pitied the poor who would be thrust out of house and home.

And then she shuddered. For had not their little worldly effects been that very night moved over on the open lot, and then carried back? How much damage must have been done! for Mercy had the instincts of a good housekeeper. Yes, Daniel had been on the lookout for her and hers. This rich marriage of Mary had brought them all many conveniences. It had given Harmon an easy death. "Mother," he had said, "I could not die if I feared that you or Mercy would ever want."

But the revelations of Friday night had turned all Mercy's comforts and conveniences into complaining witnesses of Mary's purpose. A careful study of the gray-eyed sister's face was rewarded by the discovery that she was in a high state of suppressed excitement, and Mercy, in retrospection, was forced to admit that this situation must have dated back for weeks. And yet Mercy believed Mary was innocent.

How sadly that black-eyed lady needed her lover that night. Mary had hurried from the death-bed of Harmon, and had been seen little since. Ralph was very ill indeed.

It was his worst night, Mary said, as she came to the head of the staircase to ask if Daniel had arrived.

Mr. Errington was suffering a great deal, she answered Mr. Fullmer, when she had made her appearance as he came in. She had almost fallen in his arms, he thought. Poor woman—brother dead ; husband so low ! The man once counted so hard-hearted was soft as mother to babe. He pitied this rich lady.

She had restrained herself barely in time. All men were begrimed from this West Side fire. She had supposed it must be Daniel.

Then the fire flood poured suddenly on the Chamber of Commerce and the Court House. The bell rang and the sky took a greater light. Fullmer was the only man about the premises. He began to feel the approaching danger. He suggested preparation.

Mary said "No." It came from the depths of her apartments. It was accompanied by sharp and feeble cries, alternating. Doubtless she had been too busy to give the subject proper attention. Doubtless she could not comprehend the fact that what was to happen but once in the history of civilization was happening now. She could not know that the greatest conflagration of the Pagan and Christian eras was at her gates.

So Fullmer believed, though he himself did not know of Phlegethon. He believed a fire was approaching—not a funnel of flame.

He went to the stables and hitched up the two span of horses. He took the two largest conveyances. He worked rapidly, and as he labored saw new evidences of the need of haste. He awoke the neighbors.

"Mary, dear, we must go. There is a great fire. Mr. Fullmer says it is not safe here. Can we aid you to move Ralph ? The carriages are in front." So asked the mother, worn out with disappointed hope. What is so entirely unnatural as for the offspring to die and leave its parent?

"Go," came the stern answer, with the cries of agony. "Go!" it rang out authoritatively.

"Mercy, we must go. Mary commands it." Now how was it that the mother-heart could be hurt, even while it was wrung with the greatest of sorrows. "Mary commands it!" The brooding soul did not feel that Mary had commanded her mother's services sufficiently.

What a short moment was that meeting of Mercy with the beloved Daniel. Ah! he had come! He would not leave them now! Alas! before she knew it she was in the carriage, and Daniel was not. She looked back in the unearthly light. She saw him enter the house too suddenly, she thought.

The door had pulled him in.

On every side was the evidence of panic—of great danger. She again looked backward toward the mansion and saw the neighbor's house collapsing, as though sucked into a cave beneath. Was it, then, such an onslaught as that?

She asked Mr. Fullmer: Was Daniel in danger? Were he and Mrs. Errington and Mr. Trentworthy in real jeopardy? Well, he didn't like to say, but he thought they ought to get out of that block at least.

The carriage proceeded slowly in that flying storm of sand, in that red ghost's light, in that third caravan of the fire. They were soon out of the district that was immediately threatened and reached Mrs. Trenton's house in safety.

The people in that quarter were all asleep. It was a ghastly company for the Trentons to receive, and it tried the mettle of the good woman to conceive, in one moment, that a city was burning and that a dead friend and two living ones sought the asylum of her roof. She was a heroic woman. She looked into the heavens, and the heavens were telling. She made place, and had an undertaker at the house in half an hour. There is something astonishingly clever in the wide-awake American city housewife. She has adjusted herself to heat, cold and position more nicely than any chronometer balance-wheel. She can get up and do more, and do it more cheaply, than any other potentiality in existence.

So that the body of Harmon, on a carriage-box, became the body of Harmon in temporary laying-out, ready for casket and burial at proper time. Crape was on the door. Men were to dig the grave at dawn.

Daniel and Mary and the sick man did not come.

The mother gazed upon the growing light, and put her hands to her temples in a feeble way. She dwelt entirely on Mary. Mercy could not endure her suspense. She said nothing to the busy Mrs. Trenton.

"Mother," Mercy said, "I am going back."

"Yes," said the mother, "find Mary."

And down the quiet street the girl ran, fearing Mr. Trenton or Fullmer would discover her absence. She was afraid something would happen to Daniel, and she wished to share his fate.

For a woman will leave father and mother, brother and sister, and cleave to the stranger. She will accuse herself of heartlessness to her own, and heartless she is. But how else shall she become a wife? How else shall she follow husband to scaffold? How else shall she wait at prison walls, hoping he will not forget her when the state shall purge him forth?

Mercy wrapped a shawl about her head and face. She might be some German frau, hurrying southward to her husband's beer-counter, to get the money in the till. She was safe in the growing multitude. She thought of the night of the grand wedding, and the similar journey of woe that she had made to the Ohio street mansion. "Oh! God!" she implored, "why must I suffer this twice?"—for man forever thinks he ought not to suffer. Then, as she put off her burden, the reaction of hope came back. She saw Daniel removing poor Ralph, and the stern Mary saving everything, even to the bronze goblins in the hallway.

"It is strange," she murmured thankfully, "what a panic I was in then."

But even as she peered down North Clark street, it was a mass of flame. The center of the street was on fire. The air was on fire. She looked, gasping, to the left, or east of this main thoroughfare. Verily, it must be on this side of Ohio street, over there, that those pythons of scarlet cloud made their spirals in the air.

It was Phlegethon rolling to the water works, five blocks northward of Ohio street.

The tide of pedestrians was now northward. But she had business beyond Phlegethon. She must cross it, or go around it. Daniel, her Daniel, was on the other side. She must go through it. Forward, like an endangered steed, she moved. She reached Chicago avenue, the street of the water works, but a half-mile to the westward of the pumping house. She would have gone on, but a policeman turned her into Chicago avenue.

"Go straight west!" he said, for she must be fleeing from the fire. The crowd was now behind her. She must go. "Ah! The smelting-works!" she thought. The works were on Wells street, to the south of Chicago avenue. She could get thither. Daniel and Mary and Ralph were there. Of course, Ralph could not be moved far. There was a good office over there, to be sure.

But it was an expedient of the moment—this thought. She feared Daniel was in Phlegethon. She wanted to turn back and go to him. She did not want to live without him. Like Gautama, she had seen those things she had not thought to see. Her mother had failed entirely since Harmon's illness. What other link of the past had not been rudely broken? With Daniel by her side she could have seen the

wisdom of God's present act.  But with him beyond Phlegethon, her mind was still in doubt.

Did we not all try to measure God's providence with our
own little measure ?   Did we not all try to adjust the burnt
district to our houses and lots, or to our packed trunk, ere
we attempted to believe there was a Divine hand ?

Thus Mercy, increasing in agony, went away from Daniel.  She looked down Wells street.

"Ah! ain't it a pity !" said the women, "the big smelting-
works is on fire."

"Did you hear there were forty people burned in the Con-
tinental Hotel ?" asked another.

"I saw 'em pull a roasted fireman out of a big water-pipe
over there," said a husband to the women.

"McCormick's is burned," said another.

"Oh, gracious !" said the women.

Their men worked there.  It was worse than a strike at
the great reaper factory on Rush street.

A man came past with a canary in a cage.  He was
voluble with excitement.  "I grabbed this cage," he explained, "and left $1,150 under a carpet."

This crowd, surging toward the Chicago avenue bridge,
was orderly, solemn and stoical.  No one could remark upon
a loss that would not elicit a statement of loss ten times as
great.

"I'm out of my situation," a young man would say.

"I have lost a hundred thousand dollars," a gray-haired
man would respond.

"My wife and two children burned before my eyes," a
wild-looking fugitive would shout furiously, "and I could
not even get their bodies."

And then the pressure of general contempt would fall on
him who had first complained.  So all learned to keep still.
It was deep water.  No one knew its depth.

But this west-going concourse, confident of its means of

exit into the West Side, was to behold the main tragedies of
the conflagration.  The North Side, at this point, was widening very rapidly.  At Wells street and the main river, on
Kenzie street, say, the crowd would have reached the West
Side bridge in four blocks.  But at Chicago avenue, ten
short blocks northward, the distance westward to a bridge
was eight long blocks.  They felt secure for many reasons,
but were in dire extremity for as many.  The section of the
city between Clark street and Chicago avenue on east and
north, and the two bayous on south and west, **were** thickly
filled with inhabitants.  Where factories had risen, workmen
had grouped around, two, three, four families in a house.
The houses were nearly all wooden.  The fire which was
going slowly in the South Side would get its old-time fury
when it reached this swath.  There were only two large
churches and the Kenzie school as bulwarks.  While the
multitudes had been moving carelessly at Clark and Wells
streets on Chicago avenue, the lumber piles, tar works, tenements, and flouring mills had once more given a double-
quick motion to the onset.  The people suddenly filled
Chicago avenue ahead of Mercy, coming out of Franklin,
Market, and Sedgwick streets, and the densest of endurable
smoke closed in on the scene.

That bridge ahead must stand.  That avenue of escape
must not fail.  What is that cry ?  A fire at the northward
of the bridge, caught from flying embers.  Onward the caravan pressed.  What was poor Mercy now ?  Only a unit,
only a German frau, holding shawl over head to ward away
sparks—a frau without children, without broken furniture
or cracked crockery, without wheelbarrow, buggy, truck,
dray.

Would they reach that bridge?  A woman fell by the
curbstone, and a child was born to her.  Convulsions seized
her, and she was dead ere Mercy went by.

A general fascination seized the fleeing host.  Ahead, a

half block south of the bridge approach, a large group of blacksmiths had been seen to enter a shop to save their tools —sixteen blacksmiths, a man said who had counted them. The building blazed, but the workmen did not come forth.

"Oh! they went out the other side," said a wise fugitive.

"No, they didn't," cried back a fleeing sight-seer, who was in advance. "There didn't a soul come out, and there were sixteen of 'em."

"We'll never reach the bridge!" they cried, and ran for life. Some one had blundered. It was then to be Beresina and Leipsic. They crowded up the approach. The fire was hot to right and left. It was too late. A large group of men, women and children, seeing the flames at the bridge, turned into a narrow street to the right, which proved to be a cul-de-sac, and gave them their death. How many of these victims there were is not to be known. Some said twenty; more people said forty.

Mercy went on. She had given up hope. And she was not going near to Daniel. Death with him would have been sweeter. Still she had looked at those sixteen fathers of families. The Lord willed it. What right had she to complain? She arrived at the bridge as it was well in course of the quick destruction that seemed to be in store for everything and everybody that cruel night. The group could not go back. Down the stairs she went, and under the approach by the edge of the turbid water. The Division street bridge was over half a mile away, through fire. The people were roasting down there under the approach. The weak ones were already unconscious.

Why did it not terrify her to see men, women and children biting the dust, lying thicker than in battle? Why did she go further into that oven of stonework? A boat lay beyond, where no person had believed one could go. She drew the shawl over her head more closely. She breathed through its texture. She stepped into the boat. Why did she do that?

Because an unseen hand had guided her. The wind veered for a moment. Three strong men made a dash to follow her example, unfastening the chain as they settled to the oars.

The first push brought them nearer the burning pier in' the middle of the river. Their hair answered with a crackle. Their ears rolled a little. They groaned in agony. But Mercy lay in the bottom of the yawl, and heard nothing. The water in the boat had cooled her. She was unconscious from the shock—the freezing sensation of tepid water.

The next push saved the boat-load, for the degree of heat at once lessened. They poured the black water on Mercy and splattered it on themselves. They neared a place of safety and gave Mercy to outstretched Christian hands.

Then those boatmen, grown suddenly great, according to the moment, chose their path, and transferred many others. But many of the unfortunates under that approach were so stolid with heat and suffering that they would not come out of the oven, even though life depended upon it. They lost their lives there, almost needlessly, from pure panic. There were accessible places where the heat was less intense. How many were lost is not well estimated. Mercy, with shawl over her face, said there must have been twenty.

Certain it is that this was the truly tragic spot of the fire. The loss of that bridge was the loss of a strategic point of escape. There was rapid burial by friends. There was no precise coroner's work for some days.

A man and his brother stood and received the prone figure in that boat. They carried her to the avenue. They secured an express wagon. They bore her to their home on Noble street. Why? Because they were Christian people, and all such felt a desire that they had not known was dormant in them—a desire which gave them great self-respect—a desire to reach out a helping hand to those who had been stricken.

These brothers had hoped to rescue a fair lady. A German frau, shawl over head, was thrown into their hands. They had succored her willingly. See the delight of that unmarried brother when he beholds, after all, a beautiful young woman. She is not burned. She is very low, or unconscious. They drive slowly. They carry her tenderly. They give her their best room—the parlor. They consult their own doctor, who does not refuse to come. The young man watches over her. Ah! she will be well cared for! Is not beauty a sacred thing, after all, when we, following God's evident commands, worship it so without hypocrisy?

"She is hurt from breathing hot air," the good doctor says, and bustles off on the busiest day of his life. Everywhere sad cases. Often bad cases where the patient has lost one of her two houses, and has not been near the burnt district. There were signs and portents that outdid the nights of the great Roman assassination. Five hundred babes had birthdays in commemoration of Ate.

"Bad air," hummed the doctor; "but plenty of it—plenty of it!" as the gale blew.

The young man watched this Monday night by his lovely charge. The neighbors were all interested. A beautiful lady had drifted thither from the aristocratic North Side. The street was honored. Is there anything in the boast of human equality?

There is nothing that will ever put a serf's yoke on beauty. Let Noble street do her honor. A wise thoroughfare! There shall be no regrets.

Other young men went off to the ruins or patrolled the quarter. This young man held Mercy's tiny wrist, and put his fingers to span her narrow throat. The action of her heart grew better. Her respiration became natural. At 10 o'clock she spoke.

"Daniel?" she asked, and smiled. Was it not hard that this good young man must not love her?

"No," he answered, and there came a cloud upon his brow.

"I might have known it," he said, with keen disappointment.

Of course he might. Did he suppose men had been born blind to beauty until he came on the scene?

But was he so bitterly disappointed as poor Mercy, after all?

---

## CHAPTER XXXI.

### OUT.

WHEN Mrs. Trenton learned that Mercy had gone, the good wife was frantic with excitement and suspense. She could not believe that Mrs. Holebroke would have consented to such a thing, and noticed, for the first time, the changed mental condition of the old lady. Mrs. Trenton was a brave and noble-spirited woman, and she said, when her husband remarked that he would like to go after Mercy:

"Go, my dear; it is right. Bring her back. But please, dear, be careful! Come back."

Tears were in her eyes, for the portent of the moving crowds was dispiriting. So Trenton went forth, and the entire conduct of the situation fell upon Mrs. Trenton, who begged Fullmer to stay with them as long as he could.

The crape on the door kept the refugees away during that fearful day of smoke and gale and flying sand.

The husband did not return. Mercy did not return. The mother sat inanely by Harmon's body, and gave further evidence that the sorrows and horrors of the night had unbalanced her. The good printer, growing apprehensive that he was neglecting his own household, and hearing rumors that the quarter in which his family had taken asylum was also burned or burning, was compelled to go.

The lady took him by the hand and thanked him with all her heart.

"It seems to me," he said, simply, "that you have more for which to blame than to thank me. I have brought you much trouble."

"He will come back!" she said triumphantly. "I know Edson Trenton. He told me he would come back, and he will. He knows I have trusted him with my life. It is not himself alone he will take care of."

And so, with sublime faith, she set to her great task.

Her trust was well founded. Her husband was late in returning, but he came back as he had gone out, doing his duty. He came back fighting fire.

"My dear, it's narrowing down," he said, "I think we can beat it." He looked admiringly at the long strips of wet carpet that lay on his roof.

"I have *you* here," she said. "We could fight the fire though it came here from Thirty-first street."

When Mr. Trenton saw that he must give up the hope of finding Mercy, he was confronted by the whole line of battle of the Chicago fire. It came on, over a mile wide, for a distance of half a mile of advance. Then its path must narrow. The lake shore was impinging rapidly on its right flank. Houses were getting scarce on its left. When it had reached Center street, at the main entrance to Lincoln Park, there were households there who had not seen Phlegethon. They knew there was a fire and a great wind. They were not terrified into believing it was a funnel, and it happened that their feeling responded to the facts. Good work, with well-water, actually put a stop to the flames athwart two blocks of its front on Center street.

As 10 o'clock came, on Monday night, it advanced toward Mrs. Trenton's house, with a total battle display only three blocks wide. On its right was the waste that was to be the north end of the Lincoln Park of to-day. On its left were the brave hopers, who had turned its flank at Center street and pushed it over to Hurlbut street. The gale was furious, and no longer abetted the destroyer, blowing rather directly toward the east.

Real estate had not been $100 a foot when Mr. and Mrs. Trenton bought in Chicago. They had plenty of breathing room. The ground was covered with autumn leaves, which were carefully gathered. The sidewalk was taken up and the boards piled in the park.

Preparations were made to move, if need be. But the word that came was cheerful. There was good hope that the fire was nearing its point of surrender.

From one or two precious wells the water was coming for the soaking of carpets. Houses that enjoyed strategic positions were chosen and their sides hung with these tapestries, richer to those fire-surfeited eyes than any arras or portiere that has ever breathed the air of languor and luxury since that night.

The fighters at Belden avenue had hoped their enemy could not cross that northern thoroughfare. It gained a slight hold and burned a house or two. But there its last capture was made. There it turned over its final hearthstone. There it wrecked the last of its victims. There it blasted the last hope.

At ten o'clock and twenty minutes on Tuesday night, Oct. 9, 1871, the Chicago fire labored across lots toward Fullerton avenue. She who would have been called Dame Partington when the Division street front was deployed was now a brave housewife with a chance of winning. Thump, thump, the brooms went on the ground, for these Illinois women were not afraid of grass fires.

Thump, thump, thump, and if they keep it away from that house where Harmon lies, the Chicago fire will be Out.

The lot is about seventy-five feet wide. There is a ragged fire-front of about fifty feet. They guard the house end most stubbornly. They mass their attack on that left flank of the grass fire. They turn the flank. At Eylau Napoleon let loose eighty squadrons of horse, and the lake beneath trembled so that the Russians were stricken with panic. This massing of brooms is a *grand coup*. But, when we turn the enemy, we must be careful to see he does not turn us. Rosecrans did that thing to his enemy at Stone River. While we broom back this left flank of this little billow that rolled so high over court-house, cathedral, opera-house, hostelry, and hospital, let us be sure the right flank does not prosper too easily.

Beat it hard out there; it is fighting sturdily! That picket fence—why was it allowed to stand? So scolds Mrs. Trenton. To the house, then, for the axes! How well that fence stuff burns—plenty of air, perpendicular surface, and train of connections? Yes, that is the same fiend, the same epiglottic sound of wolf, non-carnate. Chop quickly, axman. Chop! chop! It nears the corner of North Clark street and Fullerton avenue, the southwest corner. The corner is reached. The large hollow post blazes up. The front pickets are dashed away. There the destroyer must expire. His front flank had pushed forward fifty feet beyond the death-place of the left.

It is 10:30. The post burns in the center of a circle of shadowy conquerors. It chars and dies, for the brooms hit it and the axes deal it many blows.

The neighbors may claim to you that **the** Chicago fire was run to earth over there across the street in a stable. The stable, of course, is dramatic. But set here your monument. Here, by much consent, the Chicago fire went Out.

After the post had burned a leaf caught fire—an oak leaf. A maple leaf led on the spark, and one with keenest ears would still have heard the epiglottic sound of wolves. Out in the deep sand a great leaf of catalpa invited the attack. Into its leathery integument the fire buried itself. It was suffocating. Between two ribs of the leaf it narrowed gradually to a shining spark. It was now only the golden mote that reached the wisp that crossed the abyss between It Was and It Is in Patrick O'Leary's manger, three miles and a half away. Once more, as then, it prepared for some great leap of one-fiftieth of an inch.

High in the clouds a drop of rain formed and descended. The column of air that had supported this drop sprang up, and the spark breathed freer. The rain-drop, as marksman could not aim, flew at its golden mark. There was, for keenest ear, a noise not to be omitted from chronicles.

It was Ate, expiring with a hiss of hatred. Yet between that first spark, and that last spark, headed off by the converging ribs of a leaf of catalpa, and overwhelmed by drop of rain from heaven, as Pharaoh by Red Sea, what an immeasurable reach of difference! What odds whether that last house, or that last block, or that Fifteenth Ward burn or not, so far as the world, onlooking in after times, shall care? For men living in the city of the great event will to-day tell you that they know not the year of the fire. It was not for a day, a year, any more than was Shakespeare. But until the circumstances and fact of a quarter before 9 o'clock P. M. on the east half of lot 12 on the night of Oct. 8, 1871, shall reconvene, to the terror of mankind—until then, men will visit Chicago from far off lands, and when they have returned to their neighbors they will say: "I stood where It started, and I saw were It was put out."

If you go now to DeKoven street you shall see substantial brick apartment houses risen along the block. Upon the fatal spot in the rear you may behold a well-built shed of the pattern of that one which once mangered Ate, but not so high. In the front wall of the fine brick building, you will read the following, on a marble tablet :

THE GREAT FIRE of 1871
ORIGINATED HERE, and EXTENDED to
LINCOLN PARK.
CHICAGO HISTORICAL SOCIETY, 1881.

No picture of Patrick O'Leary's cottage, which stood there until 1881, was taken. The tablet was erected at the urgent request of the white-haired librarian of the society, who vows he paid for it out of his own pocket. Evidence that the generation which saw the Fire had no other curiosity concerning it! A tablet, too, not altogether exact—not altogether likely to satisfy the future. Garnish your alley, Anton Kolar, successor of Patrick O'Leary! A tide of men are to pass that way!

And set this other monument of Out at the southwest corner of Fullerton avenue and North Clark street.

And that catalpa leaf, where Ate lies buried, press it between the pages of history, and let it grow yellow!

---

## CHAPTER XXXII.

### THE HOWLING OF A DOG.

EARLY Tuesday morning Daniel laid down his gun and with the city editor started directly through the ruins toward the Madison street bridge. The city editor knew where the printing plant of the old co-operative company was stored, on Canal street, and was anxious to secure it. Daniel could not but marvel at the strange fate which had preserved this outfit. The scheme to redeem mankind through co-operative labor had failed. Whereas, at the start, no man could own more than a limited amount of the stock, it became necessary to borrow at once $2,500 in money. Thus the man with the mortgage held a very large interest. There were about $11,000 worth of material. The mortgage was not paid, and was foreclosed. Pending foreclosure the directors put the plant in the hands of a receiver, the receiver sold the plant, the directors moved the plant, and the man with the mortgage put the directors in jail. Sad end of the glorious principle of co-operation among Chicago printers! By this time there was a grand case for the lawyers, and the records were approaching completion when Patrick O'Leary's barn caught fire. The stuff itself lay in waiting on Canal street, for, while it might be dissipated in fees and other terms, it remained lead and antimony by keeping on the west side of the river.

This was the only establishment of body-type in Chicago. Singular chance by which the citizens had a paper, printed on one side, the next day. And not a bad chance for the printers, for they got $5,000 and the man of the mortgage $5,000. The lawyers would not have done as much toward getting back the $13,500 of original outlay.

The city editor was anxious to see his newspaper office.

He did not want to go alone.

"People came out of there yesterday noon," he said. "It must be cooler now."

This was true. Many persons tarrying too long about the Post-office on Monday had been forced to make the passage across to Madison street bridge. John McDevitt, a celebrated billiard player, was probably the last of these surrounded spectators. He was seen in the Post-office alleyway, apparently as safe as a dozen who escaped. He went under the sidewalk of the fire-proof newspaper office and perished. His engraved watch-cover identified his charred body.

From Congress street northward to Monroe there was not a salient ruin. The outlines of the Grand Pacific Hotel were preserved, in places as high as the fourth story. The Court-house, Post-office, a new insurance building at the southwest corner of Monroe and La Salle, the *Tribune* building and the First National Bank, at the southwest corner of State and Washington, remained, the only ruined edifices whose walls had wholly or partly preserved their shape during the term of melting heat to which nearly all the South Side was sub-jected.

The line of northern horizon was generally at the Court-house. The water-tower on the North Side and the factories on Rush street were the only visible objects known to be on the North Side. As the two men walked along the hot path of the street-car track, on State street, northward, and peered between the Post-office and the *Tribune* ruins, the great plain of the North Side spread out again as far as the eye could reach. Daniel knew this without seeing it, because he had been penned in by the flames.

"My God!" said the city editor, and spake no other word.

Central in the North Side a wooden building stands spared. It is the Ogden mansion, situated, like the White House at Washington, in fine grounds, with a small park in front. Fine history, that, the emotions of its inmates at its strange protection. Strange circumstance, that its owner should be the chief loser at Peshtigo, where in the same fatal hours a more terrible fire swept on—of which man cares nothing.

The wooden pavement did not burn. Patches of it, under blow-pipe heat, charred, but it was essentially as good as new and most of it was brand-new. Dig you down now, eighteen inches below Chicago, and you shall see it. Solemn reminder, even to the spectators of that week, that there has been another Chicago here.

But though the wooden pavement did not burn, it was a stubborn holder of heat. Midway in the ruins of the South

Side either man would have purchased escape at a fair price. The feet swelled, leather cracked, and the men thought best to seek the lake shore.

A thousand bags of cement lay nicely arranged and neatly tied. The men strove to believe their eyes. Why should cement protect gunny-bagging? It had not. The cement was solid rock—sculptured into bags.

Kegs of nails lay piled up as carefully as when put into that cellar. The very angles of the stave showed on their sides. Often nowadays a resident will show you a fused keg of nails as a relic of the fortune he once possessed.

Other adventurers, seeing Daniel and the editor, came forth. Many were sickened by the smell of the elevators and the sugar and molasses warehouses. Spices, coffees, and rags gave off their odors, with now and then a man falling from deadly fumes, as happened before Heath & Milligan's storehouse of paints and oils.

The owners of safes and vaults were early on the ground. A little group gazed at the cellar of a drug store. Far back lay a skeleton, clearly defined, as white as a grandmammy's pipe after burning in the coals.

"Poor fellow!" they lamented. "He worked all the time and slept between prescriptions. A druggist's life is a hard one."

"Yes," assented the druggist in question, who stood looking on. "That was my skeleton." Somebody was discovering the wires in the bones.

The trunks of trees were prominent and grateful remembrances of the past. On the North Side the most pronounced grief was expressed over their loss. Buildings could be erected. Trees must grow.

The transformation in the city's appearance dazed everybody. So many things had happened that were peculiar to the surprising heat of this fire that the Chicagoan was ready to believe whatever were told him. There had been a city here, a great part of which was brick, mortar, and stone. Where now were these materials ?

They had burned.

Plaster and limestone had offered to the blow-pipe the lacking constituents of Drummond light. The fire that had shown on the jeweled dome of the Court-house was not of antimony. It was lime light.

Getting their feet cool in the lake basin, Daniel and the city editor started for the long walk across the Randolph street bridge. They stopped for nothing, having learned their lesson. They tarried not to guess how that cellarful of fused log-chains could be brought forth. They passed but a moment of wonder at the emporium of the finest chinaware, where no piece was loose, though thousands of articles were unbroken. The glass of the town was in all shapes, colors and situations. One might see a keg of padlocks *glacé*.

The eloquent of the earth were already arriving and standing at the edges of the Event, putting it in fitting words. The world already knew of the catastrophe. What would it say ?

"Dan, they'll starve," the city editor said gloomily. Oh, that the world were not so bent on its own doings ! The editor felt sure some one would give something if it were only known—if he could have gotten out his paper.

They reached the bridge in safety. They saw wagons driving from the depot.

"Why, Dan," screamed the city editor, "it's food, Dan. It's been sent here already. Why, my boy, look at it. Oh ! look at that ! "

He—the stoic—he, the man who never before had been seen to express emotion—was unable to walk farther. He clung to Daniel's neck. He sat down and sobbed like a little child.

Wagon after wagon came from the depot. Bread, barrels of hams, pies—the larder of the land of plenty. "Eat, and think not, for a little while ! " said the Land of Plenty.

Oh! world that we had often reviled—world that we of hard hearts had said was deaf to the wail of the sufferer—how now can we eat for the rising of the apple in our throats? There, at the depot, stands the committeeman from every town. His badge will tell you the name of his noble community. The wheels of his train, are they not hot with the speed that has been made to stay this unparalleled Hunger?

"Eat, eat!" he cries in a rage of charity, and the gaunt specter that had skulked in Ate's path goes away forever, as we do hope Ate herself may have gone.

The dust has blown until men's eyes are no longer capable of common tears. Yet men will tell you there were wet eyes when that train-load came in.

Daniel and the editor parted company. "Come back and read proof when you have found your people," said the editor cheerily. "Always a place for you. We've got the out-fit, sure."

Yes, when he had found his people! It recalled the fearful hours Daniel had passed, and he ran once more. Southward on Clinton street he labored, vaguely hoping to get news there. How impotent he felt! How he had been defeated at every turn in this fire. Impatient feeling of all spectators that week! There, thank God! was the house, its southern side the boundary of the burnt district. He had once had hopes and fears here. That must be fifty years ago. Here he might find that Mercy was safe. Of course she was safe, he said! Oh! why had he not hurried south and west by Twelfth street? And yet Mrs. Trenton was burned out, beyond question. He had, just a half hour ago, peered past Lincoln Park on the horizon. The fire had taken it all. Well, then, Mercy would return home here, would she not?

These were his emotions as the servant opened the door. Her face made him turn pale. He thought he should fall, for he was weak. He had not slept since Sunday forenoon. He thought he should die from insomnia.

In those days it was not well known that a man could live with little sleep. It was four or five years afterward that the go-as-you-please pedestrians demonstrated that a man could exist for a week with an hour of slumber a day.

Daniel looked at that hopeless face once more. "Well, Sarah," he said, not daring to ask a question, "here I am, at last," and smiled a sickly way.

That was enough. The girl's apron went to her wet eyes. Her loud lament began: "Oh, Mr. Daniel"—the tempest grew—"Mr. Fullmer was here last night."

"Yes," said Daniel, despairingly.

"He said that Mercy, Mary, yourself and Errington were burned and were none of you at Fullerton avenue. He said that Harmon died just before the fire. And what do you think, Mr. Daniel, dear old Mrs. Holebroke is clean gone crazy."

The girl's moans, uninterrupted by words, filled the house. The house-dog, unnerved not less than other faithful friends of that stricken family, set up a dismal howl.

The exhausted young man sank upon a sofa and gazed stolidly at the loudly crying girl.

Yes, that howling of dog was always for the dead!

---

## CHAPTER XXXIII.

### BUREAUCRACY FOR ALL WHO LOVED AUTHORITY.

THIS, then, was the measure which Daniel must drink. Here were the lees. Mercy was burned. His dead must be denied to him. How hard was the fate of those mourners who must mourn without the dust of their lost ones! We have since seen a widow pay fabulous sums to the thieves who stole her husband's body. But what corse did Ate restore to loving hands?

This was Daniel's message. His mind refused to act on it. Rather did he smile and do the girl that justice which she merited for putting these household goods so quickly back in place.

Then he made her repeat all that news. He went over it methodically. At last his glimmering intelligence seized on the statement of his own death.

"You are sure Mr. Fullmer said I, too, burned up?" he asked, with eagerness.

Yes, the girl was sure.

Then Fullmer was speaking from rumor. He had not seen it. Out of this one thing Daniel gathered hope.

"Mercy will come back," he said. "Mary and Errington will not come back."

Then other important questions arose. Was Mrs. Trenton burned out? No, not when Fullmer left, but the fire was still coming toward them.

To Fullmer's. The two men grasped each other by the hand as though they had been separated for twenty years. The good man was optimistic. Daniel might find Mercy. "I have kept a sharp look-out," he said. "Don't give her up, Dan." It made Fullmer hopeful to see Daniel come to life.

Fullmer had the gossip of the neighborhood. The city offices were at the First Congregational Church, on Washington and Ann streets. Thither Daniel had better go, report the loss of Mary's body, and give a description of Mercy. That would aid more than going to Fullerton avenue.

So, while the sun shone brightly, and the thoroughfares on the West Side appeared as in a holiday, Daniel went out Washington street. At Green street he found a church open, feeding all who came. "Oh! sir, will you not cut bread awhile?" a sweet lady asked at the curbstone. How

could Daniel refuse ? Deep as was his affliction, pitiable as
were his losses, why should he not seize that knife and give
bread to the hungry ?  How to tell the needy from the
merely hungry ?  Ah ! the merely hungry stand on the curb
and cry, and speak of a charity that the world has not seen
since the other birth—in the other manger.

How to tell the needy ?  Ah ! this city has been chastened
of its sins.  Do not believe its people to be beneath all other
creatures in gratitude !

Let Daniel pass on to city offices. It is enough to see these
church people cutting the world's bread. To-night they will
be sorting out the world's garments, put upon the naked of
the North Side.

To-morrow the great pang of charity shall spare no giver
in the whole Caucasian earth.  To-morrow the encampments
on the North, on the East, shall take hope.  To-morrow shall
begin that spontaneous contribution, unequalled in extent—
sole gauge of the true grandeur of our calamity.

Ninety towns in New York $400,000.  Forty-seven towns
in Massachusetts, $300,000.  Sixty-three towns in Penn-
sylvania, $230,000.   Other states and territories, thirty-
seven in all, $1,000,000.  Other nations, England, because
she spoke our language, $425,000; Canada, her province,
$82,000; France, Germany, Austria, Cuba, Italy, Holland,
China, $200,000 more.

Each Christian on earth giving at least a penny in coin to
the suffering city. The nation showering its privileges on the
town.  The citizens of that day taking off their coats and
. sending them.  The treasure-keepers with $3,000,000  on
hand, and counted not an ounce of food or a garment in the
reckoning.

If the fire were not the event of the century in itself, then
all fair-minded men must accord the palm to this giving that
was called out.  The left hand of the world did not know
what its right hand did.  When the great city of London

gave $312,000, she did not know that the little city of Port-
land, in Oregon, was giving $10,000.

Let there be two bead-rolls written of those blessed givers,
and let the bead-rolls be put under the twain of monuments,
lest men grow forgetful, as ages roll away from acts so august, of those other acts so creditable to the human species!

On every side of this wide street now, tumult as at a fair.
Thirst and dust. Men with women on their arms. A lover
with maiden, seeking minister. Wagons, always loaded with
food. People's faces lighted by the smile of the world's love.

A queue of men and boys from the church on Washington
street along to Elizabeth, thence to Madison, along Madison
to Ada. What do they wish? To flee. Passes. All day,
all night, till noon of Wednesday. The railroads will carry
every one free, if the pass can be obtained from the city.
Church girls, without food at home, glad to work here,
sitting at tables, filling in passes. A loaf of bread and a
coat for this man. Take this lady above into the main
room. Give her a pew to lie in. She goes up-stairs and
finds her husband there. Meetings like these filling the
handsome auditorium with happy echoes. A directory of
city magnates in the rear room. Was ever office so bare of
honor?

Police to be appointed. A boy in a barn near by printing "Police" on blue ribbon. Five thousand patrols already
sworn in. Fires ordered out, except at bakeries. Water
wagons and bread wagons impressed into the city's service.
Plenty of generals on hand, with a smack of military rule
come back. A good thing, too, where expressmen have begun
to look scornfully at a hundred dollars Schoolhouses and
churches all ordered open. Delegations arriving from all
cities; some, tools in hand. Incoming of stupendous larder
of the Mississippi Valley. Barrels of chickens, turkeys, hams
Kerosene and tobacco forbidden. The price of bread put at
eight cents a loaf. George Peabody, $100,000. Alexander T.

Stewart, $50,000. Exodus, exodus! Trains of forty cars on every road, carrying forth men who two days ago were rich—to-day beggars—no, not beggars, but succored in their need. Proclamations of governors. Special session of the Illinois Legislature. General tumult of mankind to adjust the Event.

Into this maelstrom of military bureaucracy (rapidly thriving), poor Daniel Trentworthy! To him, some official of police; yes, the lake will be dragged for Mary and for all other bodies. Description of Mercy. Never mind color of dress. Description of Mary. Not known to be dead. Yes, the morgue will be established on Milwaukee avenue, at the city undertaker's. Next.

Daniel must pass on. Bah! it is his own beautiful Mercy whom they thus dismiss so summarily. He goes outside, begrudges the hours he has stood *en queue* and takes solace in the charity of the whole earth. For all men cry out when they speak of that.

Patrolmen, a half hour in service, march by, like Moriarity. An officer with a real star hides it in shame. Water-carts sprinkle throats, not streets; hackmen are meek "rescuers," doing the service of bureaucracy. The wind is again growing. The vigil for fire in every household is beginning. The city has lost $200,000,000, in goods and belongings. Not leaven is purged from household in Jewry with more fervor than fire from the hearthstones of unburned Chicago this day and night.

The ruins seethe, and terror, as in 1793, becomes the order of the day.

One hundred thousand people wonder what will become of them. Five hundred thousand people wonder what will become of Chicago. Unsentimental masons and contractors, keen and cold in their opportunity, journeying thitherward from the ends of the nation.

Good wives boiling the water from duck ponds in parks, with much fear of flux. Workmen and clerks on Canal street drinking river water strongly impregnated with anthracite coal. Everybody a convalescent.

A happy autumn sun in the western sky. Daniel looking on the fields of fire and thinking of the days'that are no more.

— — —

## CHAPTER XXXIV.

### PASSING ALONG NOBLE STREET.

"HOMEWARD!" At last, Daniel, starting for Fullerton avenue at 4 o'clock Monday morning, was now late on Tuesday afternoon, about to set out for Fullerton avenue, to see what had become of the few friends who had been left to him by this destruction of a wooden Gomorrah. There was much he desired to do. He could barely desist from again penetrating the burnt district, and going to the north lake shore. He wanted to find that morgue. But people were warned that the patrolmen at night would be very strict with wayfarers. Lights must be out about as soon as lit. There were to be no more evenings in Chicago. If Daniel expected to reach those camps on the northern prairies, he must hurry thither.

Yet it was possible that, in going north, Daniel could strike the business street called Milwaukee avenue, which cut directly into the city from the northwest. The city undertaker Daniel had heard, lived on this street. The morgue, some experienced policeman suggested, would probably be established near the undertaker's place of business.

If the unhappy young man could only find Mercy's body he might better endure his hard fate. Fullmer had told him how she had left the Fullerton avenue residence in search

of the man she loved. If Daniel could but secure her
sacred dust, no matter how charred, how repulsive to others,
he would live that he might rear a stone over her grave and
go thither to recall the features of her who was the loveliest
of Eve's daughters. His nerves were in a bad state.
His eyes were as hot as they had been on Monday in the
lime-dust of Michigan avenue.

And then, in the blindness of his grief, he recurred to
Mary. He could not find Mercy. Probably she was burned.
In that terrible heat there were no remains of human beings.
In the great soap vats, heated by coils of pipe, filled with pot
ash and fats, if a workman become engulfed, nothing is left
save maybe a half-eaten key, or a persistent metal button
frame. So in Phlegethon, which coiled iron columns
around tiny wires, which wound T-rail as the electrician
winds his silk armature. What hope to find the dead—his
fragile Mercy? Ah, that was bitter! But Mary lay in Lake
Michigan. She was Mercy's sister. She had Mercy's blood.
She had loved him. He would not think of those moments
on the grand staircase. He would be thankful that her
body would be given up, and that he might shield it from
the general burial of Ate's dead.

He journeyed far out Milwaukee avenue. At every block
he obtained less and less information. He must not go
back. The sun was descending. The quarter was German
and Eastern European. He was going northwestward.
He must strike directly north. He came to a wide and pop-
ulous street of a prosperous look, where people were neigh-
borly. It was Noble street. He turned with his ever present
feeling of defeat and entered the new route.

Now he only desired to hasten. He could not find the
morgue to-night. His face was still blackened, as there was
no water to be had by wayfarers beyond the needs of the
thirsty. To have a blackened face was a badge of residence.
It was not an interloper, at least, the householders would

say. As he walked by a comfortable residence a wan face and two great black eyes gave a start and pondered upon his carriage. It was a young woman, sitting inside by a window. She had not seen the face, and she was too weak to rise and go to the door. The games of the children drowned his footfalls, for she could easily have decided by that sound. He was out of her sight. Her heart fluttered.

"Pshaw!" she moaned, "every man I see of his age seems to be Daniel."

Her faithful friend came in. "Why, you look feverish," he cried in alarm, seizing her hand and frightened at her bounding pulse. "Here! The brandy—quick!"

"I guess I will lie down," she said, and accepted his aid.

"I urged her to sit up," he thought, regretfully. "How little I know about women!"

She lay there and rapidly regained her composure. In what a sorry plight does cruel Nature put the maid when the stranger has come between her and all she holds dear! She thinks of him all the time. She holds him next to her Lord. It is well till she speaks of him. Then she must explain the case to others—and the case is inconceivable. She disguises, avoids, denies. He who is everything is nothing. He is a stranger.

Now this maiden lay in the house of the Christian brothers—not monks—but equally good men. She had on her mind the loss of her dearest one. Yet that dearest one was the stranger, for whom she had left her own mother and the dead body of her brothers.

She was ashamed to admit the naturalness of her act, it seemed so basely unnatural. She wept.

"It is not good to cry," he said, uncomfortably. He perhaps ought to leave her. Instead, he bathed her forehead.

"Oh! sir," she said, "I wanted you to come. I have a dead brother at No. 631 Fullerton avenue, and my mother will be crazy with anguish—I know she will."

"That is very serious," said the young man, "why did you not tell my sister-in-law sooner?"

"I had just come to my mind when you assisted me to the chair. I was about to speak to you when you were called out."

"It is serious," the young man said, "because the quarter you mention is burned, and we have orders not to move out of our houses after 6 o'clock, except to go for a doctor, maybe. In the morning, however, I will go into the camping grounds on the prairie and in Lincoln Park, and try my best to find your people."

How heartlessly she had deserted her kin—how she had left that feeble mother to battle with affliction—that mother, too, who had failed so rapidly since Harmon had sickened! So Nature scourged the girl. Sometimes the funnel of a tornado strikes a field of daisies in an unsettled region, and plows the ground for a hundred feet. Strange clash of jurisdiction among Nature's overseers? Sometimes a judge of court attaches a citizen for obeying another judge of court. Bustle of lawyers in court; turmoil of emotions in Mercy, and finally, a little peace in apology for the flesh. "I expected to go back to Clark street," she said to herself.

"They are very strict, are they not?" she asked.

"It is military rule," he said.

How could she broach the subject which was of most importance?

"I went to look for my sister. A friend had remained at Ohio street to remove both her and her sick husband. I fear all three were burned."

Now she wept convulsively, and the crime stood confessed. As the children of Israel had sold their brother, so she had sold brother, sister and mother.

"I fear Daniel Trentworthy is dead!"

The young rescuer's pity gave way to the suddenness of his astonishment,

"Daniel Trentworthy!"

"Yes."

"A young man, who was once the son of a great financier, who was educated at Harvard, and left there abruptly, concealing his subsequent movements?" So asked the young man.

"Yes, but I know nothing of concealment. He is a young man, not very old—not twenty-four."

"That is my own cousin. We have sought him for five years, almost."

Strange coincidence! One of those countless episodes that uphold belief in especial providence.

The girl's face glowed with pleasure. The young man spread the news in the household. The members gathered in her room and took a renewed interest in their beautiful charge.

They had but lately come to Chicago, attracted hither by its glory. How sad this news! As sad as Chicago's glory! Inquiries, now, as to morgues, hospitals, and the search for the dead. Mercy bettered at once. She told them of Daniel's hairbreadth escape from death.

"He'll pull through yet," the family said.

And yet, the proper place for which to look was the morgue. There was a paper to-night, which promised to be of service in these matters. There would be a *Tribune* to-morrow morning.

The family could not talk enough about Daniel, and the maiden had never before had any good opportunity to discuss him. Hope led her on. She recited the smash-up in the tunnel, and gave the awful scene on the wires. The family held their breath. She dwelt upon the goodness of Mrs. Trenton, and the long illness two years before.

Yes, the maiden admitted, she had nursed Daniel, and therefore she took on new claims to the kinsman's attention. They could not see her blushes. They must surely seek these Trentons and succor them. Undoubtedly a branch of the same family, the married Trentworthy declared, and got down his genealogical treatise.

They left her with added tendernesses, addressed to her comfort for the second night. She was almost happy. She had gone to the stranger's tribe. Strange and peremptory adjustment! Then, as the street grew still, tears for Harmon, agonies for Daniel, longings for mother—desolation.

Outside, patrolmen not yet quit of their elation to be officers. Over on the eastern sky, blood-red clouds. In august line, along the four miles of bayous, bright pyramids of anthracite coal, no more to be quenched than nether fires. Angry winds and falling walls. Prayers to the Father that the gale should not turn from its present harmless course. Sleep for many for the first time since Friday night. The Event already on its journey to the far ages.

---

## CHAPTER XXXV.

### ASLEEP.

DANIEL, this solemn Tuesday afternoon, hurried onward, crossed the northern bayou at a railroad station, and entered Clybourn avenue, another important diagonal street that, like the north branch of the river, had cut its way southeastward into the North Division. To his surprise he saw the buildings here were not burned, although he was now on the North Side. However, he had not far to look to the eastward to see that same black and level plain. He followed the avenue northwestward, and was soon among the campers. It was dusk. He began to think better of the bureaucrats at Washington and Ann streets, for here, too, were bread

wagons and barrels of cooked food. There was a sound and
flash of new tinware. A buggy would serve as a rest for
boards from a sidewalk. Under this roof would lie little
children with bleeding feet—children whose escape from
death had been marvelous. Men, worn out, like Daniel, were
wrapped in blankets, asleep, such mostly veteran soldiers,
somewhat proud of their ability to forget the battles of the
previous day. Women were sobbing nervously. Why should
they not? Would not years and decades stretch out, and
never the peace and shade and luxury of that North Side
come again?

Let them sob on, and men light their lanterns, and Daniel
look eastward on Fullerton avenue. It is a long distance to
that black plain. His heart suddenly thumps. Why not
walk that way and find the ruins of Mrs. Trenton's house?
No one has seen her party. There has been no group of
refugees with a body on a window blind!

He walks down Fullerton avenue. Can he believe his
eyes? There is the very house. It is not burned, although
the fence and the yard are in that odious burned district.

"Oh! Daniel! thank God!" It is Mrs. Trenton, and the
young man is at last at home, and has a home left over his
head.

"Did you find her?" he asks, beseechingly.

"No, Daniel. She is dead. She was seen going westward
on Chicago avenue after the blacksmith shop took fire, and
none of those people got over the bridge." Mrs. Trenton
wept.

"You mean Mercy—not Mary?"

"Yes," they are both lost—that is, Mercy is surely lost.
Mary may have escaped southward, they say."

"No, Mary's body is in the lake."

The heart-broken man told them how he had lost the gray
woman. They told him, once more, how Mercy had stolen
away to search for him.

"Come up-stairs, Daniel," they said.

"Here, mother, is Daniel. Here is your son."

"Did you bring Harmon and Mary? Did you meet Mercy? Good, Daniel, my son. Sit here, Daniel, and hold my hand. Mercy has gone after Mary and poor Ralph. Say, Daniel, do you think Mary is wise to nurse Ralph so closely? I fear she will be poisoned. Daniel, do you think my chickens will get fed? That black rooster fights. I'm sure of it. Come over, Daniel, to see Mercy, and I'll put him in the pot."

She smiled grimly.

"I must be going," she said. "It's two rides on the cars. It's a long way. Mercy ought to hurry."

Daniel's cup was full. Yet this old mother in Israel, wandering in her speech, was only one of hundreds. There were sainted hearts out in the park, who had not even a board to lean against a fence, who were thenceforth, to remain dead in life. Such it was, who could not look on Ate and retain their reason.

Mrs. Trenton was afraid Daniel, too, would lose his mind. But he asked to see Harmon's body.

"I did not see him at Ohio street," he shuddered.

"We took him to the cemetery to-day," she answered.

Mechanically he started for the door. He would go to the cemetery. The good lady laid hold on him, and led him to his own room.

"There, Daniel," she said, "take this glass and drink it. Lie down. Here is water. Wash as little as possible. Sleep. There is nothing else for you to do."

True. He lay in his bed and closed his eyelids on their hot balls. He got a wet rag and laid it on his eyes. He fell into a slight doze, and awoke with an explosion of his trifacial nerve. He quieted once more, and there came a peremptory dispatch that a vertebral motor was down. He arose and turned to the wall the statue that had seen Mercy kiss him.

He was next in Sahara, and his camel was lying as an entrenchment against sirocco. Should he disembowel the faithful beast? Finally, intimations of Nirvana, nothingness. He slept.

On Wednesday, in the Fullerton avenue house, Daniel still asleep. The doctor in consultation with Mrs. Trenton.

"Let him sleep all of to-day and to-night—the longer the better. How long ago was it that his head was hurt? Two years—hum—ah!—let him sleep. It will save his reason. It is an unfortunate set of circumstances."

In the Noble street house, a girl seemingly very sick of a fever. "A slight relapse," says the physician reassuringly. "Keep her quiet to-day. She will be around to-morrow. Nothing chronic or premonitory."

And complete failure of the attempt to get to Fullerton avenue. Magnificent growth of militarism. "Got a pass from General Sheridan's headquarters? Turn back then!"

"Could you tell me if Fullerton avenue burned?"

"Where is Fullerton avenue?"

It is plain the bayonet has but just marched on the scene.

"Advertise in the *Tribune* or *Journal*," the soldier says.

Wednesday in the city and state, the Democratic Governor of Illinois profoundly indignant to see a Republican generalissimo established in the burnt district. Great heat and high wind. Many people opening safes. Vows that a monument shall be built of fire-proof safes that burned all their contents. A vow to be kept, and the hideous monument in Garfield Park to be torn down within ten years. The safes might have been fire-proof and yet not Ate-proof. Shanties erecting in the burnt district. Barracks in open squares. Fugitives already returning to Chicago. The press of the world filled with fine sentences. "It is all it has been represented to be," say the eloquent.

On Milwaukee avenue, a large barn in two compartments. To this barn, the dead, all day of Wednesday—all Wednesday

night. What is a body? Who shall say? Is this one, or
is it two? How many, then, are there? Who, too, shall
answer? How many bodies? Eighty, it is said. Who
shall deny it?

" I have found the morgue—that is, I have found where it
is," the younger Trentworthy announced that night, as the
girl sat at the window once more.

" I must go there to-morrow," she said; " did you put the
notice in the paper?"

" Yes; they said, however, that they could print only a
certain number. If it did not go in to-morrow it would appear Friday."

A rap at the door. A patrolman!

"Lights out!"

It is Wednesday ended. How strange is this new life.
How short is the day. How long is the night. How furiously the wind blows. When will the water be here! In
eight days and five hours from the burning of the works.

James Fisk's great train is this night making sixty miles
an hour toward Chicago. The Committee of the Nation has
lifted the city to her feet. The hundred thousand may pass
off the stage, if they will. The new city is born. It is
suckled by the mandate of the people.

But men are full of dormant rage. Two fools have fun
with an Italian saloon-keeper. The event has needed some
act to commemorate it. The Italian has chafed under the
common impotency. He gladly seized a great knife and of-
fers his tormentors to Ate. And hangs for it, later on. And
a negro, saved from the Court House basement, is spared for
a gibbet on a change of venue from Ate to a county along-
side Cook.

## CHAPTER XXXVI.

### THE NECESSITIES VS. THE PROPRIETIES.

" How long have I slept ? "

" Since Tuesday night."

" It is morning. What morning? I haven't been out of my head for three months more, have I ? "

" No, Daniel. You have simply caught up with your sleep, as you used to say when you were a proof-reader. It is only Thursday morning. Here is a paper. Mr. Trenton paid 25 cents for it—just think ! Daniel, there is a morgue on Milwaukee avenue. Daniel, you must go there. Isn't it dreadful ? There, I will not speak of it again."

Daniel was only too glad to go. He stood on the veranda and looked at the vast Court House afar. It was symbolical of his past. Gone, every joyful thing. Gone, everything. He thought of the complete blotting of Ralph Errington. There remained of his estate a mortgaged lot covered with ashes and a carriage with two horses and harness. Smelting works, 400 houses, wife, natural son—everything swept away. And yet, one of some thousands, so far as property may be reckoned.

He thought of his own wreck, and could not bear the thought ; and strode forth to get Mercy's body.

To Clybourn Avenue Station, to Noble street, down Noble street, past the Christian brothers, with nobody looking out, down Milwaukee avenue, to crowded alleys.

The Morgue.

Men drink a glassful of brandy before they go in there. Sublime women go there without stimulant. There has been, they say, a lady in the farther compartment already, hunting for her sister.

Daniel has said he will not falter. He has, in his time, seen the burned. He has narrowly missed being the burned. He is fire-proof—more than the safes for the moment. And yet he does not stay in there. He goes to a saloon, and drinks the first glass of brandy that has passed his lips since he was in the fire department.

He re-enters. He knows some ineradicable marks of Mercy. If she be there, that grim brandy drinker will have her!

A terrible half-hour goes by. Mercy and Mary are not in that compartment. It is settled.

A woman enters on the other side—the lady who had been there before.

"Oh, Mary! Mary!"

The man springs out of that charnel house as if he were shot from a catapult. He enters the other side. Here is fastened on his sight a white form among the black. It is the drowned among the burned. It is the only one in eighty, they say, that a friend might recognize.

But a live woman is in his arms. A kinsman, the younger Trentworthy, is grasping him by a hand, and pulling them forth, and getting them to a hack, and hurrying an express wagon to that barn.

The dead body of Mary is at the undertaker's to be put in proper form for burial at William Trentworthy's order and expense.

The living, come to seek the dead, had found the living and the dead.

"I am so sorry for you, Mercy." Daniel said, as he tried to stop her tears.

"Oh! Daniel, do not go away from me again. I know I could not live."

And this man, who had been taught by Mary that he could

18

live without any woman, although he had shuddered at the awful severity of life a half hour before, was now happy as a child to see that she could think at all of him with brother and sister dead.

"Your mother has lost her reason, Mercy," he said.

"You will not desert me, Daniel, will you?" she pleaded in answer.

Would he?

A lunch at the joyous Trentworthy's, and the pair were on their way to Mrs. Trenton's once more. They were happy, and were ashamed to be. Yet no one blamed them.

"Gracious!" was Mrs. Trenton's great oath. "Gracious! It's the most remarkable thing I ever heard of."

"What's that; the fire?" asked her husband. "Bully for Jim Fisk!" and he continued to read the dispatches. "Bravo! for Peabody! Hurrah for Stewart!"

The body of Mary arrived next day. It was buried beside that of Harmon.

The house of Mrs. Trenton, being on the edge of the camping-ground, rapidly filled with acquaintances who were without shelter. The Trentworthy brothers were desirous that Daniel should come with them.

"We have been hunting for him for five years," they said. "He is our kinsman." It meant much to those strangers in this strange city.

It had been a hard day for Mercy. She was not yet fairly strong enough to be out of bed, yet she had seen brother and sister lowered into the grave. She had listened to the wanderings of a mother. She now faced the future. How awful was the thought of returning to that Clinton street house alone! She could not do it. She sobbed and had no counsel. For she was but just engaged to be married. Her only protector could not become her protector until a proper season had gone by. And how was she to exist in the meantime? It was plain that Mrs. Trenton was already overcrowded. They, too, had lost business and the accumulations of years.

These were Mercy's troubles. Vaguely she knew that Daniel would help her. But how delicate is a maiden's position at such a time!

There was a look of grim determination in Mrs. Trenton's eye. The party was back from the cemetery. They ate their simple meal. If the truth be told, the bread and meat had come on a charity train from towns on the Milwaukee Road. No one felt proud.

"There will be a family council in the parlor directly after dinner," she said. "Mr. Trenton, pray for our especial guidance."

And thus they ate, hoping the Lord would make clearer the way.

It was a strange thing, this filing into the parlor, Mr. and Mrs. Edson Trenton, Daniel Trentworthy, Mercy Holebroke, John and William Trentworthy.

Mrs. Trenton spoke: "Friends," she said, "this is a time when the ordinary proprieties of life must be put aside. I have a matter to lay before this group, and that matter cannot wait. Mercy Trentworthy has been cast upon the world. Her mother is hopelessly ill. There is a house and furniture, but there is no one to pay the rent and buy food. There is a man, our Daniel here, who is ready, willing, and able to take care of Mercy and her mother, if he can have the right. But the objection is that Mercy ought not to marry so soon after the death of her people.

"These young folks," the brave lady continued, as her husband began to grow uneasy, "should have married long ago. Mercy's sister, Mrs. Errington, was very ambitious. She was proud of Mercy, and hoped to bring about some great match. I think her opposition kept Daniel and Mercy apart. The fact of her death ought not to continue what her life began—that is, the estrangement of these lovers. I knew Harmon. His last thoughts were as to the welfare of his dear ones.

"There now remains but one thing to do. These young folks ought to get married right off—this afternoon. Daniel owns a house on West Washington street. The couple also have the house at Clinton street. He can get a place as proof-reader again, he says, as men are very scarce. Now what do you think of that, John Trentworthy? What do you think of it, William Trentworthy? What do you think of it, Edson Trenton? Never mind, Daniel—keep still, Mercy."

That was a hard place for Mercy. Her pride revolted. Mlle. Bismarcks often put other people in bad fixes.

"I doubt if Daniel wants me," she said, and grew sick at heart, and lost all pride. Her great eyes turned upon him. "Whithersoever thou goest"—so said the eyes.

John Trentworthy rose. "I was named after Daniel's father," he said. "It was supposed that my christening was worth a million to me. It did bring me a thousand dollars, which are at the basis of my present moderate means. I am Daniel's kinsman—proud I am to find him so likely a man. I shall accept Mercy as my kinswoman. I do not see how it can be delayed."

William Trentworthy rose: "If I can't marry Mercy myself," he said, "I want my cousin to marry her."

Edson Trenton rose: "My dear," he said, like a well disciplined husband, "I will trust you with these things. I suppose there is no hope of Mercy waiting to be my second wife."

"They will be married this afternoon," the officer of the day declared. And this was the edict of the council she had convened.

The lovers could only protest that they ought to have been heard.

"Daniel," said Mrs. Trenton, "run over to the prairie.

Do you see where that long, white board is?  That is the
license-clerk's family.  Get him to write a license.  Here is
the money.  He will be glad to earn a fee.  Go, now, Mercy
is watching you.  She will marry William if you fool with
her any longer.  She's been too patient already.  Edson, go
for our minister.  He is at home."

Could Daniel tarry?

Queer weddings, that afternoon, all over the city.  Robert
Collyer will tell you of the piece of sausage that was a wedding feast, and will smack his lips unctuously at the reminis-
cence.

The clever chroniclers of small talk have recorded how an
empty parlor was converted into a handsome room, not many
blocks away, only the day before this Friday.  The refugees
marched forth to their barracks.  A soap box covered with
crimson cloth was put in the unsightly grate-hole.  On this
a slop jar, covered with crimson.  On this a fine stag's head,
left by an out-going refugee.  Branches hung everywhere.
A pair of library steps with a sheet around them for the
altar.  A scarlet cloth in front, with the illuminated motto:
"Cast Thy Care Upon Him, for He Careth for Thee."  A
large Bible and a prayer-book on top of the altar.  Four
buggy cushions wrapped in an afghan for hassock on which
to kneel.  A table with vines at edge, displaying pasteboard
presents, with monograms in lead pencil.  The wedding veil
of the married sister.  The groom in borrowed clothes, the
bridesmaid, and the first groomsman—the latter only five
feet nine, in the dress suit of a man not burnt out who was
six feet two.  Forty guests, all burnt out.  A prayer that
carried all toward God.  Warm biscuits and cold water, of
which all ate.

This wedding would have been an affair costing at least
$5,000 but for the fire.  The twain must travel toward
friends, and must marry at once.  Careful observance of all
form.  The kernel of ceremony fertile in the ashes of the
hour.

Therefore, dwell upon the good fortune of Daniel and Mercy, who had house and friends on every hand. A sudden garnishing of the Trenton mansion, Presbyterian wedding in the parlor, a wedding tour by carriage to the Clinton street house, making great haste to get the carriage back to Fullerton avenue before darkness and bayonets set in.

At Clinton street, the servant well supplied with charity food, and half mad with joy at the return of the lost. The old lady much improved by sight of her chickens, which have been jealously guarded. The rooster put in the pot for the wedding feast of Saturday.

It is a week. The event has passed by. Mankind is fairly adjusted. The fire is already twice told. Men give themselves to the stern problem of existence, and will forever read no tale of the calamity.

----

## CHAPTER XXXVII.

### "WITH CHARITY FOR ALL."

NEARLY fifteen years have passed. The spring has been blessed with frequent rains: the lawns of the city are green. It is Chicago.

Men stand before her Board of Trade, and looking upward toward the clock, declare that their hearts leap within them. Gazing toward the white clouds, the sight-seer vows that though he have gone to the ends of the earth, that office building yonder is the grandest and most beautiful he has seen.

Down Michigan avenue the throngs of carriages progress almost as multitudinous as on that day of dust and ashes. Out Washington boulevard the stone flagging glints as far as Garfield Park. Upon the northern lake shore, promises of an avenue that shall eclipse all other glories of the city.

Population, a Million in Cook County.

On Clinton, a paved street. Where Mary played the Traumerei, the sound of men, pounding. Factories, factories. Vacant lots, where once were well-to-do residences. The householders who abode there, now all two miles west.

New numbers on Fullerton avenue. But Mrs. Trenton lives not far away, her love for trees and lawn well gratified. Still a magnificent lady, with a heart for young men. "They make our city. I have always gone to some trouble to help them," she will say. And not only Daniel—but two generations—two Sunday-school classes—are about her heart, to bless her, and to declare her greatness among women.

At the Trentworthy's of Noble street—Noble street no more. Two palaces on Michigan avenue stand side by side. There live the two brothers. And how comes this great wealth? It comes of invention. In the year 1872 the city was rebuilt. John Trentworthy perfected a machine to lift mortar. It came into instant use. He next made a machine to sandpaper wood. The firm of John, William & Daniel Trentworthy was established. It flourished. John took a trip to Leadville. The firm bought a mine. The profit at selling was $1,500,000.

Daniel Trentworthy prefers the West Side. His mansion there, his cousins tell him, is out of place. He ought to be on Prairie avenue. Several of his neighbors are moving that way. He has just pulled down one of their houses and added the ground to his lawn. It makes a New Yorker smile. "A very vulgar thing," the New Yorker avers. "Eighteen feet front are enough. Parlors are entirely out of place."

But fine grounds will always evoke admiration. As in the Hebrew king's time, they will make envy.

"Will you sell your house? We want to enlarge our hotel." So said mine host at Washington.

"Send me the price of your hotel," answered the irate widow. "I wish to enlarge my cabbage patch."

A grand plan—this of Daniel Trentworthy's. It makes us wish we were all rich. How many children has he? Five? Well, well. Have any of them black eyes? Yes, there are two daughters—the prettiest little girls to be seen hereabouts. There were six. One is at Graceland.

Well—Mrs. Trentworthy; how does she bear her years?

"Gracious!" the gossiping neighbor tells you, "she looks under thirty. She has always been the handsomest woman any one ever saw. But she is a real home body. She has a great deal to do. That conservatory there, and sending flowers to sick people—that takes her time."

"Where are they to-day? The house is closed."

"Yes; this is Decoration Day. They will be at Graceland, where Mr. and Mrs. Trentworthy's people are buried."

"Mrs. Holebroke—is she living?"

"Oh, no! She died the first year they came to the big house. Mr. Trentworthy went to California and got his parents' bodies and got Mrs. Holebroke's husband's—Mercy's father's body—and they have the finest lot in Graceland."

To Graceland we must go. Yes, that is a magnificent obelisk. There are the headstones.

"John and Martha Trentworthy."

"Robert and Harriet Holebroke."

"John Fullmer Trentworthy, infant son."

"Mary Errington."

How sweet is this home of the dead to-day! "Come all ye that are weary and heavy laden and I will give you rest." Holiness to the Lord, and nobler thoughts to man. It is a sacred day with this living man and woman and his handsome brood.

There they stand, reverent, filled with thoughts that will have utterance.

It seems to Daniel Trentworthy that he has never been grateful enough to Mercy. There is something on his mind. There comes to him a desire of self-abnegation.

The man and the woman are gazing on that last headstone, "Mary Errington," which stands alone, where Mercy has piled the flowers as high as they lie on the little one's grave. She cries, as she always cries, when she touches this head-stone of the gray woman.

The man alone knows the buried Mary's secret. Never has he spoken of the matter to Mercy. Never has he heard a whisper that Ralph Errington did not go to his death by heedless inattention to his wife's warnings. Never have the man and wife spoken of it.

Has she not been a noble wife, yonder, crying at Mary's grave? Has she ever denied him aught that would make him glad?

His eye rests on Harmon's name. What would Harmon do?

It is settled.

"Mercy," the man says, in a low voice.

" Yes, Daniel."

" You know my fears, the Friday night before the fire—before Harmon and Ralph died."

" Yes, Daniel." The face was full of pain.

" Well, pardon me for speaking. But it seems to me I may have been mistaken."

A glad light leaps to her eyes. She falls toward him. It is so sudden.

" I always thought you were mistaken," she whispered. "Oh, Daniel, she was my sister. I loved her so."

They pass from the scene. There is nothing, definite or indefinite, between those parent hearts any more.

" Harmon would have done it," says the father to himself.

" I did not deserve to be so blest," sobs the mother.

Bringing up the party, two wee children, hand in hand—a picture for an artist.

The one, in ecstacy: " Oh! see what lots of people ? "

The other: " Oh! see zose pitty f'owers ! "

# THE IMMORTAL;

OR,

# ONE OF THE FORTY.

### (L'IMMORTEL).

## By ALPHONSE DAUDET.

## THE SUCCESS OF THE YEAR.

"With as much vigor of touch as his friend Zola—to whose school he belongs—Daudet is too refined ever to be coarse. His acute sense of artistic harmony leads him rather to veil the 'sores' of human nature, which his taciturn confrère revels in exposing."

This paragraph from a Paris letter in the *London Bookseller* is one key to Daudet's art; the other is his ineffable humor. No other writer now living seems to derive so thorough and so subtle amusement from the outwardly uninteresting affairs of daily life.

Daudet's manner is a continual reminder of Dickens, but the Frenchman's literary training and discerning taste give him a power of selection which Dickens did not possess. Decidedly, Daudet is the most *accomplished* writer of his day, even if some may hold him not the greatest.

Of "THE IMMORTAL," his latest work, much has been said on both sides, the judgment being determined generally by the position of the critic towards the French Academy; but the fact that 133,000 copies of the book were sold in Paris before it had been on the stands a month, is sufficient guarantee that the Parisian public find it interesting.

In this tale the celebrated French novelist "dissects" that august and ancient body, the "Academie Française," and he wields the scalpel (or shall we rather say the pen?) in a manner that must be positively painful to the dignified gentlemen who compose the famous company of "immortals." This book has made a great stir in France, and everybody in the capital on the Seine is trying to place the real names under the names of the persons who appear in the satire. To all who relish wit that is keen as a sword, descriptions that are as exact as a photograph, and stories that are extremely interesting, this book is sincerely commended.—*Detroit Commercial Advertiser.*

**Beautifully Illustrated by E. Bayard. Cloth, $1.00; paper, 50c.**

## RAND, McNALLY & CO., Publishers,

### 148 to 154 Monroe Street, Chicago.

**323 Broadway, New York.**

*The Greatest Success of the Day.*

---

# THE IRONMASTER

(LE MAÎTRE DE FORGES.)

---

## BY GEORGES OHNET.

---

*Handsomely printed, with many fine full-page illustrations on wood.*
*Cloth, $1.00; Paper, 50 cents.*

This novel, which raised its author from obscurity to sudden fame, which has been translated into all civilized languages, and which has been dramatized under many titles (notably "The Forgemaster" and "Lady Claire"), is the most pronounced success in modern literature. One hundred and forty-six editions of the book have been sold in France, and the author has realized from it some $75,000 in royalties.

"It is undoubtedly a story of admirably sustained interest, skillfully told in graceful yet forcible language. The strongly marked characters develop themselves naturally, both in their language and their actions. The book, moreover, unlike the general run of French novels, conveys a sound moral. It chastises the malice which is born of envy, and establishes the folly of that selfish pride which blinds its possessor to all consideration for the commoner clay of humanity. It shows anew how needful it is that husbands and wives alike should study each other's characters before marriage, and it enforces, in convincing language, the oft-repeated lesson, that a woman should never trifle with the affection of the man to whom she is mated for life."

"It has a strong, bold plot, and works up to an obvious moral."-- *New Orleans Picayune.*

"It is a strong novel, and one that will bear reading a second time."— *Nashville American.*

## RAND, McNALLY & CO., Publishers,

148 to 154 Monroe Street, CHICAGO.

NEW YORK: 323 Broadway.

Send for complete list of our "GLOBE LIBRARY" publications.

ZOLA'S MASTERPIECE

# The Dream,

(Le Rêve.)

## BY ÉMILE ZOLA.

**Authorized translation, done under the author's supervision by
Mrs. Eliza E. Chase.**

---

This, the latest work of the great leader of the modern "realistic school,"
betrays the same powerful hand, the same delicately analytical touch that have
made his previous works popular in spite of their drawbacks; but it evidences
also a selective taste which he has been supposed to lack. His wonderful
realism, which, when used in the portrayal of vice and crime, is revolting, when
turned to the study of innocence and purity becomes singularly sweet and
fascinating.

"The Dream" is written in the great novelist's happiest, strongest vein,
and no admirer of Zola can afford to leave it unread; while, being perfectly clean
and pure in tone, it is a proper book to place in the hands of any young girl.

---

"We do not wish to have given the impression that those who particularly like
in Zola his characteristic genius need not read his book. They would make a great
mistake not to do so. In the double transformation of Angelique, of a perverse
person becoming a devout one, then of a saint turning into a woman, psychology
is shown in every line. In all the descriptive parts Zola's peculiar power is betrayed
in the minutest details."—LE FIGARO (Paris).

---

Send for complete lists of the **GLOBE LIBRARY,**—"The handsomest of
all the cheap libraries."

## RAND, McNALLY & CO., Publishers,

NEW YORK STORE,                148 to 154 Monroe St., CHICAGO.
323 Broadway.

---

**MAPS and GUIDES to Every Country and to Every Important City in the
World; Railway and Engineering Books, etc.**

# BELFORD'S
# MAGAZINE

## EDITED BY DONN PIATT.

BELFORD'S MAGAZINE, published monthly, is devoted to politics, fiction, poetry, general literature, science and art.

In politics the Magazine will give an independent support to the Democratic party and to the present Administration.

It will advocate the extinguishment of the surplus by a reform of the present iniquitous and burdensome tariff in the direction of free trade or of a tariff for revenue only.

The department of fiction will be exceptionally full. Instead of a serial story, dragging its length through several months, and exhausting the patience of the reader, a complete novel will be published in each number, and each issue will also contain one or more short stories complete.

Col. Donn Piatt is ssisted by a staff of sub-editors, and also a large number of able c tributors, among whom are :

| | |
|---|---|
| DAVID A. WELLES | GEN. H. V. BOYNTON, |
| HON. FRANK H.    RD, | SARAH B. M. PIATT, |
| PROF. W. G. SU NER, | EDGAR FAWCETT, |
| J. S. MOORE (Parsee Merchant), | JOEL BENTON, |
| HON. JOHN G. CARLISLE, | ELLA WHEELER WILCOX, |
| HENRY WATTERSON, | REV. GEORGE LORIMER, |
| HENRY GEORGE, | E. HERON-ALLEN, |
| JULIAN HAWTHORNE, | COATES KINNEY, |
| EDGAR SALTUS, | JAMES WHITCOMB RILEY (Falcon), |
| JOHN JAMES PIATT, | SOULE SMITH, |
| THOS. G. SHEARMAN, | GERTRUDE GARRISON. |

BELFORD'S MAGAZINE is a first-class medium for advertising, as the publishers guarantee a bona-fide circulation of at least 70,000 copies per month.

---

### Price, $2.50 a Year, or 25 cents per Number.

---

# BELFORD, CLARKE & CO., PUBLISHERS,

### CHICAGO.    NEW YORK.    SAN FRANCISCO.

www.ingramcontent.com/pod-product-compliance
Lightning Source LLC
Chambersburg PA
CBHW020848020726
47497CB00005B/1312